Advance Praise for the Bear in a Muddy Tutu

"From the first page to the last, Cole Alpaugh had my attention. His zany and colorful characters and style of writing put me in mind of one of my favorite authors, John Irving. I suspect that I have found my next new favorite author."

—Michelle Hessling, Publisher, *The Wayne Independent*

"Pick up *The Bear in a Muddy Tutu* if you enjoy taking a literary journey that is twisted, peopled by characters who are social misfits, caught up in events that range from bizarrely tragic to merely sad. Reminded me of *A Confederacy of Dunces*."

—Molly Rodgers, Library Director, Wayne County Public Library

"Reading *The Bear in a Muddy Tutu* is like running away with the circus. You won't regret the emotional ride or the fantastic people you meet, but you might regret not getting to stay longer."

—Regan Leigh, writer/blogger

"A deftly written story driven by raw and vivid characters and rich with evocative language and colorful descriptions. With every page another layer is peeled back as this fascinating, magical tale unfolds—sad or humorous, but always thoughtful. Alpaugh's writing does not rely on cheap tricks or predictable plot points, but slowly pulls you in and compels you to stick around for a while. Rest assured, in *The Bear in a Muddy Tutu*, you will constantly be surprised by what happens next."

—Rhiannon Ellis, author of *Bonded In Brazil*

THE BEAR
IN A
MUDDY TUTU

COLE ALPAUGH

CAMEL
PRESS
Seattle, WA

Published by Camel Press
PO Box 70515
Seattle, WA 98127

Cover design by Sabrina Sun

Contact: info@camelpress.com

ISBN (Paper): 978-1-60381-825-4
ISBN (Cloth): 978-1-60381-826-1
ISBN (eBook): 978-1-60381-827-8

Printed In The United States of America

For Tylea, Kat, and Regan.
And for my amazing wife, Amy,
whose dancing would be
the envy of Gracie.

Acknowledgments

Special thanks to the editing talents of Catherine Treadgold, and to the energy of my agent, Dawn Dowdle. And to Stephanie Nebel for showing so many people what is possible.

Chapter 1

Billy Wayne felt like he'd grown wings, a couple of bone and feather things ready to fly him away from this lousy place. His head ached a little, like it always did. But it wouldn't for much longer, not when he got these wings working.

"You walk out that door and you ain't never allowed back in, Billy Wayne Hooduk!" his mother shouted, the recliner under her bottom groaning from the massive weight. But Billy Wayne knew better. He was all too familiar with the mumbled pleadings in her tortured dreams. For a thousand nights he had cringed at the far edge of her bed, which reeked of the talcum powder she used on the sores under her breasts. He'd listened in the dark to her fear of him ever leaving, each word another pound of burden pressing down on his chest. Who would do the laundry and the shopping? Who would use the pumice stone on her corns? Who would help her out of bed to the toilet and wipe up her mess?

"I'm a fat old lady and I'm going to die alone in my own filth!"

Billy Wayne—who had baked his own birthday cake and bought his own thirtieth birthday present two weeks earlier—stopped on the top step, just on the other side of the storm door. He turned and squinted into the darkness. He could see the back of his mother's chair, her blubbery right arm draped over one side, a wad of tissues dangling. A soap opera flickered beyond the lunch tray he'd left for her. Billy Wayne recognized that the moment he dared turn his back and walk down the cracked front steps of his mother's house in Asbury Park, New Jersey, his life would change forever. He swore it would. It was his time. Once he had gone, nothing could bring him back, especially not his mother's threats.

Billy Wayne put down the small green Samsonite suitcase he was carrying to open the book that had caused these turn of events, this new chapter in his life. The book was due back at the library in three days, but the nice lady behind the library desk would just have to order a new copy. Libraries must get all their books for free since they let you read them for nothing. And this book had become Billy Wayne's bible, more precious to him than it would be to anyone else. Billy Wayne needed it. It had surely been written for him.

How to Become a Cult Leader in 50 Easy Steps had caught his eye as he was browsing in the Religion Section. He'd fumbled the skinny book off the shelf, knowing right away that he had been meant to find it. He opened to the first chapter, and there it was in black and white:

"How do you know you are the Chosen One?"

Billy Wayne read on.

"Do you hear voices in your head when nobody else is around?"

"Yes!" Billy Wayne was alone between the stacks, shaking his head. "Almost all the time."

"Have you noticed that people have come to rely on you more and more?"

"The bed pan," Billy Wayne said with a mixture of wonder and disgust.

"Do you feel the suffering of the sick on your back?"

"Oh, God." Billy Wayne was almost in tears of ecstasy and revulsion. "I have to sponge her privates."

"Have you been persecuted for your beliefs?"

"She threw all my *Screw* magazines in the trash and said I was a dirty sinner boy," said Billy Wayne in a hushed voice.

"Are you ready to rise from the ashes and take your place as the Chosen One?"

Billy Wayne's hands were shaking as he closed the book and clasped it to his thumping chest, letting the epiphany take full hold. Sweat dripped down his back, making his shirt stick to his skin.

"I am ready." All these books about Islam, Christianity, Judaism, Buddhism and the Rastafarian movement were stupid fakes, Billy Wayne thought. He ran his hand over the shiny cover of this marvelous book as he turned it over and over. He didn't expect to find an author's photo and so he wasn't disappointed. Did the Bible have photographs?

He opened back up to the first chapter. "Repeat these words: I am God."

"I am God." Coming from his mouth the words sounded hollow and whiney.

He tried again, deeper, with more authority: "I am God." *Better*, he thought, *much, much better*.

"How does saying those words make you feel?" he read.

Billy Wayne squinted in concentration, making an all-out effort to come up with an honest answer. He was overwhelmed with the notion that he must answer sincerely, not taking the usual shortcuts. His mother had nagged him about shortcuts—how he never finished anything he started, if he even got around to starting in the first place. Having enough money to supplement her disability checks was all she'd ever aspired to. As a teenager, Billy Wayne had written down all the names of the neighbors he was going to approach about cutting their lawns—all little square plots of grass that would take a few minutes each. He copied three dozen names from mailboxes and the phone book, but then he was distracted by a toy store flyer. Billy Wayne's new list was for all the cool new toys he planned to buy with at least some of the money he was going to earn. A day later, he grew bored of the toys he thought he had wanted. And the whole idea of waking up on Saturday mornings and mowing lawns seemed like so much work. What was in it for him, anyway? Billy Wayne spent his weekends behind sticky bowls half filled with brightly colored milk and a few remaining soggy bits of sugary cereal, entertained by violent cartoons.

Billy Wayne was barely a teenager when he came to accept his mother's assessment regarding the hill of beans he was destined never to amount to. Billy Wayne liked beans, especially smothered in catsup and honey, so the abuse rolled right off his plump back.

How did speaking the words "I am God" make him feel? Standing amid all the shelves of books—dispensing advice on dieting, having better sex, and making tons of cash selling real estate with no money down—Billy Wayne came up with what he considered an accurate assessment: "They make me feel big."

Billy Wayne Hooduk dug through his jeans pocket, found his library card, and handed it to the nice lady at the front desk. He stood nervously in front of the circulation computer as she scanned the bright yellow card and the bar code on the book. Tucking the receipt inside the front cover, she handed it back with a smile.

"It's due back in two weeks," said the kind library lady.

"God bless you." The words caught in his throat as he took the extraordinary book from her. What was supposed to be his first loving benediction came out a mumbled thank you, for all of his newfound confidence had already washed away. Billy Wayne turned from what was surely now a disparaging smile and ran for the door, heading home to pack his Samsonite and try out his new wings.

Chapter 2

The steady onshore breeze stacked the dark clouds into a wall less than a quarter mile from the Jersey shore, the wind forming an invisible barrier to lightning-filled cumulus clouds trying to push east. Billy Wayne sat on a boardwalk bench, enjoying the warm sunshine, while thunder rumbled behind him. It was a powerful feeling having all that energy right over his shoulder. He imagined he could summon it if necessary.

It was the last Thursday in May, and only a few people were stretched out across towels on the deep white sand. A bevy of kites were flapping in the distance, and a troop of industrious kids were busy digging a hole large enough to park a dune buggy in. *Or maybe they were preparing to trap a dune buggy*, Billy Wayne thought.

He gazed across the wide expanse of beach at the gray ocean, his Samsonite between his knees and the pages of his holy book open on his lap.

"I am God," Billy Wayne practiced. The cool sea breeze that slapped at the pages was refreshing on his face.

Billy Wayne had parked his '63 Dodge Dart at a meter right behind his bench. His mother was just four miles away, but the three small towns wedged in between were enough of a barrier for Billy Wayne to bask in his independence from everything but the parking meter. He cupped a damp nickel in his left hand, ready to drop it in should a cop happen along. He had eleven hundred dollars stuffed, tucked, and hidden in five different places on his person. He'd learned the method for protecting against muggers during a segment of *Good Morning America*. There was no telling how long it would be before his followers would start turning over their life savings, so he was prudently trying to conserve every last penny. Proselytizing was not going to pay off anytime soon. Billy Wayne knew he needed to keep reading.

Step number three from *How to Become a Cult Leader in 50 Easy Steps*: "Appearance and grooming: it is extremely important to wear a suit and tie when first recruiting followers. People must see you as authoritative. Picture yourself a school teacher who is also a door-to-door salesman. Your face and hands should have a nice tan, which can easily be applied. After establishing your following, appearance and grooming can and should be ignored. Think existentialism here. You will be seen as more spiritual with greasy tangled hair and body odor."

Billy Wayne adjusted his clip-on tie. Each time he'd summoned the courage to approach what appeared to be a lost soul, he lost his nerve. He'd been left standing awkwardly on one foot, stuttering a squeaky apology and cowering away, armpits dripping with sweat.

He looked down, examined his pudgy hands, and made a resolution to stop biting his fingernails.

Step number four: "If you are in shape and have a muscular physique, skip ahead. If you are fat, then you need to practice what is called 'Successfat.' 'Successfat' is a belief system wherein the fatter someone is, the more successful he has been in life. Most of the great kings and rulers in history have been terrible gluttons. This is you! Rise above your waistline! Don't slouch and continually pull your suit jacket over your great belly. No, a true Successfat celebrates his corpulence, patting his or her bay window without chagrin. Smile wide and warm and throw those meaty paws out and shake hands like you're sealing a deal, because you just may be!"

Billy Wayne sat up straighter and let his suit jacket fall away to his side to proudly display his fat belly. He smiled broadly, reaching out to shake an invisible follower's hand.

"Hey, what's your problem, buddy?" came a startled female voice in front of Billy Wayne, who immediately recoiled his hand as if electrocuted by the passing bikini bottom. "You fucking sicko!"

Billy Wayne flinched, expecting to be hit, but the woman was more than two benches away by the time he dared open his eyes. Her legs, glistening with suntan lotion, were made even longer by the inline skates. The bikini bottom he'd touched was cut way up over her tan hips. Billy Wayne guiltily watched her jiggling rear end grow smaller. Then he grabbed his suitcase and book, retreated to his Dart, and backed out onto the empty street to search for a cheap motel. Being God required careful fine-tuning. He needed to read and work on his recruiting skills.

On the lookout for the most faded paint and missing signage letters, Billy Wayne swung the Dart into the spot nearest the Belmar Arms Motel office door.

"It's forty-nine dollars and no hookers," said the leathery old man behind the counter. "Cash only."

Billy Wayne pulled off his right shoe and removed a moist pile of twenties and fifties. He peeled off two limp fifties and pushed them across the counter. The desk clerk eyed the bills but wasn't prepared to pick them up.

"Sorry," Billy Wayne said. "The rest is in my underwear."

"Room twelve." The old man snatched a key out of a large coop of mail slots and slapped it down next to the bills. "And no hookers."

"I swear." Billy Wayne grabbed the key and headed back out to reposition his car in front of door number twelve.

The soap in the tiny shower stall smelled like a urinal cake, but the near-scalding water emptied his sinuses and cleared his head, which seemed to hurt a little less since he'd left home. Billy Wayne twisted both knobs to "off" and leaned out of the curtain to listen for his mother's phantom voice. A puddle formed on the moldy tiles as he strained to hear; thirty years of incessant heckling was going to take some time to eject from his head.

Billy Wayne resumed lathering, wondering how long it would take before he was free from the haunting demands that had overshadowed every event in his life, including the only time he'd ever made love to a girl.

"Billy Wayne," his mother had said. "You get right off that dirty tramp!"

It had been four years ago, just before his mother had lost the ability to climb the stairs to the second floor of their house. Even then, she'd had to struggle, taking a long rest on the landing then using the railing to hoist herself up one step at a time.

Billy Wayne had snuck his girlfriend in through the kitchen door. At forty, Betty Katz was more of a woman than a girl. And since he'd had to pay her twenty-five dollars, she didn't exactly qualify as a girlfriend. But Billy Wayne wanted his first time to be special. He didn't want it to take place where she'd first suggested—in the backseat of his Dart, down behind the closed drugstore.

"You got a real nice house," Betty said, as Billy Wayne pulled her quickly toward the stairs, the music from *The Price is Right* wafting in from the living room.

"Shhh." Billy Wayne hurried her up the stairs to a small bedroom his mother kept ready for when her sister came to visit. "In here."

Behind the closed door, Billy Wayne tried to relax a little. He smelled her wonderful perfume and hoped it covered any bad smells he might be giving off. Betty was thick around the middle, and her large bosoms resting on her belly made her almost pumpkin-like. But her skin was so clean and soft that Billy Wayne nearly swooned in anticipation of what was about to happen.

Betty snapped her gum coyly, twisted a finger in her curly brown hair, and seemed to be waiting for Billy Wayne to make a move.

"What should I do?" Billy Wayne stood directly in front of her, looking her over from head to toe, clueless as to where to begin or how sex really worked. The thin material of her flowered blouse barely covered her breasts; the powder-blue stretch pants showed off every voluptuous curve and cellulite divot.

"Get my twenty-five dollars," Betty whispered, low and sexy. Billy Wayne could smell the menthol cigarettes on her breath, and it made him ache, his hardness trapped against his thigh by his Wranglers.

"It's all there." He shoved a wad of ones and fives at Betty, who tucked them into the front of her bra. She slipped past Billy Wayne to sit on the narrow single bed, then crab walked her way up to where his aunt's pillows waited.

"Come lay on me," Betty said, rolling her stretch pants and underwear down to her ankles and giving Billy Wayne his first look ever at a woman's privates other than his mother's. The hair was black and full, and there were creases that he didn't understand at all. He suddenly wasn't sure where his penis would go, just hoped it would fit into the proper place when he climbed on her.

"C'mon, big boy," she cooed, and Billy Wayne unzipped his jeans and stepped out of them one leg at a time. All his underwear had been in the wash, so his penis was now hidden only by his shirttail. *This is the first woman to see my penis other than Mother*, Billy Wayne thought, looking down over his round belly to where his penis flashed in the space between buttons.

Billy Wayne climbed onto the bed one knee at a time, lunging up toward Betty. Her legs were now spread wide, inviting, and Billy Wayne caught the scent of her wonderful odor. The fragrance was nothing like when he sponge-bathed his mother. Betty smelled like black licorice, and like something sour, too.

"Put this on." Billy Wayne nearly panicked at the little square wrapper. Put it on what? Put it on her? Was it cream? *Oh, God.*

"Here, I'll do it." He was immediately relieved. She tore open the wrapper with her teeth and pulled out a condom, reaching down to expertly roll it on Billy Wayne's penis.

"Oh, Jesus." She was the first woman, other than his mother, to touch his penis.

"You like that, don't you? Isn't that nice?" Betty stroked his sheathed penis. "Put it inside me, Billy Wayne."

As he'd feared, Billy Wayne could not find the mark, prodding too high, and then too low, poking a place that elicited an almost angry response out of Betty.

"Sorry," Billy Wayne whimpered, and Betty settled matters with her right hand and a quick shift of the hips.

"That feels good, doesn't it?" she asked in his ear, and Billy Wayne nearly swooned again. *This is sexual intercourse with a woman*, Billy Wayne thought to himself. *I'm having sexual intercourse.*

"You have to move," Betty said after a minute or two had passed. "Like this," she pulled and pushed on his hips, sending them into the slow rhythm of lovemaking.

The bed creaked and moaned under their combined weight. Billy Wayne was nearing his first ever orgasm with a woman when his mother's voice found him.

"Billy Wayne!" He could still hear her words dripping with revulsion and loathing. "You get right off that dirty tramp!"

Conditioning told him to obey, to do as he'd been told. He began to turn toward his mother, to tell her he was sorry, but it was too late.

"Oh, God," Billy Wayne moaned, ejaculating as Betty tried to pull out from under him, looking for something to cover herself with.

Four years later, Billy Wayne stood with his face turned up to meet the hot spray of the motel shower, erect penis in his soapy right hand, his mother's voice echoing in his head.

Chapter 3

Clean and refreshed from his long, hot shower, Billy Wayne gripped the wheel of his Dart as it rose up over the sparkling water of Manahawkin Bay. Seagulls lined the safety railing of the bridge, some squawking and preening, but most just watching the cars and trucks speed past on their way to Long Beach Island, a twenty-mile-long strip of land just off the southern New Jersey coast.

Bill Wayne passed a big surfboard shop with pictures of beautiful women and muscular young men plastered to its gigantic windows, then had to slam the Dart's brakes to avoid hitting a dozen people in the crosswalk under a red traffic light.

"Fuckhead," a teenage girl yelled through the sun glaring windshield, inches from his front bumper. His heart thumped heavily at the sight of her wonderful, bleach-blond hair flowing over her shoulders and her white t-shirt. Over his car hood Billy Wayne could see a lime green bikini bottom peeking at him as she slowly ambled toward the sidewalk and back out of his life.

He steered the car in the opposite direction of the girl, paying close attention to the busy intersections. The ocean was off to his right, a block away, hidden by tall dunes. Where to find people in need? Bars were an obvious choice, but along this stretch of road there were only a few souvenir stores, seafood restaurants, and increasingly expensive looking homes. A few blocks later, Billy Wayne slowed his car as he approached sets of tennis courts, pulling into a diagonal spot two spaces from where an ice cream truck was parked. A dozen small children had formed an erratic line, some on tiptoes, bouncing as if they had to pee, dollar bills in their hands. *Too young*, Billy Wayne thought, but maybe they had older brothers and sisters not far away. Tennis courts and a regular ice cream truck stop offered decent potential for recruiting followers. Billy Wayne pushed his hips forward to dig for the pen in his pocket. He wanted to write down the street number for future reference.

Billy Wayne was fishing deeper in his front pocket for loose change to buy an Eskimo Pie when a tap on his car roof startled him so badly he cried out, banging his knees sharply on the bottom of the steering wheel.

The police officer had dismounted his bicycle and was scanning the inside of his car through the passenger window. He frowned at Billy Wayne. "Drive away, buddy. Just put it back in your pants and drive away."

Billy Wayne's hands were shaking as he backed up. He cast one last brief, longing glance at the group of children and the colorful menu of ice cream treats on the side of the truck and pulled back into traffic.

Off to his left he caught peeks at Barnegat Bay, but the ocean remained hidden as the miles slowly passed. At the far end of the island, the traffic thinned. Homes became mansions, and sand started to creep out into the street from tree-filled lots.

Despite having grown up ten blocks from the Atlantic Ocean, he'd never actually been in it. Not even ankle deep.

"Where there's ocean, there's sand," Billy Wayne's mother had complained. "No good ever comes from the sand."

Billy Wayne's father had kicked him and his mother out after she'd come down with an unexplained pregnancy the year he started kindergarten. His mother, it turned out, had been impregnated during a brief fling with the pest control man who had been hired to do something about a nest of termites eating away at their house in Eatontown, New Jersey.

Billy Wayne had an almost mystical memory of the termite infestation. He'd been standing over a wide crack in the foundation when the termites decided living with the poison wasn't going to work out. The pudgy five-year-old had been poking a stick and killing a few of the termites that were emerging from the crack one by one, when the flood began. Hundreds, then thousands, then maybe millions of termites poured from the crack and took flight. A swarming, silent brown cloud of insects hung in the air just over his head, expanding like a great balloon, perhaps pausing to decide which way to go. Little Billy Wayne stood there looking up, mouth gaping in amazement as the mass of vibrating wings hovered like a genie just out of the bottle. After the last straggler emerged from the foundation, the cloud slowly elongated, seeming to rev up and drop into gear. With afterburners fired up, they blasted off due south, over the neighbor's houses, disappearing somewhere among the rooftops and brick chimneys.

"Holy shit!" he said.

Billy Wayne's mother was just stepping out of the kitchen door, the bug-killing impregnator right behind her. "Filthy-mouthed boy." She slapped the back of his head. But the slap didn't diminish what he'd just witnessed, and he could tell she wasn't really mad, anyway. In fact, Mom was acting a little strange and loopy as she walked the bug guy down the sidewalk to a truck with a gigantic green insect bolted to the roof. What kind of bugs had the man been killing in his parent's bedroom, and why had the door been locked with them both in it? What did Mom know about killing bugs?

A few months later, Billy Wayne and his pregnant mother would be taking roughly the same path as the expelled termites, due south toward a rental house in Asbury Park, since there was no way his father had been responsible for the fertilization.

Nobody ever sat down and explained the truth to Billy Wayne about what had happened. What he knew now came from years of eavesdropping, sitting at his mother's bloated feet under the kitchen table, invisible, a bored little boy listening to her long-distance confessions to relatives scattered in far away states. It was a collection of pieced together snippets of blubbering phone conversations to cousins, aunts, and nieces who seemed to welcome word of other people's misery.

His father had been rendered spermless from a motorcycle accident when Billy Wayne was two. He'd lost control of his treasured Harley when its front tires lost grip on a patch of sand deposited at an intersection by recent rains. It was one of those accidents that happened in the blink of an eye. One second he was fine, the next he was being held down by one paramedic, while another tried to free his crotch, which had become impaled on some broad's Cadillac radio antennae. The prized testicles of Billy Wayne's dad had been indelicately skewered, rendering him forever infertile.

After a few beers, James Robert Hooduk would express the opinion, loud and clear, to everyone within earshot that it was no great loss, anyway, since the one kid he knew about was a whiny lump of shit. You had a kid because it was what you did when you got married, like it or not. The Harley was the real loss. By his second six-pack, Jim Bob vowed to cut off the piece of shit insurance agent's balls if he ever saw him again. He repeated this vow to the mailman, also the paperboy who came to collect once a month.

It wasn't yelling and fighting that scared Billy Wayne, but the deafening, angry silence from his father, who loaded the boxes his mother had packed into the back of his pickup without a word. His dad drove back and forth from the rental his mother had found, depositing their lives on an overgrown front lawn. The man who towered over the little boy, spitting out curses at everyone from the mailman to the baseball pitcher on television, had stopped cussing. Billy Wayne saw it all bottled up above that burning red neck, maybe about to explode. Exploding would have been ten thousand times better, Billy Wayne knew. Better than being thrown away along with his mother. Better than being sent off to live alone in some strange house where that bug man might come find them. Billy Wayne had understood bits and pieces, enough to know that the bad man had done something terrible to his mother's belly.

Billy Wayne helped his crying mother pack, filling plastic garbage bags with his clothes, rolling up crayon drawings that had hung on his walls. He knew that if he was just a little older, he could have come up with the perfect thing to say to keep his father from sending them away.

"I don't wanna move away, Mommy," Billy Wayne said as he dragged a bag of toys into the kitchen. The ladder from a fire truck had punctured the bag, scratching a wavy line in the linoleum, which got his mother started on a whole new round of sobbing tears.

"We don't got a choice." She eyed the trail of sand that had also escaped from the torn bag. "Go make sure your closet is empty. We ain't comin' back for nothin'."

Billy Wayne's mom hated the way sand felt on her skin, would spin a dish towel into a whip to snap every bit off his clothes and bare skin if he'd been playing anywhere near it. She complained how it kept reappearing on your kitchen floor and how it caused your husband to lose his manhood, along with every last bit of kindness.

Allison Hooduk had confessed her sins to her sister over the phone, and Billy Wayne listened to every word, having stealthily crept around the living room couch to get the best angle for eavesdropping. They were barely settled into their new home, a small Cape Cod that had spent most of its life as a shore house rental. It was located too far from the beach to stay occupied. The distance from the beach suited Allison Hooduk just fine.

"Jim Bob wouldn't never have found out about the baby if it weren't for the sand that caused him to crash and lose his you-know-whats," his mother confided.

Billy Wayne was confused, trying to figure out what important things his father had lost, and why no one had gone out and searched for them.

Quiet again, and Billy Wayne craned his neck toward where Momma sat spread out on a chair at the kitchenette table, the long black phone cord coiled like a skinny snake around her arm.

"I just don't wanna go on livin' most of the time," she said. His mother's words scared the little boy. Who would take care of him if she wasn't livin'? His dad hadn't even answered the phone when Billy Wayne got the nerve to call him. Even a dad that yells at you was better than one that never wanted to see you.

After the baby came, and then died right before its first birthday, Billy Wayne watched his mother go from chubby to really fat. She stopped doing things outside and always told him she was too tired to play. She had been making Billy Wayne a grilled cheese when the baby slipped under the soapy water in one plugged-up side of the kitchen's double sink. The other sink was jammed with greasy pans, dirty dishes, and an old rubber duck that had gotten away from the baby. His mother had been rushing from the kitchen to the living room and back; some real important event had been going on in her soap, enough that she kept shushing Billy Wayne.

Billy Wayne had been confused by his mother's screams and crying but did manage to pull a chair over to the stove and twist the knob to "off" before the smoldering sandwich caught fire. He wanted to tell his mom it was okay, that he'd help her make another, but she just kept crying and rocking his wet naked little brother, all squeezed up tight in her arms.

Late that night, Billy Wayne's mom dragged him out of his bed, and the site of her wild hair and puffy face scared him badly enough that he didn't dare ask any questions.

"Come," was all she said, and he pulled on his dirty jeans and sweatshirt from the clothes pile as she turned and walked out of his room. He was tugging on one sneaker at a time, hopping on one foot then the other, as he watched her scoop up a wrapped bundle of rags from the kitchen table. She headed out the side door without looking back to see if he was done dressing.

Billy Wayne followed her down the dark, narrow sidewalk along Second Avenue. As they crossed Emory and Grand, Billy Wayne was glad there were no cars because she didn't seem to bother looking anywhere but straight down. They crossed Heck and Bergh streets before coming to the light at Kingsley. She never broke stride, stepping in front of a big black sedan that had to swerve to miss them, the driver hammering his horn and swearing something out his open window. His mom just kept going, and Billy Wayne could now hear the waves and see the low clouds that were lit by the reflecting street lights along Ocean Avenue.

Clutching the bundle of rags to her chest, Allison Hooduk led her son across the last patch of pavement and onto the deep sand. Halfway to the water, she dropped to her knees with a whimper. Billy Wayne sat down next to her, frightened for his mother, still not knowing what she was holding, but knowing it must be mighty important to have made her come down into the sand. Mighty important.

"Dig a hole, Billy Wayne," his mom finally said in a voice he didn't recognize. It was like the croaking of a frog, all thick and wet. But Billy Wayne obeyed. With his small hands, he pulled sand toward him in great scoops between his legs.

A half-hour later, exhausted, his hands burning and stinging from the coarse sand, Billy Wayne could dig no deeper. He'd reached wet clay about four feet down.

"I can't go no more," he whispered through dry lips, as he stood in a hole up to his shoulders. He was thirstier now than he'd ever been in his life, and his back ached like crazy.

"Come on out." His mom reached to pull him up. Allison Hooduk laid the bundle gently in the sand in front of her and slowly peeled back the layers of baby blankets to expose the impossibly white face of her youngest son.

"Is he dead, Mom?" Billy Wayne asked in a hushed voice, crowding against her shoulder to look down at his brother. His throat was raspy and dry, and it hurt to swallow. His brother looked like a sleeping doll, except that his eyes were open just a little bit. Billy Wayne had a sudden urge to reach down and push them closed but was afraid to touch him.

"Yes, that's right," she answered. A pair of seagulls circled overhead, probably checking to see if there might be an early breakfast down there.

"You want me to put him in the hole?"

"Yes, put him in the hole." She covered the baby's face back up. "Put him all the way down, real careful."

Billy Wayne did as he was told, laying his baby brother at the bottom of the hole, on top of the wet clay, small avalanches of sand cascading over the sides as he worked. The baby fit perfectly at the bottom, without any cramming, and Billy Wayne was relieved about that. He'd feared having to bend his little brother to make him fit.

"Go ahead." His mother indicated she wanted him to push the sand down and fill the hole.

"What do we do now?" Billy Wayne asked, but she was already turning away, struggling to her feet. "Momma?"

"You just finish up."

Billy Wayne hurriedly pushed the sand into the hole, not wanting to be left alone out there by that dark ocean and all that sand. He was almost in a panic as he swept the last bit flat, jumped to his feet and started running back toward where he thought his mom would be. His feet kicked up sandy rooster tails as he made his legs go as fast as they could. The feeling of sinking started to overwhelm him. The sensation of being pulled down by the sand, or something underneath the sand, drew yelping cries from the little boy, who was terrified of being sucked down and buried like his brother.

The seagulls continued circling overhead.

Whenever Billy Wayne was forced to endure sand, unpleasant visions of that night came back to haunt him. The mature, grown-up Billy Wayne, who knew sand was just sand, pushed thoughts of that dark night away, as he trudged through the deep white granules toward the lone figure of a boy he'd spotted on today's new mission.

"You got a dollar, mister?"

Billy Wayne had parked his Dart in the sandy lot of the Barnegat Light at the very northern tip of Long Beach Island. He wore his best suit and carried an important looking yellow legal pad recommended in step number seventeen of his book. The pad was to convey a sense of importance and substance to a prospective disciple. If not for some important reason, why else would someone be carrying a legal pad? A pen or pencil was optional.

"Fifty cents?" the boy tried again. Billy Wayne steered toward him, fishing in his pockets as he slowly approached, legal pad tucked beneath his double chin. But the only money he had on him was the wad of tens in his wallet and whatever was stuffed one sock, sometimes cramping the muscles in the arch of his foot. His heart raced at this unexpected opportunity, and he could feel the sweat glands in his armpits go into overdrive. He'd studied up on suggestions for peeling what the book called Odd Ducks away from the pack, but had only had time to glance at the section on Lone Ducks. He had read that even though loners might seem like easier targets, they tended to have their guard up in anticipation of fending off the mean people who were always just around the next corner preparing to hurt them. People at the edges of larger groups, trying but failing to fit in, were much more approachable. They wanted more than anything to be accepted into just about any group.

These people might seem a bit dim, but their eyes were wide open, and they were drawn to any smile that welcomed them like moths to a bare bulb. These people longed to be pulled into something bigger than themselves; they were ready.

"Relax," Billy Wayne whispered to himself, holding the legal pad tightly in his left hand while attempting to keep his right hand dry by wiping it on his pant leg as he walked.

The boy sat in the shade of the enormous lighthouse. The lower third of the Barnegat Light was painted white; the rest, up to the metal crow's nest that surrounded its large windows, a rich burgundy. The sand walkway leading to the base of the building was deep and white, with an old, sun-bleached split rail fence to keep visitors off the dunes. Small trees and grasses held the dunes together, despite the harsh weather this exposed area endured. Most of the vegetation was a healthy green, showing new growth from the mild spring and recent rains.

"I have a ten dollar bill if you'd be willing to hear me out for a few minutes." Bill Wayne offered his hand for a shake. The boy, no older than fifteen, looked up at him, scoping out the best escape route at the same instant, but held fast.

"My name's Reverend Billy Wayne." He displayed his whitest and brightest smile, pulling his hand back casually to show there was no offense taken. "I s'pose in this day and age a young person needs to be especially vigilant 'bout who he lets near, am I right? World's gettin' crazier and crazier, it seems."

The boy shrugged his shoulders and Billy Wayne relaxed a little. So far so good. *Take it slow*, Billy Wayne reminded himself and then did a quick mental review of step number twenty-four of his book: "Most young people respond to the 'Us versus Them' scenario. A child is alone for a reason; either he's escaping an angry parent or older sibling or he's having trouble with a teacher or the kids at school. Show you understand, and that you, too, have suffered the same unfair persecution. Soon you'll develop a bond that will lead to loyalty and dedication."

"You remind me of myself when I was your age," Billy Wayne began, but the kid's bulging eyes at the impossibility of this statement made him backtrack. "I mean, I spent a lot of time alone when I was young. My dad used to drink and beat the pants off me."

"You ain't a homo are you?" the boy asked earnestly.

"Ah, no, son, I ain't a homo, last I checked." Billy Wayne regrouped his fake smile. Why did people keep asking him that? "If I swear I ain't a homo, can I take a load off?"

"Yeah, whatever."

Billy Wayne dropped to the sand with a grunt, leaning back against the white cinderblocks of the lighthouse foundation.

Okay, this is good, this is very, very good, Billy Wayne thought, although both his shoes were now half-filled with goddamn sand.

"I'm Tommy," the kid said.

"Nice meetin' ya, Tommy." Billy Wayne adjusted his coat to proudly display his belly while trying to hide the fact that his legal pad was blank. He'd have to write some things down and busy it up for the next time. Maybe some math problems would look good.

"Tommy, you believe in God?"

"My mom does." Tommy pulled a crumpled green soft-pack of Marlboro Menthols from the back pocket of his cutoff jeans. "She believes God is who put my good-for-nothing father and her piece of shit son on this earth to torture her each and every day."

Us versus Them, Billy Wayne thought as the boy lit a cigarette and blew a stream of smoke out both nostrils, then turned his head away. Billy Wayne had read that when someone turned just their head away from you, it meant a level of trust had been achieved.

"Wow, so you know what I'm saying about my dad, huh?" Billy Wayne said. "Parents can be pretty screwed up."

"You can say that again."

"My mother was pretty tough, too. I couldn't hang out with my friends. Seemed like I always had to be doing homework and never got to watch TV."

Billy Wayne didn't blush one bit at these lies. He, of course, never had any friends to go anywhere with, stopped doing any sort of school work at an unusually early age, and was always welcome to lie down on the living room couch and watch soap operas to keep his mother company. He was pretty much free as a bird, as long as he kept his mother stocked with cans of Coke and bags of sugar cookies from the dollar store. She sometimes even paid Billy Wayne a quarter for slathering her feet in Vaseline Intensive Care lotion, rubbing real hard between her toes.

"So you became a preacher?"

"Yes, I guess you could say I found my calling." Billy Wayne was trying to figure his next move, maybe see if the boy was hungry and buy him a cheeseburger or something. Bringing out the big guns and announcing he was God didn't seem the right tactic to use with a kid. Not yet, anyway. Although Billy Wayne was feeling more and more at ease as a counselor.

"Hey, you hungry at all? Let's go grab a bite and talk over a burger or somethin'. Be my treat."

"I got no place else to be." The boy hopped to his feet with ease, while Billy Wayne had to grope at the side of the building to rise from the deep sand. Christ, his shoes were *more* than half-filled with this goddamn sand. The dark-haired boy was taller than Billy Wayne had estimated and a lot broader in the shoulders. *He has the makings of a fine first disciple*, Billy Wayne thought. And the kid actually had some manners, gesturing for Billy Wayne to go first down the narrow sand path that led back to the parking lot.

Billy Wayne was feeling like a fisherman, coming back to port with a big trophy catch hauled in from the high seas. He felt better than he'd felt in weeks, maybe months. Heck, maybe ever! This might not be so hard after all. It was just about being able to talk to people, being yourself.

"My car's up here or we can ... Ouch!" Billy Wayne screamed, stars flying across his vision and his knees buckling from the staggering weight that had banged across the back of his head. Billy Wayne lurched first one way, then the other, as though trying to stand up on a floating lounge chair in a swimming pool. The world was rotating but his eyes couldn't keep up, and he realized he was going down just as another heavy blow cracked down on the top of his skull, sending him sprawling in the sand.

"Fucking homo," he heard from somewhere in another room or maybe another planet, what with all the stars and blackness. He tried to blow some of the sand from his mouth, but it was all coated and stuck to his tongue. Billy Wayne then felt he was being levitated and realized the kid was lifting him by his belt. The muscular boy rummaged through his front pant's pockets and then dropped him to snatch the wallet from his back pocket.

Billy Wayne's ears were receiving a high pitched ring and it felt like a sizzling-hot needle had been plunged into his right temple, but he was still able to hear the boy unzipping his jeans somewhere up above. A warm stream of piss started at the back of Billy Wayne's neck and then drew a line up the back of his head, finally finding his right ear. The boy's piss sent the ringing underwater, dulling the pitch, which actually made the sharp pain subside a bit.

Then Billy Wayne lay there alone, only moving enough to begin taking inventory of the damage. His vision had returned and he could see the very top of the lighthouse, just above the gray fence and stubby trees. His feet moved and he wiggled the toes on his bare left foot; he'd apparently lost one of his good shoes in the attack and would have to find it.

His book said how important it was to have good shoes. Billy Wayne concluded he was probably okay, except for the salty taste of sand and piss and one thumping headache. He used the front of his incisors to scrape the sand off his tongue, spitting out little clumps.

Jesus was a martyr, Billy Wayne thought. He sacrificed his life for his beliefs and to redeem us from the original sins of his forefather, Adam.

Step number twenty-six in *How to Become a Cult Leader in 50 Easy Steps*: "When life gives you lemons, make lemonade! When suffering your own seemingly monumental setbacks, take into consideration that the original cult leader was beaten, stoned, whipped, and nailed to a cross. Now, as you stand there feeling sorry for yourself, has your day really been that bad?"

"Yes," Billy Wayne groaned as he found his way to his knees before trying out his legs. He resisted the urge to remain kneeling, whimpering there in the sand for the rest of his life. The smell and taste of urine was horrible, and the wet sand sticking to his arms and face was itchy. He knew his mother would let him come home. He could tell her how sorry he was for leaving, that he couldn't live without her. He could promise to be a good boy from now on, to stop being foolish. She'd have to take him back because she needed him.

"No." Billy Wayne leaned forward to punch the deep sand. "I'm not giving up."

Billy Wayne let a new wave of nausea pass before rising to his feet and stumbling down the path toward his car, spitting tiny grains of sand as he went. He spotted his lost shoe on the other side of the split rail fence near the parking lot and strained to squeeze his fat torso through to reach it. The shoe was also damp with piss. Billy Wayne decided another long hot shower should wash this day away. Maybe buying a gun would help him avoid another one like it.

Chapter 4

The phone book in the Belmar Arms Motel was so fat, its soft spine and pages rubbed so smooth by age, it acted like liquid in Billy Wayne's lap. Each time he attempted leafing through a section, it tried pouring itself onto the floor.

The old guy planted behind the counter watched Billy Wayne's struggle. "Book is old like me. Ain't got no bones left."

The stub of a pencil and scrap of paper Billy Wayne also held made it even harder to corral the phone book. His head was tender in two spots, but the headache had mostly passed, and he was determined to continue his mission properly armed.

"If you're looking for a massage girl, you best make certain it ain't for no house call. I'll kick your butt right outta here, and don't even think about a refund."

Billy Wayne had decided the old clerk wouldn't be the best person to ask about buying a gun, so he'd opted for the Yellow Pages.

Everything Billy Wayne knew about guns had been learned from cop shows. His mother sometimes mentioned them, but only to tell Billy Wayne he might as well go down to the corner store and buy a gun so she could kill herself. When he was little, he pictured a real store down on the corner that stocked these special suicide guns, with curved barrels that aimed the bullet back at the shooter. He imagined the proprietor wore a sinister black cloak, face hidden deep within the dark hood so nobody could tell which person from the neighborhood was the owner. Maybe, while he gave you your change, the man would reach out with your dollar bills clenched in a white, bony skeleton of a hand.

Billy Wayne found a sporting goods store that promised guns and ammunition of all sorts and sizes, and jotted the street and town on a slip of yellow paper torn from his legal pad. The listing was in the Yellow Pages at the back of the book and included two lines advertising how they served the brave men, women, and families of Fort Dix. Billy Wayne considered asking the old clerk for directions but decided to make this journey on his own. Now that he had a plan, he needed to stop relying on others. He knew Fort Dix was maybe a half hour away, somewhere off to the south.

Billy Wayne followed road signs and found the turn for Tom River with gratifying ease. But after an hour of hopeful turns, Billy Wayne's Dart had begun to overheat and was nearly out of gas. Giving in to asking for help became much easier, and he found a group of teenage boys hanging around the front steps of a convenience store in a place called West Tuckerton.

"You can't miss it," the boy said of the sporting goods store. "Left out of the lot, then the second right. Then just keep on going."

"It's kind of in the middle of nowhere," added another boy, and Billy Wayne misinterpreted the snickering from two others, used to having teenagers laugh at him for no reason other than his presence.

"Thank you, boys, and God bless." Billy Wayne backed his Dart out of the space to another round of snickering.

He drove his old Dodge Dart down the long, straight road, all his windows open to let in the salty air.

As suspicious as Billy Wayne currently was of teenage boys, it didn't dawn on him that they might be sending him down a long, dead end road into the flat, grassy marshes for a laugh. He drove over the last small bridge, which stood about six feet above the water and muck, scanning the gray horizon for any signs of a bigger road that might lead to a town and a sporting goods store. The only sign of anything other than nature was the gravel drive running off to the right, returning on his left after it appeared to make a large loop. He also noticed a weathered wood sign painted with the words, "Fish Head."

"Fish Head Island," Billy Wayne guessed and then drove down the other side of the bridge onto the island, using his blinker to turn right. He was deciding whether to risk getting stuck in the mud turning around or to just drive all the way around the loop, when he came to a spot where the bay opened up to the ocean off to his right. He stopped his car to watch several specks race and bob across the horizon, finally recognizing them as jet skis.

It was in this remote place that Billy Wayne began to feel something foreign, a sense of unease. Other than the times he locked himself in his bedroom, he had rarely been alone, always in calling distance of his mother. Every peaceful moment was always tarnished by the cringing awareness of his mother's impending plaintive demands. Billy Wayne was a beaten dog when it came to enjoying peace and quiet. He mostly winced through those calm moments, too jittery to ever enjoy them.

He parked his Dart and stepped out into the morning sun, which rose up over this calm section of water. Facing due east, he saw a fairly narrow channel out to the Atlantic, where strips of land reached from both the left and right across several hundred yards of glassy water. Off in the distance was a gigantic tanker ship, big and dinosaur-like, silhouetted by the glare of the sky.

For as far as Billy Wayne could see, there wasn't another human being other than those hidden inside the far-away tanker, now that the jet skiers had disappeared. Billy Wayne could almost taste the solitude, his senses sharpening like someone who had been deaf but could suddenly hear. He was certain there was something very special about this place.

On Fish Head Island, the sky was a blue-gray dome, a steel cathedral overhead. Billy Wayne thought he'd been sent to this place by a power greater than a juvenile delinquent; there was an undeniable spiritual aura, notwithstanding the crumpled condoms underfoot.

There simply had to be an important reason he'd been led to this bleak but glorious spot, busy only with darting seagulls and tiny fish breaking the surface of the bay to escape bigger fish. Billy Wayne felt for the little ones under assault, leaping into what was to them an airless world for momentary freedom. He'd suffered a thousand dreams of being chased by something with awful teeth and scales.

Billy Wayne regretted wearing his best shoes but felt compelled to explore, especially since there seemed to be no dangerous teenagers lurking about. He reached back into the car for his yellow legal pad, just in case, and took a walk down a path through the sea grass off to the right. He was a little surprised at all the trash in such a remote area; then he remembered watching a television show with his mom about places in Hawaii where all the garbage from Japan would wash up, making that tiny slice of paradise look like a garbage dump. Maybe this was the same thing. Maybe even Heaven had a big pile of soiled mattresses and non-biodegradable debris stacked up against the Pearly gates, flotsam and jetsam from mortals below.

The path was interrupted by a narrow canal that seemed a little too wide to hop across. Litter was strewn throughout the sea grass, from faded Dunkin Donuts boxes to mashed beer cans and nasty, poop-streaked diapers.

The path continued on through slightly taller grass on the other side, and Billy Wayne stood for a moment to calculate his chances. Throughout his entire life, this was the exact type of challenge he'd avoided, opting for safety. But that wasn't how he was going to live the rest of his life. Things were different now, and he could feel the power and strength of his new purpose-driven existence.

"I can do it." Hearing his own words encouraged him even more.

He took a few steps back to allow for a running start, clutched his legal pad so as to not flap and create drag, and twisted from side to side to limber up his back and legs. Billy Wayne eyed the landing, bent his knees and said, "On your mark, get set, go!"

The last step before take-off was more slippery than expected. Instead of taking a graceful leap out and over the narrow canal, Billy Wayne's feet were suddenly headed skyward. It was like slipping on a banana peel the way people did in cartoons or in old slapstick movies. Billy Wayne entered the warm, salty water head first and was practically pile-driven through the three feet or so of water, deep into the brown muck. Letting go of his prized legal pad, he sank both hands into the slime all the way to his elbows before gaining enough leverage to extricate his head. Despite ears filled with years of decaying flora and fauna, Billy Wayne heard the loud sucking pop as his head was freed from the bottom of the canal. He splashed and flailed to his knees. On all fours, Billy Wayne arched his back to get his chin above the water line and gulped a mouthful of air, gasping for breath.

"You okay, buddy?" a man's voice called down from somewhere behind him.

"Help," was all Billy Wayne could manage. He froze, trying not to shift his knees or hands for fear of sinking deeper into the mud and back under the stinking, horrible tasting water.

"Hang on." Billy Wayne heard the man step into the water, sending a series of miniature waves to break against his raised ass. The man straddled Bill Wayne from behind, reaching under his chest to pull him to a more stable sitting position, and Billy Wayne was grateful to have his face clear of the churning brown water, where he imagined there must be a thousand poisonous snakes.

"Gimme your hand, boss." Billy Wayne blinked away mud and looked up to see a wrinkled and splattered tan uniform. Not a cop, but some sort of ranger reached out to lock hands with him. The ranger guy had a scruffy, unshaven face, and Billy Wayne was immediately envious of the big gun strapped inside a holster and hanging from his hip. Leaning away, the man pulled Billy Wayne to his feet, then steadied him for the three sloshing steps to dry land. First one then the other shoe was sucked off, claimed by the muck at the bottom of the canal.

Released from the man's iron-like grip, Billy Wayne struggled out of his muddy suit jacket and stood in floppy socks that had been pulled half off.

"Warden Flint." He reached his muddy hand back out for Billy Wayne to shake. "What were you doin'?"

"I, uh, came down for a walk." Billy Wayne tried to come up with a reason other than his divine vision, which seemed completely ridiculous at the moment. "I was trying to pick up some trash floating there in the water and I lost my balance."

The icy suspicion in the warden's eyes softened a bit.

"Billy Wayne Hooduk." He took the warden's hand in a muddy clasp, his composure coming back in uneven little pieces. "I hate to see such a beautiful place all trashed, you know?"

                         ❧   ❧   ❧

Flint had an uncanny ability to put a face to a name, and a slightly blurry catalog of faces ran across his vision as if he were flipping through a deck of baseball cards. Despite the thousand liters of cheap Russian vodka he'd consumed over the last couple of decades—and how much a face changed from boyhood to manhood—Clayton Flint knew he'd had some dealing with this pasty, fat little man from the moment he opened his round mouth. The eyes were set too

31

close, the nose was too small in contrast to the chubbiness of the cheeks, and the chin was barely discernable.

Finally, it was the mouth that gave the face a name, or at least told him where he knew it from. The prissy, goldfish-like round mouth was the same as the boy's mother's. The little bastard had sulked outside the locked bedroom door, whining for cereal or something, while Flint was pinning his kooky mom to the mattress for one of their half-dozen afternoon romps, back when he ran his commercial pest control business. Sure as shit, standing there before him was that same little turd blossom.

For a moment Flint stood lost in memories of the days when there had been real purpose to his pest control efforts. Those neighborhoods were chock full of lonely and misunderstood housewives, and he provided a little shot of real Flint, yes, sir.

But then Flint's brow furrowed at a memory just outside the reach of his vodka-soaked capacity. Something bad was attached to the memory of Mrs. Hooduk ... What the hell was her name? Flint worked his brain, searching through letters of the alphabet. Her name, he decided, began with an L or an A. Somethin' like Lisa?

"I got some fairly clean rags up in my truck," Flint offered. "That shit'll stink up your car somethin' bad."

"I'd sure appreciate it, Warden." Billy Wayne's suit was plastered to his fat body, his white shirt ruined for sure, probably his suit as well. He blew his nose on his sleeves, and mud came out in slimy little clumps. Billy Wayne fell in line behind the ambling Flint, the toe portions of his stretched out socks flopping as they trailed behind his heels.

"Allison!" Clayton Flint nearly shouted and coughed real quick to cover up his revelation.

"Pardon?" Billy Wayne said absently, padding across all the God-forsaken pointy things hidden under the mat of sea grass.

"Watch your step here," Flint said. "Some broken glass up 'round this spot."

The little man cringed behind him.

Allison Hooduk had been a first-class basket case, for sure. She was from one of those Eatontown termite jobs. Jesus, those neighborhoods were a gold mine. Chase the bugs out of one house and right into the next. Couple weeks later, you got a frantic call to come spray the same damn swarm under a different roof. Any good pest control expert, Flint could tell you, knew how to make even the most roach infested crack house absolutely insect free by herding them right on over to the neighbors. Ka-ching!

The Hooduk job, Flint now recalled, had involved a nest of termites that hadn't really gotten going into the wood, although he'd explained the dire need for a full treatment. The lady of this house had the sweetest round mouth, and real meat in all the right places. This pest control expert liked some flesh to hang onto when the lights went down, yes, sir. And the Hooduk woman was quick to let Flint know the coast was clear as far as the husband was concerned. That was how Flint knew he was gettin' the nod: when the wife made it perfectly clear what time mister so-and-so was due home, and that mister so-and-so was not inclined to come home unexpectedly.

But that fat little pain in the ass of hers was another story. "Mommy, I'm hungry. Mommy, I'm thirsty. Mommy, how come the door's locked?"

"We're killin' bugs in here, hon."

"But I'm hungry now!"

"You go right ahead and fix yourself a peanut butter on bread," Allison Hooduk huffed, as Clayton Flint humped away doggy-style, which was his favorite way to do a woman with such a nice wide behind. He loved the waves he caused in the fat, as he slapped his groin against her large raised buttocks. Sometimes he'd reach forward and grab hold of a handful of hair and yank it back a little. Had he done that to *her* hair?

"What's that bumping noise, Mommy? Who's jumping on your bed? I'm hungry!"

He'd gotten paid for the job and was perfectly in the clear until a month or two later. That's when he started getting those crazy-ass calls on his answering machine.

"Please, you gotta call me back," was the gist of her first message, and had Clayton Flint not just come from a very successful and satisfying afternoon job at another lonely broad's roach-infested home, he just might have. It wasn't beyond him to go back and lay some more pipe, but the pipe was good and done for the day. Instead, he erased the message and forgot about it, until another flood of whiney calls came in a week later. Allison Hooduk had some nutty idea she was knocked up, or some such bullshit, and was trying to pin the blame on his sorry ass. Flint became very wary of answering his telephone, as well as any knocks at his door. Best let those things work themselves out on their own.

But now, Flint wondered with dread what had become of the woman and the alleged baby.

"You got any younger brothers or sisters?" Billy Wayne seemed to flinch at the question, the jumpy little bastard.

The two had reached Flint's pickup with the mist blower mounted in the bed. Billy Wayne took a grease stained towel from Flint, wiped his hands, and then used it to scrape away some of the muck that had begun to coagulate.

"I'm an only child. My mother and father divorced when I was little, and my mom never really moved on. It hit her pretty hard."

Oh, shit, Flint thought. He prided himself with not having a single guilty bone in his body and hadn't anticipated growing any new bones at sixty years of age. So where was this guilt coming from? Too much time alone in the marsh, he figured. Too much poison had made its way into his fragile system.

Billy Wayne looked to be faring a little better now that he had his socks off; he was examining a couple of tiny scratches on the soles of his feet. He'd dumped what appeared to be a wad of soggy cash from each sock, squeezed out some brown water, and shoved it into his pants pockets. He accepted a second towel from the warden, eyeing his gun like he was jealous. Flint surely enjoyed men feeling jealous of his big gun.

"Never had no children of my own," Flint said. "What line of business you in?"

"I'm a preacher of sorts. I came down here to enjoy some quiet time just between me and Him." Billy Wayne didn't want to admit that the boys had tricked him into following the road down here.

"Is that so?" Flint stuck Billy Wayne right into the nutcase category. He'd never had much use for any kind of religious folk.

"And I couldn't help feelin' terrible about all the trash people leave behind."

Flint pulled him back out of the nutcase category for the time being.

"Hey, you mind me asking what type of gun you have there?"

A medium-sized grin cracked Flint's thorny, sun-weathered face. Warden Flint paused for just a second, then clicked open the passenger side door of his official-use truck, grabbing a shiny new bottle of Russia's not-so-finest from a toolbox on the floor.

"You like guns, boy?" He twisted open the screw cap, offering the bottle to the chubby little man. There was some good in most everyone, Clayton Flint decided. And with the sun now halfway up in the sky, a man didn't need an excuse to tip back a few to soften his fall.

Chapter 5

Billy Wayne and Warden Clayton Flint each sat on their own grease-stained towel spread over black mud and passed the bottle of cheap Russian vodka back and forth, gulls swooping in from time to time to check for French fries or whatnot.

With the end of the bottle near, even a dedicated drinker like Flint was drunk off his uniformed ass. And as drunk as he was, he was getting a kick out of the muddy little guy drinking from the bottle just like a high school kid sneaking a smoke out in back of the gymnasium. He'd check behind them real quick, eyes dartin' all around before tippin' the bottle, and then hand it back fast like it was a hot potato. Sure seemed like he had some sorta hell looking over his shoulder. Flint had half a notion it might be that loon mother of his.

"You are not." Flint gagged on his pull from the bottle, coughing and laughing. "God?" Vodka sprayed from his nose, burning, causing his eyes to tear up.

"Yes, I surely am." Billy Wayne shook his head with drunken sincerity.

"So, lemme get this straight." Flint was amused just the same as he'd been from the fifty other drunk men in bars over the years who'd suddenly decided they, too, had become God, Jesus Christ, or even Satan himself. Hell, he'd probably told people he was God a few times but had been too far gone to remember. "You just woke up one day and shazzam, you're God Almighty?"

"Well, there was a process," Billy Wayne said.

Flint really didn't want to hurt the guy's feelings. It seemed he'd already screwed up the poor bastard's life by knockin' up his goony mom. *Ah, but there was some fine junk in that crazy broad's wide trunk*, Flint thought.

"You ain't got a church?"

"No," said Billy Wayne. "Not yet."

"And you ain't got a congregation?"

"No, but I'm workin' on it."

"What are you gonna preach about?"

Billy Wayne just sat there looking at Flint, a drunken glaze over his eyes.

"Guess that's the tough part," Flint said.

Clayton Flint had only been inside a church four times in his life and all were for professional reasons. The Methodist church in Wanamassa had carpenter ants from the basement up to the damn steeple. Getting up into the steeple was a bitch on his sore back, and there was no way in Hell he was going to part the legs of the broad with the keys. The woman did have a little shape on her, but she wore a mustache on her upper lip even a shot of DDT couldn't scare off.

"I never been to church." Flint held the nearly empty bottle out in front of him as if to inspect the contents. "Never saw no need."

The bright overhead spring sun cast harsh shadows around the two inebriated men. The marsh and ocean beyond lost some of their color this time of day.

"I just got beat up by a kid," Billy Wayne blurted out, taking a small sip from the bottle. "And he robbed me."

"Fucking kids," Flint said sympathetically. "No real good ever comes from kids."

"And then he pissed on my head." Tears began to well up in his eyes. "Nobody ever pissed on me before."

"That's rough." Flint felt more like a heel than ever about nailing his mother and not answering his phone. She did have a fine set of knockers, though, with them jumbo nipples that looked like friggin' plates. "I pissed myself more times than I can count but never had nobody else piss on me. I seen it done in skin flicks. Made me wanna barf." He burped long and hard and threw up a little in his mouth, spitting it out next to his towel. He was casual, as if it happened all the time.

"I need a gun like yours."

Flint was now lying on his side, propped up on his left elbow, his long legs extended in the sand, crossed at the ankles. He reached down with his right hand to pat the .44 Magnum on his thigh. He hadn't discharged his sidearm in at least five years, since a raccoon had come charging up out of the marsh while he was on his back under the truck. He'd been using coat-hanger wire to reattach the tail pipe when the son-of-a-bitch came hissing and stomping out of the grass like it was a pissed-off wolverine. He'd seen a television show about those crazy fuckers; you didn't wanna be cornered by them for the life of you.

Flint's first reaction was to wonk his forehead on the undercarriage, while his second was to unbutton his holster and pull out his loaded forty-four. He had a clear and easy shot right down between his legs—a little low and he'd shoot off his pecker from that angle—as the rabid actin' coon made its final insane charge. After blowing the animal to smithereens, Flint wriggled out from under the truck and poked its body with the toe of his boot. There probably wasn't enough left of its head to consider shipping off to be confirmed for rabies, even if Flint had been inclined to do so. Why bring any unnecessary attention on his quiet sanctuary? And then there would be all the friggin' paperwork.

Instead, Flint picked the coon up by the tail, walked back to the edge of the swampy marsh, and swung the dead animal in two big arcs before flinging it as far as he could. Little bits of blood and gore parted from the spinning raccoon as it sailed out and splashed down. Flint knew there weren't any insects to eat or cart off the corpse, what with all the poison he released into the immediate environment on a weekly basis, but the marsh had a way of consuming, of slowly rotting away, anything it got its hands on. And Flint had looked down at his own hands out here at the edge of the swamp. He'd put them all over this poor bastard's momma, and now look what they'd done. Fucking guy thought he was the Lord above.

Flint struggled to his feet, stumbled sideways into the rear quarter-panel, and then slid along his truck for balance to retrieve a fresh bottle.

"Boy, you'd be better off with something that has a little less kick than this girl." Flint rubbed the side of his big holster as if it were a beloved pet. "Somethin' tucked away for emergencies."

"Bringing the word can be dangerous," Billy Wayne said earnestly, digging at the sand in front of him with his white feet.

"Okay, so you need a small gun and a good place to find people who need to be closer to God, am I right?"

"That about sums up my life right now."

"Well," Warden Clayton Flint began, "you just happen to be about half an hour from Valhalla. Ever hear of Valhalla?"

"Something to do with Vikings?"

"I ain't talkin' 'bout fucking Vikings." Flint dropped back down on his stained towel next to Billy Wayne, too exhausted to crack open the new bottle just yet. "I'm talkin' about a magic place adorned with gold, where people go to find treasures, anything they could ever possibly want. Right down the Parkway a couple of exits; it's a place called Atlantic City."

Chapter 6

A plump housefly landed on Graceful Gracie's tongue, preened its wings, walked in two tight circles, and then seemed to fall asleep standing. Gracie did not expend the energy to pull her tongue back into her toothless mouth. For a bee, yes, but she let the fly have its peace.

The line of traveling circus trucks rumbled forward, as they always had and always would, in Gracie's world. It was hot and the old dancing bear's belly ached from the meaty things she'd discovered in the trash earlier that morning, just before being told to climb into her cage. Gracie had known the meat was spoiled, but self-control was not a bear-like trait. The absence of this trait had left her nose with tiny scars from the dozens of times she'd tried stealing from the disagreeable tiger's food dish. The roll of fat around her middle, despite all the hours dancing, was from pilfering the guard dog's dinners. He'd be off barking and threatening, while Gracie would be slinking away with a stolen plastic bowl of beef kibble.

Bears might be fat, but dogs were stupid.

And now, during this long leg of the circus' journey to Atlantic City, Gracie had the runs. She shifted her back legs, careful not to disturb the fly on her tongue, watching the truck behind her through the bars of her cage. The old lion and bad-tempered tiger rode on the back of that one, one cage stacked on top of the other. If their cages were next to each other, the cats would fight and complain the whole way.

The Pisani Brothers Circus caravan made a sweeping right turn up the slight hill of an entrance ramp—animals and people sliding a little to the left—and engines were gunned to speed up on the new stretch of highway. Speeding up was a relative term for a line of decrepit circus trucks, since they really could only manage about half the speed limit.

The five container trucks wore exquisite American graffiti, acquired from artisans in towns called Sopchoppy, Monkey's Eyebrow, and even Shoulderblade, Kentucky.

"Suck my Monkey's Eyebrow," read the side of one truck.

Two flatbed eighteen-wheelers carried the rides and animals on their oxidizing backs, followed by a dozen other pickups and passenger cars, all of which would have looked right at home at a demolition derby. The procession crawled across the flatlands of South Jersey on the AC Expressway, blatting a choking blue smoke from leaky engine blocks, a frustrating bulwark to silver-haired card-sharks and all-you-can-eat aficionados.

And then it was apparently time to swap positions in a game of follow the leader; the lion-and-tiger truck driver pulled into the passing lane and began to slowly overtake Gracie's truck. The car drivers weren't the least bit happy about this new development and were all horns and flashing lights in the passing lane's growing line. The cranky tiger in the top cage arose from his bedding and did circles of his own, agitated by the ruckus below.

As the passing truck was side-by-side with Gracie's, she turned her yellow eyes toward a driver who had brought his shiny car to within a foot of the rusting back bumper of the tiger truck. Even with her not-so-great eyesight, Gracie could tell the driver was spitting mad and wanting to get past the truck right at that instant. The driver, who to Gracie seemed an awful lot like the tiger up above, had opened his window to bark insults. Gracie did not understand human language much, but sometimes you got the gist.

The tiger did understand, roaring back a snarling reply.

Not satisfied with mere words, the tiger backed its ass against the rear of its cage, and Gracie nearly smiled, despite her rueful tummy. She knew what the tiger was up to, had seen the long, sleek muscles extending and then contracting under its coat. The tiger shimmied one last time, arched its back, and then let go a thick, almost orange stream of urine. The pee was caught by the wind, turned into fine droplets by turbulence, and sprayed down onto the windshield of the tailgating car.

The driver tried rolling up his window with one hand, while reaching for the wiper switch with the other. The man's car swerved, and its right front bumper thumped Gracie's truck hard enough to startle her, even though she'd been watching all along.

In the commotion, Gracie accidentally swallowed the fly who'd been dozing on her tongue. She felt a frenzied buzz and queer tickle in her throat, but it was too late for the fly. Its death made her sad. But that's how it was with a traveling circus, even for a fly hitching a ride. You're going along all peaceful and fine, getting comfortable with your day, and maybe bravely considering the prospects of tomorrow.

Then something swallowed you whole.

Chapter 7

On the fourteenth floor of Atlantic City's once luxurious Lucky Dollar Hotel and Casino, Acapulco de la Madrid Cordero coiled the long vacuum cleaner cord with hands and fingers gnarled from arthritis. The ancient, threadbare carpet was as clean as it was going to get, and the hunchbacked Mexican wanted off this evil floor as quickly as possible. The owners might fool guests into believing this was the fourteenth floor, but Acapulco knew better. Eleven, twelve, and then fourteen? *¡Eso ni pensarlo!*

And he could feel what lurked in the closets and shadows of these rooms and halls. Just two weeks ago, he'd observed the ambulance workers remove an 87-year-old man from room 1412 on a stretcher, zipped up tight in a body bag. Acapulco had watched the pretty newsperson on television, later that night, following along well enough to understand police blamed a bad heart. But Acapulco had no doubt what had made the man's heart stop working. It was surely the work of *el Diablo*.

Acapulco had come to America with a small group of neighbors from towns around Chihuahua, crossing the Rio Grande into Texas, following the directions from relatives and friends already employed in Atlantic City. Despite the long hours of pushing brooms and vacuums and emptying endless trash bins, he thought this work was wonderful because it wasn't out in the sun. Acapulco felt blessed not to be hunched over bean plants, trying to grasp and twist frijoles all day long with his afflicted hands, the blazing sun making him feel like a forgotten tortilla on the back corner of a griddle.

Acapulco didn't need to be told to be invisible while going about his job. Being invisible was instinctive among the older Mexicans who came to work in Atlantic City with no papers, hoping to make enough money for their own food and then to send American dollars back home for their families to spend at *la tienda de comestibles*.

What these rich Americans did with their money shocked Acapulco during his first days at the hotel and casino. It was physically painful for him to watch the elderly gringos with papery, translucent skin sitting on high bar stools, coveting big cups filled to the brim with shiny coins. They'd sit for hours, feeding coin after coin into what he saw as the hungry mouths of fancy slot machines. But Acapulco would always share in the elation of the winners, first being startled by the bells and flashing lights, then smiling warmly and compassionately at the person who'd just gotten their money back from the evil, money-gulping contraption. Acapulco would absorb as much of the radiating good fortune as he could before disappearing back into his invisible labor. His wallet was empty, but his heart was rich.

Acapulco and his fellow Mexicans never resented the well-to-do white people who came to risk their money in these machines. They understood the draw of *la loteria,* although the coin cups these wealthy people started out with would have made fabulous jackpots in Acapulco's hometown. Acapulco would even light candles to honor the ones who died from staying on the fourteenth floor. There were no poor people in heaven, and they'd all meet again someday. All were God's children, even if some spent their last years in musty maroon jackets with crooked name tags, hunting cigarette butts and polishing elevator buttons.

From the long hallway's one small window, Acapulco had a bird's-eye view of the caravan of colorful trucks making the sharp turn into the Lucky Dollar's expansive parking lot. He lingered in this spot much longer than he normally would, there in the company of *el Diablo*, watching *el circo* bump over the curb in search of a place to park. He dangled the long cord from the handle, then stepped back into the shadows as what he first thought was a fat, naked white man rushed past him with one of the hotel ice buckets. Acapulco could hear the robot-like sound of the dollar bills being eaten by the vending machine next to the elevator, the metallic thuds of candy bars and rustle of chip bags.

The man, who Acapulco now saw was wearing small white underpants, collided with his vacuum cleaner as he hurried back down the hall, letting out a frightened, high-pitched cry. He looked directly at Acapulco but didn't appear to see him, just frantically searched the shadows for anything that might wish to hurt him. His eyes were bulging, filled with fear that Acapulco understood all too well. The man lunged clumsily away from the old vacuum, nearly toppling it, ice bucket clutched to his chest like a baby. Acapulco knew what it was like to be in a strange place, surrounded by things wanting to get their hands on you and drag you down into terrible places. He was certain this man felt *el Diablo* in many places besides this hallway. He was sorry for him, and even said a quiet prayer.

Acapulco grabbed the vacuum cleaner with his aching fingers and pushed it toward the elevator.

~o ~o ~o

Two old, stooped men climbed out of the first circus truck in the Lucky Dollar Hotel and Casino parking lot, began directing traffic and barking orders. Brothers Enzo and Donato Pisani were nearly eighty years old, bitching and cussing their flaring arthritis after too many hours without stretching. Each had suffered dozens of broken bones in pursuit of their dangerous trade and had developed skin tougher and more leathery than Alligator Woman. Both had, at one time or another, donned wigs and lipstick to fill in for the World's Ugliest Woman. A buck was a buck, after all, and pride was the last vestige of the weak man. The Pisanis were both tough old goats, although their hearing was good enough to register most of the other names they were regularly called.

While the Pisanis gestured like over-the-hill traffic cops, the mechanics checked a pencil diagram for where the rides were to be erected. The animals were parked in shade, as long rolls of hoses were unwound, and an outside faucet was tapped to get the panting beasts cooled down. All were drills that had been repeated a thousand times before, always with the same snarling old man voices competing with the cage-weary animals and rattling of hundreds of feet of unassembled tent poles and fencing.

The two main tents—each with three sets of collapsible bleachers facing inward to create a perimeter for the performers—would take half a day to erect on the sweltering black pavement. Work on a dozen or so smaller tents, for games and other sideshows, would be tackled last.

The mechanics bolted together the kiddy rides, which included a mini-coaster, train, merry-go-round, motorcycles, trucks, and spinning swings. The work was rushed in order to be done in time for the city inspector to stop by for the usual bribe.

The sideshow tent occupants, billed as The Freaks of Nature, varied over time. Attractions such as The Fattest Man Alive tended to have heart attacks more often. Even The World's Strongest Men were occasionally beaten beyond recognition by drunken challengers. Pinhead would get an infection that wouldn't go away, Albino Man would fall asleep in the sun, and Alligator Woman would find a miracle cream.

But then there was the core of the circus. Acts such as The World's Ugliest Woman, who would never run off with a boyfriend, and The Flat Man, with his debilitating phobia of being more than an inch or so from solid ground. These people were more or less the soul of the circus, acts the Pisanis wouldn't have to replace any time soon. The juggler and the clown could always leave to work children's parties, like a journalist could always leave the front lines of a war. Employment options were few and far between if you had part of a congenital twin riding shotgun on your hip. And once a Freak of Nature found a home where their ailment made them ordinary—and no remedy would ever be found— they became a permanent member of the Pisani family.

The Human Cannonball and the lovely little contortionist named Amira arranged makeup trays and hung costumes from hooks in the ceilings of trailers. They made sure their stands, special lights, and cannon were unloaded safely. The surly woman in charge of games made certain there were ample balloons and red star targets for the pellet guns and that the supply of Taiwan-made stuffed animals had not all split their seams. Ropes were pulled and poles were hoisted, and the hot-top parking lot became a bustling community. It was a family routine, repeated in town after town and state after state.

Slim Weatherwax let his stiff-legged dancing bear out of her cage to stretch and poop, while the cat trainer tried to get his animals to swallow bits of liverwurst with heart pills wrapped inside.

"You people must have brains as good as new, bein' that you never seem to use 'em!" Enzo Pisani hollered at everyone within earshot. "Where the hell's Slim? Slim, come get your goddamn bear's nose outta my crotch 'fore I get my shotgun!"

Chapter 8

"The first piece of shit who gets caught with a fourteen-year-old local gets strung up by the balls from this rope." Enzo Pisani dropped a thin coil of nylon rope at his feet. The brothers had called the usual pre-opening meeting in the bleachers of one of the main tents. "Bugger their wives and grannies all the goddamn much you want, but I'll rip the nuts off the next one of you who messes with a kid. Understood?"

Pinhead, named for hundreds of scalp and face piercings—several were always infected—held up his hand, but the surrounding freaks elbowed him and nudged his piercings, so he put it back down. His wisecrack about whether hand jobs should be considered sex had sent both old Pisanis right over the edge last time.

"I want zero trouble from the law," Donato Pisani said. "No fights, no boozing, and if anyone gets in trouble outside this parking lot, you better pray to God I don't find out you told them you worked for us. Got that?"

There was enough general mumbling for Enzo to continue. "We open at three tomorrow with games and rides, right after the little shits get outta school. Performers who don't need makeup will take first shift on games, while you barkers are on shit patrol until it gets dark. Enrique's cannon goes off at eight, followed by the main events. I know you ain't got any questions, so get the fuck outta here and finish settin' up."

"Hold up!" Donato shouted, and the barkers and ticket sellers who'd already made it out of the tent stuck their heads back in to hear the old man, lit cigarette hanging from his lips. "This is a good gig we got here, people. This one could be gold if some dumbass doesn't screw it up. We got a

48

permit for two weeks, and there's word 'bout another circus on hard times down in Delaware lookin' to sell two Africans."

"We gettin' slaves, boss?" asked one of the two mechanics.

"African Elephants, you fuckwit," Enzo shouted. "And you know what that means?"

The barkers who had afternoon shit patrol cringed.

"Means we could be in the big time soon," Donato answered. "Means we triple the head count and make some real money.

"Now get the fuck outta here!" ordered Enzo, and they did.

Chapter 9

Billy Wayne had even less experience with guns than he did with women. He'd never touched a gun, or even seen a real one other than the game warden's and those strapped in police holsters. But just like with women, it turned out that anyone could possess a gun with the right amount of cash.

Convenience was also something money could buy. An extra eighty dollars bought him the privilege of shopping in the back room of a pawn shop, where "preferred" customers could make purchases without the hassle of paperwork.

It took Billy Wayne almost an hour and a half to find the Parkway and then the Expressway, crossing the long marshy flats into Atlantic City. There was something magical about the place. Not so much the tenements and abandoned cars, but all the names were the same as on the Monopoly board in his bedroom back home. He sometimes played for hours against himself, since the game had too many small pieces for his mother's sausage-like fingers to manipulate, and the game board didn't fit right on her TV tray. Billy Wayne built houses and hotels, owned railroads, and forced himself to pay to get out of jail. He sometimes wondered if Betty Katz liked Monopoly and maybe would have played with him.

Steering with his left knee, Billy Wayne reread the directions written in the squiggly, drunken script of the game warden, as he guided his Dart down busy Atlantic Avenue searching for the U Pawn-It Store sign. He certainly didn't expect to see so many black people. Billy Wayne was nervous around black people, especially those who sounded like they might be from Haiti. There were more Haitians living near his mother's house than all the other foreigners combined, and Billy Wayne didn't trust them one bit. It was the tone of voice from the women who waited for their laundry to tumble dry. They sat with their hair wrapped in dingy cloth, smoking harsh-smelling, unfiltered cigarettes, and eyeing him like he was a suspicious piece of meat. Billy Wayne's mother had told him about voodoo and how these women might decide to snatch some of your hair and make a little doll with it, if they caught you looking at them. Once the doll was made, they'd stick pins in your eyes and twist your legs all the way around—whatever they wanted. Billy Wayne walked past them as fast as he could, his hands cupping his eyes as if he were trying to see through a dark window. The women had laughed at him, but they'd never gotten any of his hair.

He also didn't expect all the Mexicans and circus people at the hotel he checked into—him and his shiny Smith & Wesson .38 Special, a box of bullets stuffed inside his Samsonite. The Lucky Dollar Casino had a weekly room rate of $125, which gave Billy Wayne plenty of time to unearth some disciples and begin his new life.

Now he was packing heat and feeling wonderfully safe, a swagger in his step for the first time. No more panicky fast walking for Billy Wayne Hooduk. The feelings associated with becoming a gun owner were both surprising and edifying. Billy Wayne feared nothing, despite the exotic salsa music and strange cooking smells seeping out from behind the doors as he hunted for room 1427. Having such stored power at his finger tips—should he unlatch his suitcase and load his gun—heightened his senses, lengthened his stride. He was James Bond. He was Superman.

The carpet underfoot was so worn it had no real color remaining, and half the lights in the hallway were dark. The gold-and-white-flowered wallpaper was frayed and peeling near the sconces, giving Billy Wayne the impression of an old wild west saloon, upstairs where the loose women serviced cowboys, like in the movies. All the muffled Spanish swearing gave it a Tex-Mex aura, like a saloon at the Alamo,

Billy Wayne fancied. He was Davy Crockett, or maybe Sam Bowie ... no, he was Billy the Kid!

Texas or Atlantic City, this was the farthest Billy Wayne had ever been from home. The farthest he'd been from his mother. And as he turned the room key and stepped inside, some of Billy Wayne's exaltation shrank a little, drained away by the sight of the small, boxy, steaming-hot room.

He unpacked his Samsonite—filling one drawer with his four good shirts and two pairs of slacks—and cranked the dial on the air conditioner to high. He wrapped his new gun and bullets in a towel from the bathroom, then tucked them back into the suitcase. Then, worried the maid would hunt for the missing towel, he unwrapped the gun and bullets and stood at the foot of the bed, turning in a slow circle, holding the gun as if ready to blast away.

Billy Wayne dropped to his knees and shoved the gun between the mattress and box spring, as far as he could reach.

Satisfied, he stood and carefully removed his dark blue suit jacket, the back and armpits sweat-soaked, and used a wooden hanger to hang it in the narrow closet. He unbuttoned his best shirt and folded it on the bathroom counter, with plans to rinse it out later. He draped his pants over a chair next to the bed, then flicked on the television and stood scratching his testicles through his white underpants. The tube warmed up and showed a snowy Phillies baseball game.

Not able to follow the action and not really liking baseball anyway, Billy Wayne sat at the foot of the bed and flipped through his book.

Step number thirteen in *How to Become a Cult Leader in 50 Easy Steps*: "Always be alert for opportunities to display your eminence. Put out a small fire, deliver a baby, or stop a purse snatching. Purchase a container of pepper spray and a small fire extinguisher and consider a midwifery course at your local health clinic or community college."

He was sure he'd never be able to deliver a baby without passing out or throwing up and was afraid that if he started a fire, it might get out of control and he wouldn't be able to put it out. He'd gone through a bit of a fire-starting stage as a teenager and didn't want to risk tapping those old compulsions. Having the gun was already a better rush than setting things on fire, even without shooting at something.

Stopping a crime sounded intriguing and much more likely now that he owned the weapon. Billy Wayne fantasized about walking into a bank during a holdup. The lone masked robber would have forced everyone to the floor, waving his own puny gun, much smaller than Billy Wayne's. When the robber demanded Billy Wayne get down, he would just stand there, glaring, refusing to obey. He'd show off a deadly, quiet strength, just like when his dad had kicked him and his mom out. Instead of cowering on the floor with all the others, Billy Wayne would reach into his holster, pull out his .38, and take aim.

"Go ahead," Billy Wayne would whisper harshly, "make my day."

And every person in the bank would love Billy Wayne Hooduk. He would be an instant hero, bigger than a movie star. His picture would be on the front page of all the newspapers. He would use the reward money for a down payment on a secluded cabin out in the Pinelands, where people would beg to come and stay, just to be in Billy Wayne's presence and listen to his preaching, whatever that might be. He made a note to start trying to fill out that section of his book, since his time was getting closer and closer. Ascension, was what his book called it.

The empty ice bucket in the bathroom reminded Billy Wayne of the humming machines next to the elevator. He grabbed the brown plastic bucket and leaned back into the closet to rummage for change and dollar bills in his pockets, snatched the key off the dresser top, and headed for the door. Billy Wayne paused, looking down over his pale round belly toward his dingy briefs, then back across the room to where his pants were draped over a chair. He decided it wasn't worth the trouble; the elevator wasn't that far. He pulled open the door, ice bucket held like a football, and scurried toward the vending machines.

The ice dispenser was unplugged; a note had been torn from over the bucket cradle with only the top left corner and a piece of tape remaining. All six little lights glowed red to indicate the Coke machine was also empty. Billy Wayne went to work at the snack machine, feeding dollar bills and pressing buttons for three Snickers bars, two small bags of Doritos, and chocolate covered pretzels. Carefully packing them in the ice bucket, he turned to hurry back to his room but stumbled on an upright vacuum cleaner abandoned in the hallway, its cord a long gray snake coiled, dangling from the handle. Billy Wayne searched the deep shadows all around, almost expecting something terrible to step out and reach for him. Then he scampered barefoot toward his room, ice bucket clutched to his chest. The muffled music was louder and food smells more pungent than earlier; they seemed to close in on him. His hands were shaking as he fumbled to get the key into the lock and wondered why he hadn't thought to bring his gun.

But the food made him feel better, and his thumping heart slowed back down with each bite. Chocolate worked like a medicine, his mother had told him, although he couldn't remember exactly what it did. In the bathroom he drank two glasses of water, went back and swept crumbs from the bedspread and plopped down.

Room 1427 was clean enough, but everything was threadbare, and every sharp edge looked as if it had been gnawed on. Billy Wayne stooped forward to twist the volume all the way down on the television. Dropping the book to his side, he collapsed back on the orange bedspread, letting the cold air drift over his body, imagining these rooms filled with lost souls just waiting for someone to love and adore. They were waiting for someone like him.

The ceiling was a rough popcorn texture with flecks of glitter, now yellow from cigarette smoke. Tiny cobwebs drifted back and forth in the moving air. If you squinted, the ceiling became a moonscape, or what sand looked like after a rainstorm.

Above the hum of the air conditioner, Billy Wayne heard a new noise coming from outside his window, a familiar music from his recent stops along the various boardwalks. The whistling calliope notes rose and fell, their dancing melody both childish and hopeful. The sound always reminded him of old cartoons his mother didn't approve of and the ice cream truck his mother would never let him run out to meet. Listening to the calliope was like listening in on someone else's childhood, and it made Billy Wayne's bloodshot eyes fill with salty, self-pitying tears that formed dark spots on the orange spread.

Billy Wayne was suddenly a depressed and uncertain God. He was a pasty, overweight God, with thinning hair and itchy balls.

"But I am still God," Billy told the wafting cobwebs. His voice was wavering and unconvincing. It was a good thing he was feeling too fat and tired to get up and reach under the mattress to load his new gun.

The calliope sang him to sleep.

Chapter 10

Enrique the Human Cannonball stood naked in front of the full-length mirror in his cramped trailer. He sucked in his paunch and flexed his small round biceps, striking a series of poses that allowed him to admire his physique as well as stretch his muscles prior to performing. His gray chest and pubic hair were a stark contrast to the artificially deep black hair on his head and lip. He reached for his nose clippers and mustache comb, pulling a bare bulb lamp close to make a few snips and adjustments.

"Enrique is a beautiful man!" He stepped back and then glanced at the clock. Seven minutes to showtime.

Enrique knew that the danger of being a human cannonball wasn't in being blown up, since the only gunpowder used was for theatrics. Shooting a person from an authentic cannon would result in almost certain death, what with an explosion big enough to fire a two hundred pound projectile. It would, at the very least, blow the legs off the person involved. The propellant was compressed air under the platform where the performer stood. The platform inside the cannon was blasted forward by releasing the air, which was compressed at about two-hundred pounds per square inch. The platform stopped at the mouth of the cannon; the human cannonball did not.

Even with the much less dangerous compressed air cannons, roughly half of all the big name human cannonballs had been killed plying their trade. The most common accident occurred from either missing the net, or hitting the net and bouncing back out for a high-impact landing. And despite how nets had improved over the years, increasingly elaborate cannons were sending performers farther and farther. Some of the top acts flew more than sixty yards. At that distance, the margin of error shrank, especially on windy days.

Enrique wasn't concerned about the wind as he stepped into one leg of his spandex uniform. One leg was red and the other blue, matching the stripes on the fifteen-foot tall cannon. Wearing no underwear accentuated his manhood— a tip from his papa. A large white letter E was emblazoned on his barrel chest, and a shiny red cape, reminiscent of Superman, trailed behind.

Enrique pulled on the thin leather helmet he'd painted bright blue and adjusted the chinstrap. The helmet wasn't meant to protect his brain from impact, but rather to protect his hair from being ripped out when he crashed into the rope netting, seventy feet from the release point. A deep pull from a pint bottle of Kentucky bourbon, and he strode through his trailer door and out into the New Jersey evening to the scattered chants of, "Enrique, Enrique ..." *Now this is already Heaven*, he thought, smiling broadly.

A barker known as Sir William, done with shit cleaning duty, was stirring up the crowd of a hundred or so onlookers for this free show, clapping steadily and chanting, "Enrique, Enrique, Enrique ..." The human cannonball show was a last noisy draw to get customers into the main event tents. There were two medium-size tents because one large tent couldn't be safely tethered in most parking lots. Plus, one big tent was nearly five times the price of two middle-sized ones. Enzo and Donato also emerged from their trailers, scanned the crowd, and gestured impatiently for Enrique to hurry the hell up.

Enrique waved to the crowd in the shadowy parking lot with genuine appreciation and climbed the ladder up the side of the cannon with flare and gusto. He loved the showmanship, the over-the-top dramatics. Enrique was Elvis at that moment. He was Liberace and Evil Knievel rolled into one glorious, red-caped package. He had been born a performer, and being the center of attention was what he lived for, what he would proudly die for. The spotlight was never boring, and being adored for his bravery could never be tedious, even after ten thousand shows. He dropped feet first into the dark, round opening, elbows supporting him to blow some final kisses to the families who were caught up in the show and were now all chanting his name and clapping, ensnared by the spectacle.

Enrique waved a last wave, then pulled both arms in at his sides and allowed his body to slowly slip down the steep, seventy-five degree angle, to the platform below.

Inside the cannon sounds became a hollow echo, as though he was underwater. Enrique recognized the squeaky hinge of the toolbox holding the road flares, as Sir William began the ignition process. He heard the barker strike the flare to life, could hear the hiss of the flame and smell the rotten egg stench of the smoke as the crowd screamed and cheered, fully captivated. Enrique smiled, knowing this was going to be spectacular. Sir William called out, "Ten!"

Thick white smoke reflected the red fire overhead as Sir Williams counted, "Nine ... eight ... seven ..." and Enrique listened for the sound of the flare sparking the comically fat fuse. It caught with a crackling flourish and raced toward the base of the cannon, purposely setting off a stash of small bottle rockets that were sent whisking out in an arc over the parking lot.

"Six," counted down the barker. "Five ... four ..."

Enrique reached up with his right hand and crossed himself.

෨ ෨ ෨

Acapulco de la Madrid Cordero stood next to a sparkling clean second floor window of the Lucky Dollar Hotel and Casino, damp rag in one hand, a bottle of Windex in the other. The window, directly overlooking the ruckus below, was nearly struck by one of the darting bottle rockets. Acapulco pushed the window open a few inches to allow sounds into the silent hallway. The smell was wonderful, like fresh hay and warm cotton candy. The man who had climbed into the mouth of the cannon would have made a fine Mexican wrestler, Acapulco thought.

The last two bottle rockets set off in the parking lot to the right of the cannon exploded over the heads of a flock of seagulls that had surrounded an overflowing dumpster. Acapulco watched the flock rise in unison, squawking and complaining, heading east toward the ocean where they could safely circle over the water until the coast was clear.

Not two seconds into their escape attempt came another, much bigger explosion directly in their path. The flock scattered as one of the humans suddenly took flight. This human was a flash of blue and red, with just one big red wing trailing behind. Much of the flock was able to avoid the flying human, but several took a direct hit, themselves exploding into big white and gray puffs of feathers.

The crowd seemed to marvel at this part of the show and began to clap and cheer even harder. How many of them had ever witnessed a human cannonball, let alone the part where the performer blasted his way through a flock of exploding birds? It was certainly new to Acapulco, although he also sensed something might have gone wrong.

The human cannonball was tumbling in midair over the parking lot, waving his arms wildly, getting them tangled in his cape. Pin-wheeling and tumbling were not terribly aerodynamic, Acapulco guessed, which probably contributed to the human cannonball's failure to reach his net.

Two old men dropped to the pavement just as the human cannonball passed over their heads. The man in the funny blue helmet bounced once and slammed into the tiger cage.

Both old men looked relieved not to immediately find anything that seemed seriously damaged, as they patted their bodies, each lifting to one elbow. Not as comforting, perhaps, was the angry roar that came from directly behind where they lay. The roar silenced the screaming crowd. The onlookers wanted to believe it was all part of the show, that a brave tiger tamer was waiting in the wings, about to crack his long whip as he haughtily marched out over the exploded prop birds and cringing old men.

This was a show!

No whips or wooden chairs in its face, the tiger let out what might have been the greatest roar of its life, letting every beast within earshot know he was king of this paved jungle. The tiny gray hairs on the back of Acapulco's neck stood at attention. He crossed himself with the hand holding the bottle of Windex.

The tiger dropped to his haunches, zeroing in on the two feeble humans directly in front of him. His jaw slowly dropped open and saliva seeped forth in the form of two thin strands glistening in the spotlight. The tiger's ears turned forward and twitched; one paw reached in slow motion, followed by the other. It prepared for the kill.

The two old men craned wrinkled necks to look over their shoulders; then both instantly looked away, as if bracing for impact. The tiger leaped forward as if jolted by electricity, pouncing on their bodies simultaneously, crushing them so fast that neither could muster one last pathetic scream.

The tiger looked impossibly heavy, and bit and bit, and both men were surely dead before the single shot rang out and stopped all the biting. The sounds of tearing flesh and splintering bones were replaced by the screams and pounding steps of retreating circus goers as they ran away from the gory scene in the parking lot—the dead tiger, the two mangled corpses, and the crumpled human cannonball.

The fat man who had nearly trampled Acapulco's vacuum cleaner up on the fourteenth floor earlier was the only live person not running away. He was boldly stepping forward, still holding what looked to be a .38 Special out in front of him, pointing it at the dead tiger. Like frightened animals after the danger has passed, people began to pop up from dark corners, behind tent flaps, and from around the sides of trucks.

The gunman strode confidently up to his kill and nudged the flaccid beast with the toe of his right shoe. The bullet had pierced the old tiger's pelt just behind the shoulder, entering its chest cavity and creating a large red bloom on the fur over its heart. The gunman looked up and greeted the cowering circus folk with his best, most friendly and all-knowing smile, as they emerged, hollow-eyed, like zombies from the grave.

"My name is Reverend Billy Wayne," he said in his best, most God-like voice. "I am God and you have all been saved."

Acapulco shuffled on to the next window and pointed the bottle of Windex.

Chapter 11

Billy Wayne Hooduk acted like he knew exactly what he was doing and exactly where he was leading the caravan, as the circus rolled out of the Lucky Dollar parking lot. They left their dead behind.

Step number eighteen in *How to Become a Cult Leader in 50 Easy Steps*: "Always act as if you know exactly what you are doing. The more precarious the situation, the more stone-cold absolute you must be in handling the predicament. Ambivalence breeds contempt; confidence is king!"

Billy Wayne Hooduk puffed out his chest, feeling the slight breeze tickle the few hairs not sweat-pasted to his scalp. If his mother could see him in his shining moment, she'd be reminded of the statuesque men adorning the covers of the romance novels she occasionally read in binges. The idea of ripping open his shirt danced through his mind on wings of adrenaline, and he would have done it if not for the seventy pounds of dimpled fat clinging to him from the neck down, chapter on Successfat or not.

Billy Wayne's first pronouncement was a simple nine words completing the chain of events triggered by the cannon blast. He stood at the edge of the spotlights shining toward Enrique's missed net, then took a casual sideways step into their full brightness. "I am God and you have all been saved."

After the police had finished interviewing enough people to confirm it had all been a tragic accident, they had given them a perfectly clear and unmistakable order: "Pull up stakes and get the fuck out of our town."

Billy Wayne re-emerged from the rear entrance of the Lucky Dollar Casino with his Samsonite in one hand and his guidebook in the other. He strode up to the lead truck's passenger door and climbed in as if he owned it, leaving his Dodge Dart behind like a rusty, unwanted toy. He relished the idea that he now had the power to send someone to collect it later. Billy Wayne made his second declaration from high atop the black pavement of the parking lot: "We turn left."

And they did.

The remaining loyalists—some had grabbed their belongings and fled into the brightly lit Atlantic City night—abided Reverend Billy Wayne's order and turned onto Ventnor Avenue, slowly rolling northeast up the narrow strip to Atlantic Avenue. They followed the giant green signs toward the Expressway, which took them west, away from the glow of the city. They exited onto a north traveling road, and Billy Wayne watched for signs toward West Tuckerton, where he knew they'd find the road to take them to their new home.

Great Bay Boulevard was a pavement made of shells and polished stones that led travelers almost due south, over dozens of canals and tiny islands, across the marshes and protected wetlands. The road spliced a nearly prehistoric, yet bland, ecosystem of bubbling mud and rotting flora toward a piece of New Jersey that few people ever saw, despite the well-maintained and smooth access.

The black eastern sky over the ocean had broken to purple, as the caravan made a final left turn off the boulevard. The drivers of the largest trucks tested their faith, slowly creeping up and over the rickety bridge onto Fish Head Island.

"Ain't gonna make it," the driver of Billy Wayne's truck said, resigned and matter-of-factly, and just a few hundred yards away, the exact same words might have been spoken with a drunken slur by Warden Clayton Flint.

❧ ❧ ❧

Warden Flint was perfectly happy sitting on the back step of the shack that doubled as an official department office and his home, smoking cigarettes and taking pulls off a bottle of cheap Russian vodka. What brought him joy was the absolute silence he'd caused to go along with the lack of a single flying or otherwise biting bug, despite being smack dab in the middle of what would normally be called bug central.

Flint was in charge of protecting the fish and game inhabiting a plot of roughly twelve square miles of percolating land and water. He was also responsible for a weekly hump out to the county seat to fill up the hundred gallon drum with either temephos or malathion pesticides. His truck was equipped with a mist blower, whose powerful blast ejected insecticide into the airstream, killing either the larvae or adult pests. Some three decades back Flint had begun the job with great resolve and ambition, making absolutely certain to treat every square foot of his territory. He even went so far as to check the wind gauges before setting out, ensuring the drift would come from the right direction and taking particular care to mist the small eddies and ponds after rains.

As the years wore on, the circle of treatment grew smaller and smaller, until a few months ago, when he stopped bothering to drive the truck anywhere after returning with the poisons. He still had to drive out to headquarters, fill the tank, and then sign and file the required paperwork in order to show he was doing his job. But there was nobody to check how the poison was disbursed, nobody to care.

Back at his post on the marshes off Great Bay Boulevard, he simply cranked the mist blower motor, opened the valve, and went inside the shack to relax in the air-conditioning. He would cozy up with a magazine featuring huge boobs and off-color party jokes, while a deadly fog engulfed the shack and surrounding wetland.

What difference would it make? Days after you stopped spraying, the mosquitoes, green heads, horse flies, no-see-ums, and black flies came back in full force. And the only people he was protecting were the day crabbers who came down from nearby cities with chicken legs on strings and long handled nets. These people were unbelievable pigs to the very last one. Every carload was good for a dozen cans or bottles tossed into the canal, left bobbing next to the floating potato chip bags and sandwich wrappers. The kids who came down at night kept their engines running, air conditioners and music blaring. They noticed the bugs about as much as they did Flint's occasional episodes of exhibitionism, which he only engaged in when drunk and regretted when sober.

"People are pigs," Flint said into the night, taking another swig of Russian vodka, referring to the litterers, and a little to himself. He let the bugs feast away on the city slickers, and it served them fucking right.

When it came to bugs, Flint could sit on the back step of this shack naked as a jaybird at any hour of the day or night, if the urge so took him. With a full hundred gallons of insecticide injected into the ecosystem of the immediate area on a weekly basis, not a cricket chirped or a fly buzzed. Any frogs—had they been able to tolerate all the poison—would have long since packed up and moved on for lack of food, as had the fish in the canal and any terns or ducks in the tall grasses. Everything with a heartbeat was dead or driven off, except for the game warden.

"Slow actin'." Flint held the bottle of what he knew was his own poison out in front of him, tilting it toward the yellow light filtering through the nearest window.

Warden Flint had come to love his silence, which was now being broken by a line of slow moving trucks that had rolled past the driveway to the fish and game shack. The trucks made a wide left turn toward Fish Head Island's bridge. Flint watched as one by one the truck headlights tilted up into the black sky, each vehicle crawling across the old wooden bridge that must be shaking and swaying from the enormous load.

"Goin' in the drink." Flint took a long swig off the vodka bottle, as each vehicle tested the dilapidated structure. Flint shook his head each time one made it across, counting one after the other, and then losing track of what and why he was counting. Miraculously, the bridge survived, and nothing but angry red taillights stared back in the distance, disappearing somewhere behind the tall grasses of the outermost island of Flint's jurisdiction.

Flint leaned back against the door of the shack, meaning to close his eyes just for a second, maybe figure out a plan of action for doing some investigating regarding these new developments out on Fish Head. Lots of things to be done, Flint thought, yawning and rubbing his stubbly face. He tilted the bottle in his right hand to see how much was left and then brought it toward his face, sloshing the rest down in one final, wet gulp.

Flint entered that satisfying spinning time, when all the pains and worries had left his reach, yet he sensed he was still alive. He imagined this was how a man felt when his life turned out good, with a stash of money in the bank, a real house, and maybe a decent woman. It wasn't so much the alcohol that he'd become addicted to, but the chance to catch a glimpse of this good life, if only for a minute or two before passing out. And what did it cost him? Less than four bucks a bottle, and the occasional hangover to kick him in the balls the next day.

But tonight, his moment or two in the good life was different. He was a kid again, back at the arcades he used to haunt with his friends in Seaside Heights, burning through quarters, sharing smokes, and passing around French fry filled paper cups drowned in catsup. It was the music, Flint decided. His drunken head lolled to one side against the back door, ear turned like a satellite dish to collect the sounds drifting on the gentle sea breeze. A kind of music a kid never even thought of as music. It didn't play on the radio or at birthday parties. You didn't hear it in grocery stores, or coming from behind the band room door at school. It was music that meant one place and only one place to Clayton Flint. Music that smelled of cotton candy and caramel apples, and the baby wipes moms used to scrub their kid's hands. It smelled of pepperoni pizza, sour garbage cans, and cocoa butter glistening on the untouchable skin of the older girls in stiff new bikinis.

The music was a link to the past. The rising and falling whistles of the circus calliope became a lullaby for Warden Flint in the otherwise silent night.

Chapter 12

Fish and Game Warden Clayton Flint was used to treating hangovers. It was a matter of picking one's self up off of the floor and trying to avoid too many obstacles en route to a fresh, unopened bottle of inexpensive Russian vodka. *God help you if they ever stop manufacturing cheap Russian vodka*, he thought, shielding his eyes from the brutal morning sun and groping for the shack's rusty doorknob.

Flint's back was a knot of razor blades and broken glass, which shot sparks of bright white pain up his shoulders and neck, onward to his thudding brain. He stepped blindly into the sparsely furnished, one-room building and decided his first task would be to pull the shades. His second would be finding the short, dorm-sized refrigerator. He yanked the door open so hard it nearly toppled forward. The clanking glass jabbed at his skull, and he flicked his tongue across dry lips, tasting a hint of the vomit that must have interrupted his sleep at some point.

Flint fished out the first tall, skinny bottle his hand came across and cracked open the blue screw-top. He took three long gulping pulls and then paused with his drinking arm half-cocked, waiting for the heat to find its mark. Flint's stomach clenched at the first hit of booze, but the alcohol flooded into his bloodstream within a minute or two, and the world got a little less shaky. After another couple of short swigs, Flint's crippling headache started to release its grip, the way he imagined an octopus would release an inedible bowling ball.

He opened the back door, stepped out onto the small deck, unzipped his trousers and fumbled with his penis. He waited for his cranky prostate to allow him to empty his full bladder, tears building up in his eyes as he willed the urine to come. And just as it did come, with all the relief God could grant a tortured man, his blurred vision registered all the trucks parked on Fish Head Island.

"Last night," Flint said out loud, foggily recalling the line of trucks off in the night. Something about circus music, too. The stream of pee dwindled down to single, strained drops, and Flint shook three times and adjusted the bottom half of his uniform.

"Duty calls." Flint was surprised not to hate the idea of having a little duty to perform around this place. Other than that odd little man he'd fished out of the canal and a couple of boys he shooed off for plugging gulls with a .22, not much duty had called in recent months.

The warden slapped his face with cold water from the little kitchenette sink, strapped on his badass forty-four magnum, and took a few extra quick hits off old Mister Ruski for good luck. He headed out the door to answer the call of duty.

Chapter 13

A lion roared, or maybe just hacked something up, someplace disturbingly close.

Warden Flint's pickup thumped over a deep rut, apparently made by one of the flatbed trucks loaded down with a kid-size roller coaster, and slid to a stop next to where Billy Wayne Hooduk was holding court with two men and a kid.

The kid, Flint saw upon closer inspection, was actually a tiny man with a pencil mustache, standing no more than belt high. One of the other men turned out to have full, torpedo-like breasts to go along with a scraggly beard. The third person had hundreds of metal piercings that puckered, stretched, and did other unnatural looking things to every square inch of his head and face. The man with tits was far less disturbing than the one with earlobe material dangling to his shoulders.

There was actually a fourth; Flint nearly tripped over the crudely built stretcher holding a supine man who seemed glued as low to the ground as he could possibly get.

"Sorry," Flint told the guy on the ground.

"No problem," Flat Man answered, tilting his head for a look up at the warden. "Happens all the time."

The fact that the circus had come to town was doing nothing to improve Flint's hangover.

Billy Wayne, though, appeared to be in great spirits, breaking away from his odd group to greet Flint as he climbed out of his truck. The hairy-faced man or woman smiled at Flint and blew a theatrical kiss before sauntering off around the big truck.

"I suppose you're wondering 'bout all this." Billy Wayne beamed. Flint noticed the troupe had already set up at least

70

four small tents and a couple of cooking fires that sent spirals of blue smoke into the skuzzy gray sky.

"They can't be here." Warden Flint slammed his door and leaned against the front quarter panel of his truck. "You might very well be God, but this land is protected marsh."

"It's a beautiful place, in its own way." Billy Wayne looked out beyond the hulking vehicles. "It's almost like coming right down to the end of the world."

Flint closed his eyes and rubbed both temples with his thumbs in tight, hard circles, the pain coming back in heavy waves. "It don't matter what you think it might be the end of. There ain't no overnight camping, and there sure as shit ain't no circuses."

Billy Wayne turned and slowly walked toward an opening between two of the flatbeds. Flint followed his footprints in the mud. Billy Wayne led them across the gravel drive, and they stopped at the edge of solid land to look out at the inlet toward the Atlantic. Flint wanted very much to turn back and crack open a bottle of his good medicine stashed on the passenger floor of his truck.

"Can't do it, Billy Wayne. Just can't do it." Flint sensed something different in the fat little man he'd pulled out of the canal a few days earlier, the son of that crazy loon. Something had gotten hold of him, or he'd gotten hold of it. Hell, somewhere he'd gotten hold of an entire friggin' circus.

"It's come to me that sooner or later we all arrive at a crossroad." Flint stood listening quietly. A few gulls did a quick flyby but found nothing interesting and rode the slight breeze south. "I came face to face with my personal crossroad not half a day ago."

Flint said nothing, just listened to the strange howls and grunts and swears coming from the men and animals behind them. It was high tide on a full moon, and the briny water surged up to cover what was normally dry ground here on Fish Head. Flint was partial to this cycle of the tide. It filled the canals and carried away a good bit of the trash. It covered the mud flats and things didn't smell so much like death and rot.

"It ain't an easy thing," Billy Wayne went on. "The entire course a man's life takes depends on which direction he decides to turn when he reaches that crossroad. Sometimes we're walkin' toward a thing and sometimes we're running away from it. I think you know what I'm talking about."

"I know you people ain't supposed to be down here with all this stuff." Flint's voice didn't hold any real conviction.

"Of course we aren't. Just like a man such as yourself probably wasn't meant to spend year after year in a rundown shack, lookin' out for seagulls and snapping turtles. But somethin' in your life brought you to a crossroad, and this was your choice, am I right?"

Clayton Flint shrank from the question, feeling accused by the son of a woman whose life he'd wrecked pretty darn good.

"I don't know what you're talkin' about," Flint said.

"Maybe you do and maybe you don't." Billy Wayne tried to look Flint in the eye. "But I can look you straight in the eye and see you understand that sometimes we need to take a leap of faith. To do something that seems all wrong and against the rules. But we know in our heart of hearts it's right. That it's something we have to do. You follow me on this?"

Like the tide, Clayton Flint's hangover crested under the morning's glare. Looking out over the calm water where he'd stared a million times before, he again heard the plaintive voice on his answering machine telling him about a baby he'd put in that crazy broad's belly. He sure as hell hadn't done a very good job with that particular crossroad. The voice on his machine had been one of the reasons he'd sold his truck with the big green plastic bug screwed to the roof. The voice was probably the only reason he sold the tanks and sprayers and told his landlord he was taking off to find greener pastures. There were a half-dozen openings in the newspaper classifieds for state jobs down by the shore. Jobs for fish and game, which he knew a little about 'cause he hunted and fished, but there were also a couple listings for insect control. And insect control without the carnal temptations was just what the doctor had ordered for Flint. Getting out from under the dreams he kept waking up from, starting all new and fresh. Clayton Flint may not have had a guilty bone in his body, but something had gotten inside him enough to let him know he was done with lonely housewives.

"You know what I'm askin' of you?" Billy Wayne folded his arms over his round belly, rolling a small rock under the toe of his shiny old shoe.

Flint shoved his hands deep in his front pockets, still looking out over the water, hearing Allison Hooduk's voice louder than ever.

"What I got here is a group of lost souls." Billy Wayne nodded back over his shoulder to where his lost souls were now frying bacon in a big iron skillet and tossing a flat, deflated football someone had found in the grass.

The fish and game warden's crusty old heart wanted more than anything to know what had become of Allison Hooduk and the baby she'd called and called about. He'd been hiding in these marshes and mud flats for too many years. As stupid as it sounded, he could half believe some sorta higher power had brought this fat little man back into his life. Was it some sort of punishment? Was he supposed to make things right? His thumping head was about to explode from the questions and voices. His past hadn't just caught up with him. It had caught up and wrapped its hands around his sorry neck.

Clayton Flint took off his faded, state-issued cap and folded it over in his hands. The cool breeze felt good on his balding head, and he wiped his brow on his forearm sleeve. The same state seal logo had been engraved on the badge he'd lost a few years back. Well, not so much lost as skipped out across the inlet water not far from where they were standing. He'd been drunk, of course, and especially down in the dumps that night. He vaguely recalled saying something about quitting, right before sending the round badge skipping across the top of the water, where it disappeared into the blackness. He also recalled waking up the next morning right there in the mud. A tern, its black head shaggy as if it was wearing a wig, had eyed him with disgust from a few feet away.

"I quit," Warden Flint had repeated to the bird, but it squawked at him and hopped away.

"I'm just asking for a place to do what seems right." Billy Wayne dared look the warden square in the eye.

Off in the distance, a lion roared again, or maybe just hacked up something else. Someone swore and someone else laughed. Music he didn't recognize faded in and out on the breeze, and Flint could smell the bacon sizzling over the fire. He struggled to put his finger on what had been missing, and it came to him slowly as he turned to watch a small pony with colorful cloth pieces woven into its shaggy mane trot down to the water's edge. The pony lapped at the salt water but then shook its head and backed away, not happy with the taste.

There is suddenly life here, the warden thought. Maybe it had been missing because so much of him had died inside, or maybe it was all the pesticides. Perhaps this wasn't the sweetest life, like salt water to a pony, but Clayton Flint decided the circus needed to stay.

Chapter 14

Lennon Bagg smacked his Jeep Wrangler's dashboard with the palm of his hand, cracking the plastic vent hinge but in no way improving the functioning of the struggling air conditioner. Snapping the fan lever from high to low and back again also didn't help.

The radio still worked, so he turned the dial until he found the closest thing to rock and roll.

Bagg was a reporter for the *Atlantic County Beacon*, a mid-sized daily newspaper based in Pleasantville, New Jersey, ten or so minutes west of Atlantic City, with seven small bureaus spread out around the county from Buena to Egg Harbor to Brigantine. Bagg was in no real hurry to get to this particular spot news assignment. A news event that a few months ago would have sent him flying out of the parking lot, breaking a dozen traffic laws, and risking life and limb in order to get to the scene as fast as possible. A few seconds could mean everything, especially if he was ahead of the photographer, because Bagg also took pictures. Although it was far and away better to witness events firsthand—humans being incredibly unreliable and inaccurate witnesses—getting the story was usually a simple matter of piecing together bystander and cop accounts. But while you could recreate events with words, once a jumper jumped or a fireman doused the fire, the best photo opportunity was gone.

The dark cloud of malaise that had come over Bagg was the same one that enveloped the entire newsroom. *The Beacon's* publisher and executive editor had called a mandatory meeting for all editorial staff a week earlier to announce that the distinguished, award-winning, eighty-seven-year run of the paper was coming to an abrupt end.

"It's just about over, folks," their Ukrainian-born publisher, Semen Gnatenko, said with what appeared to be a truly heavy heart. "We have maybe two weeks, the accountants tell me. You all have been a part of my family, and this is the saddest day of my life."

Mr. G, as he was affectionately known, had tried everything from raising advertising prices to slashing the hell out of advertising prices. He had tried pushing his editors to get the investigative reporters to uncover dirty political secrets; he had tried pushing the same editors into having the reporters cover up the dirty politics to keep everyone happy. Mr. G had tried everything, which eventually resulted in subscribers, business owners, and all the local politicians distrusting the content of his newspaper. Roughly half the letters to the editor these days were filled with profanities and threats against the news staff.

Not that anything the publisher could have done stood any real chance of working. Even the top newspapers in the country with Pulitzer Prize winning reporters and nationally syndicated columnists were failing, one by one. It was the Baaton Death March of words, a Trail of Tears. It was a My Lai without the cover up. Newspapers were sick elephants, dropping away from the herd as if heeding the call of mythical dying grounds. Like a last heavy bundle of papers tossed from the back of a delivery truck with a banner headline saying "Farewell," the elephant dropped to the dirt next to the bones of its ancestors.

The staff of the *Atlantic County Beacon* listened, some crying. This was the only working life most of these people had known, Bagg included. There was no escape from the back of a dying elephant. If you were lucky, you just moved to the back of another, buying yourself a little more time. Bagg and the rest exited the newsroom, left the meeting in shock, squinting into the afternoon sun on what should have been a beautiful spring day.

To Bagg, though, his stint with the newspaper was just another segment of his life to mourn. And this mourning was a piece of cake compared to the last five plus years following his divorce and the disappearance of his little girl. Mom had loaded her on a plane bound from Philadelphia International Airport to somewhere else, probably far, far away. The police were sympathetic at first, but sympathy meant nothing if it wasn't followed by action.

"She's with her mother, right?" a detective had rhetorically asked Bagg.

"She's been gone three weeks," Bagg had said. "I have a court order."

But to these cops, the rolled up court order in Bagg's hand, with the official looking raised seal and explicit wording dictating who had custody and when, might just as well have been a supermarket sales flyer.

"We have season passes to Sesame Place." Bagg had lowered his head into his hands, slumping in a chair in the detective's small cubicle. Family photos lined the walls of the miniature office. In one, the detective flashed a huge grin while towering over his son, who awkwardly held out a string of brook trout. Both wore baseball caps with the same insignia. In other photos, the same boy flashed a thumbs-up while sitting in a go-kart and a chubby-cheeked baby girl, a pink ribbon clipped to a tuft of fine blond hair, was cradled in the arms of the detective's wife.

Bagg's entire life changed when his daughter was stolen away. He'd dealt okay with the divorce and, although it hadn't been his idea, he hadn't fought it. There had been plenty of fighting already. He was pretty sure his wife had slept with one of her coworkers, and that was something you could never take back. Maybe they'd been in crazy mad love when they'd first married seven years before the divorce, but if someone asked Bagg about the love of his life, he'd immediately think of his daughter, Morgan.

Morgan Bagg was almost five years old and just about to finish Pre-K when she went missing. Bagg learned that when a parent stole away a child in New Jersey, it wasn't called kidnapping, but it sure felt like it. That summer was going to be perfect, with weekends spent at Sesame Place, and the joint-custody arrangement gave them a full week together in August. He'd collected tourist brochures in diners to plan the best week ever. Trips to a wave pool, the shore, and a real cave. And they'd catch movies any night they weren't too worn out.

Bagg had coached Morgan's soccer team, which was a little like herding puppies up and down a miniature field. Morgan had wanted to play again, especially after she and her teammates had been given trophies at the team pizza party following the last game.

The trophy was still on her bedroom dresser at Bagg's apartment. Bagg knew it was there, although he hadn't looked at it in more than five years. He'd stayed in the same apartment so she could always find him, but Bagg couldn't go back into that room. He kept the door closed but would sometimes stop outside and just lay the palm of his hand on the wood door. Once, when he'd gotten drunk off a bottle of cheap gin while watching an old black and white movie on television, Bagg had lumbered down the hall and pressed an ear to his daughter's bedroom door.

He'd stood propped against the door, tears running down his stubbly face, the gin bottle dangling from one hand. Bagg had held his breath and listened as hard as he could. And from what seemed a million miles away, Bagg had been certain he'd heard the ocean. Waves breaking over a sandy beach and seagulls squawking, bickering above.

Bagg's legs had gone weak and he'd struggled to keep his ear to the ocean as he slid down the door. He had sat there crumpled on the floor listening, gin pooling around the seat of his pants as the bottle slid from his grasp.

"Where are you?" Bagg had whispered, but there had been no answer and he'd eventually fallen asleep, taken away by the ebbing tide.

There, in a puddle of juniper scented alcohol, Bagg had dreamed. Dreamed his ex-wife had shown up with their daughter as scheduled. After helping with dinner, Morgan had lain on top of her father during the next two cartoons then brought up the same dozen reasons bedtime wasn't as important as the next show.

As it had always been with his daughter, time slipped away practically unnoticed. Then came that quiet time just after the cat had fallen asleep but the hamster had not yet awakened to activate his maddening squeaky wheel. Teeth had been brushed after a last chance on the potty, followed by the fluffing of pillows and the tucking of blankets. This was a broken home, which made the rituals all the more important.

"I have a brand new story," Lennon Bagg told his little girl, as he sat on the edge of her bed, somewhere near her pudgy and scuffed knees encased in the too-small footy pajamas. Despite some squeezing and sucking in of breath, these jammies had not been replaceable. So what if she could no longer zip them anywhere near her chin?

"I don't want a new story," Morgan said, sounding a little worried that her dad might not be teasing. "Our story is perfectly fine."

"A story about a friendly witch who only kidnaps naughty children."

"Our story is about a circus," she said.

"Okay, it's about a circus."

"And there's a bear!" she squealed.

"Of course there's a bear. A proper circus has a bear."

"A dancing bear?"

"Who's telling this?" he asked.

"Okay."

"So there was this circus, and there was a happy dancing bear named Sally," Bagg began.

"Sadie."

"Okay, Sadie. But she wasn't always a happy dancing bear. In fact, she'd been taught how to dance by a very bad man, in a very bad way."

"He hurt Sadie?"

"Well, he was very mean to her, yes. He had this long whip made of braided black leather, and he would lift it above his head and snap it forward, making a sound just like a crack of thunder." Bagg told this part in a soft voice, empathizing with just how frightening the whip must have been. "That was how the man taught her to be a dancing bear. And whenever there was a lightning storm, Sadie would huddle in her cage and feel very sorry for all the other bears being made to dance in the world."

"I'm a little afraid of lightning, too," Morgan told her father. "Did Sadie want to run away?"

"Yes, she really did. But Sadie was afraid to run away. She'd been taken away from her mother as a very young cub and had never learned to catch fish or find berries. Imagine what it would be like to be stolen away from your family and forced to live among bears?"

"So she stayed with the mean man."

"Yes, that's right," Bagg said. "And she learned his dances while he snapped his whip at her paws."

"Did she wear a tutu?"

"Yes, a pink one. The very nice magician's assistant made it for her because she understood that even a girl bear should not dance without any clothes on."

"Daddy!"

"It's true!"

"Tell me about the magic."

"Well, Sadie and the magician's assistant spent a lot of time together because neither was allowed to explore the towns the circus traveled to," Bagg explained, and there began the first yawns and rubbing of eyes as the story settled into its less scary parts. "And Sadie thought the magician's assistant was really wonderful. She had made her such a beautiful tutu and could do almost all the tricks the magician knew. The kind lady made flowers appear out of a little black stick, although they didn't taste like flowers to Sadie."

"Sadie ate the plastic flowers?"

"How's a bear to know?" Bagg shrugged his shoulders as he always did. "Anyway, the assistant could turn a quarter into a puff of smoke and make a torn-up dollar bill whole again. But Sadie's favorite trick the assistant performed for her—you see, the assistant really wanted to be a full-time magician—was turning objects into lovely white doves."

"What kind of things could she turn into doves?"

"Well, she turned a man's watch into a dove."

"And what else?"

"Um, she turned a little boy's half-eaten candy bar into a dove."

"Ew! That didn't happen!"

"She turned a woman's broken pair of sunglasses into a very beautiful dove."

"So she could turn anything into a dove?"

"Well, she could try to, but she was still just a magician's assistant, not a real magician."

"Did Sadie want her to turn something into a dove?"

"Well, yes, I suppose you could say that," Bagg said. "You see, Sadie thought it must be the most marvelous thing in the world to be a dove. Doves, as you know, are very pretty animals and nobody ever thought a dove was going to bite them. And even the meanest of mean people would never think to crack an awful whip at a dove. Why, that would just make a dove fly away."

"Nobody would ever be mean to a dove."

"Yes, nobody would ever be mean to a dove."

"So what happened?"

"Well, one night, when the mean bear trainer was off doing mean things with other mean people, Sadie slipped out of her collar and went to visit the magician's assistant. In her bear language, she asked the magician's assistant to do a magic trick for her."

"What trick?"

"To turn her into a beautiful dove."

"Did she?"

"Well, the magician's assistant was very worried. She didn't think she could. After all, turning a bear into a dove might just be the greatest magic trick ever performed."

"So she wouldn't even try?"

"She didn't want to disappoint Sadie by failing, but she could see all the sadness in her eyes. Who could turn down a dancing bear on the verge of tears?"

"Dad, what are crocodile tears? Mommy said I cry crocodile tears."

"Hmm." Bagg paused. "They're pretend tears."

"Crocodiles pretend to cry?"

"Maybe they cry to make other animals feel sorry for them, so they can get close enough to eat them."

"Sadie would never do that."

"Off course not," Bagg said. "So, the magician's assistant pulled out the magician's special black handkerchief and tried to cover Sadie with it."

"It was too small!"

"Yes, it was too small. So she had to go find a magic bed sheet to cover the great big bear."

"And she said the magic words?"

"Abracadabra ziggity-zam," Bagg held his hands up over his daughter, who covered herself like Sadie, except for her eyes. "If your heart is filled with love, may the magic powers make you a dove!"

"Did it work? Did she turn into a dove?" Morgan lowered the blanket beneath her chin.

"No, she did not."

"But ..."

"Not right away," Bagg interrupted. "You see, there's a lot more to turning a bear into a dove than just a wristwatch or wedding ring. The magician's assistant repeated the words four more times, then added a little sparkly magic dust, and voilà!"

"Voilà?"

"Yes, the bed sheet suddenly dropped to the floor, all crumpled up, where a big bear had been sitting patiently, hoping and wishing."

"There was something under the sheet, right?"

"Yes, but it wasn't a dove."

"Oh, no!"

"But it was a creature meant to fly, just the same. And even though it wasn't a beautiful white dove, it was still quite lovely."

"What was it?"

"Well, out from under one corner of the big bed sheet poked a tiny little antenna, followed by another," Bagg said in a low voice. "It prodded the air on the other side of the sheet, twitching this way and that, making sure the coast was clear. And then one orange wing appeared, followed by another."

"A butterfly!"

"Yes, a butterfly! And the butterfly swished her beautiful orange wings and danced up into the air in the magician's assistant's tent."

"Did she fly outside?"

"Oh, certainly she did," Bagg told his daughter. "The magician's assistant, who from that moment on became a full-fledged, top-of-the-line magician, opened her tent flap and allowed Sadie to fly into the night, far from the mean trainer, to where there were endless meadows of flowers."

"And she danced from flower to flower?"

"Yes, Sadie the dancing bear ..."

"Dancing butterfly!" Morgan squealed.

"Sadie the dancing butterfly lived happily ever after, dancing from flower to flower."

"Will you tell me the story again?"

"Tomorrow night, honey," Bagg said, leaning down to kiss his daughter.

Had that been the last time he kissed her? Had she been too busy getting her papers and crayons stuffed into her backpack when he dropped her off Sunday afternoon? She had worn a plain white short-sleeved shirt and jean shorts. Pink and white sneakers with a picture of one of the Disney princesses; he couldn't remember which one. Morgan's brown hair was short, had just been cut. A tiny freckle on the left side of her nose, which you could only see close up. Her eyes were blue. A little girl; she looked like a little girl.

Bagg now sat behind the wheel of his Jeep, not really any better or any worse than he'd been when Morgan first went missing. He'd found that as the parent of a stolen child you daydreamed a lot. When fragments of happy memories appeared out of nowhere, you tried to hold onto them, even if it meant getting honked and sworn at while sitting at a green light by someone who didn't have a giant hole in their heart.

"Wake up, shithead," the female driver shouted as she pulled around Bagg, laying on her horn, almost hitting him as she swerved around and in front of his Jeep.

Calls had come into the newsroom reporting a bear attack at one of the local golf courses, and Bagg was daydreaming at stoplights instead of getting his ass to the scene.

"Sorry." Bagg shifted the cranky gears and rolled forward. He just wished he'd had another minute or two to spend with that last memory of his little girl.

Chapter 15

Graceful Gracie was hungry and tired. Her tutu was in tatters, all tangled with burs, and kept snagging on sharp twigs. The gentle old black bear loved the pink tutu her man had given her more than anything in the world. He'd scratched her ears and rubbed her chest to make her okay with having it snapped snuggly over her lower belly, but he didn't need to do any of that. It was beautiful and smelled like flowers, and she was happy to show it off. No complaints about the extra scratching, though.

The human cubs who came to watch her adored her pink tutu as well; they made lots of happy noises. There were bright blinking lights when she rose up and danced on her hind legs. Sometimes, Gracie's man would dance with her and feed her peanuts, although now that she didn't have teeth, she could only swallow them whole.

This man was kind and gentle to Gracie and she loved him very much. She knew what it was like to be forced to wear a muzzle, which had pinched her lips and made her chest hurt because she couldn't breathe. The muzzle wasn't necessary. No matter how badly her first owner had treated her, she wouldn't have tried to bite him. Not even when the man put her in that awful little cage where she was forced to stand on her back legs, making her hips ache like they were on fire. The ground turned red hot when the music came on, and she had to hop and dance to keep from burning. Gracie had learned that when the music played, the ground was going to get hot, so it was time to dance.

But Gracie had gotten old. Her stomach sometimes hurt for days and she couldn't eat. And when the bad man tried to force a tube down her throat, she feared she really might bite him. She didn't bite, of course, but she also didn't keep the liquid in her belly. The bad man had kicked her, snapped the whip across her face, and yelled that he was going to get rid of her. Gracie couldn't help that her stomach hurt so badly.

Her new man loved her, and she danced for him even when she was sick. This new man smelled terrible, with layers of grease and old urine—Gracie knew his mother had never taught him to properly lick himself—but he didn't make her wear a muzzle and he never hit her with a stick. He even woke Gracie one night, stumbling against the lion's cage and tripping and falling over metal tent stakes. The man had come to her cage and talked sweetly to Gracie, telling her a story in his human language.

Gracie was curled up in one corner, just watching her man with her yellow eyes, ears cocked, ready to listen to his lullaby, when she heard the chain rattle and the lock click open. Her man let out a grunt as he climbed into her home and began stroking the soft fur of her jowls. Gracie closed her eyes and the man stopped rubbing and settled down in the straw beside her, his smelly back to her. Gracie lifted her big right paw and pulled him close, and her man made a low murmur as she began licking away some of his filth.

Graceful Gracie's safe cage and kind man were now lost. She was lost. Her tutu flapped like a broken kite, taunting the bad animals who were gaining on her. Gracie lumbered as fast as she could, with the yapping, angry animals in chase. She ran across an open field of perfectly groomed grass that looked like a gigantic carpet. Groups of strange men carrying bags and skinny metal sticks ran to their little white cars when they saw her charging toward them. *I'm lost*, Gracie wanted them to know, *and I'm being chased. Help me!* But the men in their brightly colored clothes—which Gracie envied, despite her current situation—were driving and running away from her.

Gracie knew this was all her fault. When the man who was shot out of the big blue and red machine flew into the tiger cage and broke it open, Gracie was scared and tried to hide under a truck and wait for her man to come find her. But then the truck roared to life, and a big herd of screaming cars and trucks with horrible flashing lights were after her, and she ran from her hiding place.

Grace scurried through the night, trying to escape the lights and hard ground, which hurt her old paws. She ran until she came to a shoreline of muddy salt water that smelled like dead fish and rotten grass. Gracie stopped to catch her breath, turning to look over her shoulder at the giant mass of buildings and the lights shining up on the clouds. Off in the distance, she could hear the screaming cars still looking for her, so she stepped into the cool water one paw at a time. The mud soothed her paws and she was tempted to just roll there in this sudden goodness when one of the screaming cars came wailing around the big building toward her.

Gracie pushed out away from the shore into the black water and the bottom fell away quickly. Tucked somewhere in a far corner of her mind, where cub memories were stored, Gracie had images—like old Polaroid snapshots—that flashed across her vision. In them, Gracie was swimming across a pond with her mother, reaching her young paws out one after the other in easy, sweeping movements. Gracie decided there must be something good about swimming, since she had done it with her mother so many years ago. She swam in long even strokes, resting a few times by just treading water and arching her back to keep her nose in the air. And after a while, her paws found mud again and she pulled her sopping body up and out of the bay, giving a great and mighty shake that nearly knocked her over.

There was tall grass here. Gracie walked into the thickest patch, made a few circles to mat down a bed, and fell asleep in less than a minute.

The sun and complaining seagulls startled her awake a few hours later. She looked around for her food dish but then remembered where she was and a little bit about what had happened. Her pink tutu was streaked brown with mud and she hoped her man could make it clean for her. With a grumbling tummy, Gracie peed and pooped a great watery mess, then set off to find her man, heading away from the water and away from the bright sun.

Roads filled with cars seemed to intersect every option, but none of these cars were screaming that terrible noise or shining those flashing lights, so Gracie sprinted across the pavement each time the coast was clear. It was on the first patch of perfect grass that the angry barking had begun. Gracie's old muscles were sore from the swim and she didn't know how long she could run, so she either had to find help or a sturdy tree.

Running past the startled golfers, Gracie smelled the wonderful food even before she spotted the building the smoke and scent were coming from. Gracie felt energized by the idea of breakfast; she recognized the beautiful smell of hotdogs and hamburgers and the tasty buns they came in. Gracie's dry mouth filled with drool, and a rush of adrenaline drained away her fear of the pursuing animals; she turned on them, rising as tall as she could, letting out a thunderous roar, and baring her mighty gums.

"Get away from me now!" Gracie thundered in her bear language at the pack of three mutts that had been nipping idiotically at her back paws and muddy pink tutu. The dogs nearly bowled each other over hitting the brakes, and their plaintive barks turned to yelps as Gracie transformed herself into a monstrous ballerina.

"Go!" Grace bawled and the dogs obeyed, leaving her with yummy hotdogs on her mind.

The snack bar was empty of customers, but the grill was going and only one human was foraging around in the cold box in back. Gracie pushed through the screen door and headed right for the grill, lifting herself onto her haunches and carefully brushing the two dozen sizzling hot dogs onto the floor, singeing just a few hairs in the process. Gracie dropped back down and began wolfing the hot meat, burning her lips and gums a little. But it was oh so heavenly good. Gracie barely noticed the woman who stumbled into her, fell onto her hairy back and started screaming bloody murder, as Gracie licked every last bit of juice off the floor.

Screaming humans were nothing new. Male humans regularly snuck up behind their females and pretended to push them too close to the bars of her cage. The females almost always screamed, as if they were in danger. The game had hurt Gracie's feelings at first, until she realized it was just how humans played.

The screaming woman, who had fallen on her then rolled beneath the grill, was leaving her alone, so Gracie checked the kitchen for more treats. Nothing was as good as the hotdogs. The candy bars were okay, but tasted much better when human cubs took the wrappers off for her. The loaf of bread made her thirsty; she was trying to open a frustrating container of water when she heard the familiar screaming of the bad cars. Gracie's heart sank and her stomach turned sour as the awful fear flooded back. Those cars that had chased her last night with spinning lights had somehow found her.

Gracie went for the broken screen door at first, but that's where the cars were loudest. She backed away, searching for someplace to hide. Scrambling back into the kitchen, she nosed open a cabinet. The space was small, but she got quite a bit of her three hundred or so pounds into it, with only the back half sticking out. There were boxes of cleaning supplies under there that made her want to sneeze, but Gracie held it in.

The old black bear, with her pink tutu clad rear end sticking out of the snack bar cupboard, sensed that she would have to be as quiet as a mouse if she ever wanted to see her man again.

Chapter 16

A cop car blew past Lennon Bagg's Jeep and rocked it with turbulence, lights flashing and siren blaring. The sight of the speeding black and white stirred something in Bagg, and he couldn't help but feel a rush of excitement.

The radio calls from the police dispatcher had themselves piqued his interest. Apparently, an enormous black bear had attacked a pack of dogs, then smashed through a concessions building door and went after a young woman. By the grace of God, the woman had escaped with only minor injuries.

A black bear down in these parts would have made one heckuva long trek, Bagg thought. There was a good chance it had crossed the Delaware somewhere up in North Jersey, or maybe came all the way down from New York. Whatever the case, he'd never heard of a black bear breaking down a door or attacking dogs. Maybe if a dog cornered it. But smashing through a door ... from hunger? Rabies?

Bagg began writing the first paragraphs of his story in his head. Glancing down, he was surprised to see that the speedometer had edged over eighty miles per hour. The back nine holes were now zipping along the left side of the two-lane highway, and Bagg backed off the gas pedal, searching for the stone archway entrance to the Absecon Golf and Country Club. With no pay increases in the newsroom for the last couple years, Bagg had grabbed a few freelance assignments from the sports department by covering some Saturday gigs. Most of the work had been high school football games, but he'd also written up a few high school golf matches at fifty bucks a pop. Writing about golf was much easier than football, where you had to log every damn play, and the weather was crappy every other game. Golf was a spring sport that was cancelled if it rained hard, and you could write your entire story from the 18th hole in about thirty minutes.

Bagg pulled in under the big AGCC sign and followed the narrow drive around past the clubhouse, continuing along a service road to where an ambulance and the cop car were parked. The concessions building was a low, one-story structure, no more than twenty by thirty feet, with a covered patio and a half dozen round metal tables and chairs. Everything was painted a fresh coat of white and stood in stark contrast to the lush green fairways. Bagg was no golf fan and had never swung anything but a bright blue- or red-handled miniature golf club. But there was something special about the bucolic settings, the meticulous gardening, and the grounds keeping that went along with golfing. Golf courses reminded Bagg of Walt Disney World, with the topiaries and tulips and small signs instructing visitors to go this way and that. Bagg wasn't a golfer, but he certainly envied their playground.

The Absecon police officer who had roared past Bagg's Jeep was at the back door of the ambulance huddled next to a woman holding an ice pack to her forehead. With them were an EMT and two crisply dressed men in collared shirts and shiny leather golf shoes. Bagg cranked his emergency brake and shoved his reporter's notebook into the tan Domke camera bag that carried his Canon T90 and short zoom lens. He untangled his press pass from his stained tie as he walked toward the group, while keeping an eye on what must be the bear-occupied snack shack.

"The back door is solid and is always kept locked," one of the men in golf shoes was telling the young cop. Bagg knew a couple of the town cops, but this kid looked right out of high school.

"Is Fish and Game coming?" Bagg asked, joining the group in the shade of the shiny, hulking ambulance. He flashed his dangling press pass and added, *"The Beacon."*

"Ted Shamsky." One of the golfers stuck out his hand and showed his bright and perfect set of teeth. "I'm the pro. S-H-A-M-S-K-Y."

"William Montrose." The other man took his turn shaking Bagg's hand. "Spelled just like it sounds. I own Carpet World, in case you've seen the commercials."

"Their ETA is an hour, maybe more." The young officer didn't seem the least bit pleased to be interrupted. According to the gold nameplate over his shirt pocket, his name was Officer Gates. Skinny, with big ears and black frame, military-issue eye glasses, he looked an awful lot like the world's richest computer nerd with the same last name, but didn't seem to be in any sort of mood to discuss the coincidence.

"We got the bear cornered in there." Officer Gates lifted his chin to indicate the snack shack as he scribbled notes on a pad much smaller than Bagg's.

"So the bear attacked you?" Bagg asked the pretty young woman who was dressed in sharp white slacks and a light blue button-down top. Her name tag said "Bonnie," and she sat on the top step of the ambulance. The EMT, whose blue shirt had "Jake" written in script over the left breast pocket, sat next to her, saggy rubber gloves dangling from his fingertips. Jake looked disappointed that the victim had no treatable injuries, which was probably why he'd pulled out the ice pack. "When in doubt, grab an ice pack," was a motto Bagg had heard at countless accident scenes. With nothing more to do unless the bear started mauling people, Jake seemed to be concentrating on breathing in the girl's perfume.

"Yeah, I just got the grill going and was coming back from the freezer when this huge bear appeared out of nowhere right there in the kitchen." Bonnie was talking too fast, her voice genuinely shaking. "It stood up on its back legs, snarling, and its teeth were like this long." She took the ice pack from her head to use both hands to show how big the bear's teeth were.

As if to punctuate her demonstration, a metallic clanging rang out from deep inside the snack shack.

"Holy shit!" The cop unholstered his gun and pointed it down at the brown divots of the tenth hole tee area where they stood. The snack shack was maybe a twenty yard chip over a deep oval bunker.

"It musta got rabies or is just plain crazy out of its mind." Bonnie shook her head, and each member of the group turned toward the dark place beyond the broken screen of the front door.

"How'd you get away?" Bagg pulled out his notebook and flipped to the first blank page.

"Gosh, I don't really know. I just ran screaming. I thought it was following me. I could feel its awful breath on the back of my neck as I was pulling open that door." She pointed. "It was like I knew I was about to die."

The EMT took the opportunity to comfort the pretty woman, reaching one rubbery hand around to rest on her shoulder, taking an obvious peek between buttons at her lacy bra.

"I'm going in." Officer Gates apparently recognized this as his big chance.

Gates stepped away from the group and keyed the microphone clipped to the epaulet on his left shoulder, the mic cord curling down to the radio hanging from his belt.

Officer Gates tilted his head toward the microphone. "Unit Sixteen to Dispatch."

"Dispatch. Go ahead, Sixteen."

"I'm ten seven to take a ten sixty-two. All other units code four." His voice was hushed.

"Ten four, Sixteen," said the dispatcher. "Let me know when you're back in service."

"Code four?" Bagg understood that the cop was telling his dispatcher he was out of service to take a report from a citizen, but why code four? Code four cancelled all other responding units. And why the secrecy? Why was the cop practically whispering this stuff?

The cop turned to the golf pro. "Take Mr. Montrose up to the clubhouse. Go back along the eight and nine holes and stop anybody from coming down here, okay?"

"You bet, officer!" The pro seemed more than happy to be given a job away from the cornered bear.

"You three ... inside the ambulance!" Gates was talking to the EMT, Bonnie, and Bagg, but Bagg wasn't budging. Instead, he fished the Canon out of his camera bag and loaded a fresh thirty-six exposure roll of Fuji film.

"I'll come with you," Bagg told Officer Gates, as the EMT helped the sweet-smelling Bonnie to her feet and back onto the single gurney locked to the floor.

"Yeah, baby!" Jake the EMT mouthed at Bagg as he turned away from the girl. Apparently things were looking up for him. He winked at Bagg and mouthed, "Nice tits."

Gates eyed the expensive-looking camera and also seemed to decide things were looking up. Perhaps he was planning how to pose for tomorrow's front page newspaper photo.

"C'mon." The cop held the black gun out in front with both hands. Bagg let his Canon lead the way, as he followed the cop down into the sand trap and back up toward the snack building.

"Just stay behind me," the cop whispered. "Out of my line of fire."

"Yeah, I'm right here," answered Bagg, as the pair crept onto the patio and made their way between the round tables. Bagg noticed the sweat dripping down the back of the officer's neck, despite the cool afternoon and the nice breeze. In fact, the entire back of the cop's uniform shirt was drenched in sweat.

"Busted right through the screen," Gates said to Bagg, as they looked at the hole where the animal had obviously busted right through the screen. Bagg reached around the cop to pluck a torn strip of pink taffeta snared on the broken wire.

"What do you make of this?" Bagg whispered, offering up the taffeta.

"Fuck if I know." The cop bent down, about to squeeze through the jagged hole in the screen.

"Wait." Bagg grabbed the cop by his black leather belt with his left hand. With his right hand, Bagg reached for the doorknob and pulled the door slightly ajar.

"Right." Gates straightened up, took the doorknob and slowly opened the door.

The building had two rooms. The front portion was divided in half, with space on the near side for golfers to place orders, while orders were taken from the other side of a high counter running the length of the room. At the far left side was one of those hinged countertop doors you saw in bars that the employee lifted and ducked under.

Against the wall behind the counter was a grill, with huge steel vents disappearing into the ceiling. It was hot, and the smoke from charcoal-black pieces of what was probably old meat was silently being sucked into the vent. In the middle of the back wall was an open doorway leading to the kitchen and prep area.

The cop looked around, blinking, as both men let their eyes adjust to the dark room. Gates then stepped inside in big, slow, almost comically arcing strides, as if stepping across a river on rocks a little too far apart. He held the gun at arm's length, the barrel darting from spot to spot in quick, twitchy motions.

The first section of the front room was clear. No wild bears whatsoever.

"We gonna keep goin'?" Bagg asked, and the cop, who'd seemed frozen, jumped a bit at his voice. "This bear's awful quiet for being crazy rabid."

"Shhhh," Gates hissed. "C'mon."

The pair ducked under the counter; Gates had his gun darting and dancing again, while Bagg wished he'd packed a flash. It was too dark in here for a good photo of a thrashing, crazed bear.

"Look," Gates whispered, pointing the gun down to a greasy wet spot on the linoleum floor. Bagg noticed that the gun was shaking and the officer's hands were glistening with sweat.

"You hear that?" Bagg asked, as a low uneven rumble seemed to come from the next room where the food was prepared. They were hunkered down below the grill, about five feet from the kitchen doorway, listening.

"It sounds like snoring," Bagg said.

"No, it sounds like a bear," Gates answered in a sharp whisper, spittle flying from his mouth. "Now, shut up and stay behind me."

"Still sounds like a snoring bear," Bagg repeated under his breath, as Gates edged forward. Bagg had gotten a look at the cop's too-wide eyes, which showed mostly white. Talk about crazy rabid.

From the arched doorway to the kitchen, the two men stood side by side, shoulders pressed together. One was armed with a gun; the other, a Canon T90 single lens reflex camera with a short zoom lens, not recommended for indoor use unless used with a flash. Bagg could feel the heat radiating off the cop. It felt like a sick heat, the kind that comes from someone with a really high fever, or someone who has a bad infection deep down inside.

≫ ≫ ≫

Gates spotted the bear, semi-hidden and waiting for its opportunity to pounce. He pinned the end of the Glock 9mm sight on the beast across the room, and suddenly the newspaper guy crowding him in the doorway became invisible, or wasn't there at all. Instead, Gates could sense his father's eyes, could hear the condescending laugh meant to show off for his asshole friends.

Officer Gates could feel his heart trying to burst out of his chest, and his mind slipped back to the first time he'd ever hunted, his father kicking him hard in the leg when he didn't get out of bed right away. He'd been ten years old and it was opening day of deer season. He had been forced to climb up a ladder formed by two-by-three boards nailed to a tree trunk and sit shivering in a stand. Gates remembered being frozen to the bone, miserable and wanting to leave. But he had been stuck sitting on an upside-down bushel basket on a platform his father had built years before, some twenty feet up in the tree's crotch. Gates had been peeing over the side when a big eight-point buck came walking along the game path that his dad had built the stand above. He reached for the Browning twelve gauge his father had given him, brought it up to his shoulder in slow motion, and pointed the barrel down at the buck.

It was a clear shot. The young Gates stood with feet spread at shoulder width, the stock tucked tight in his armpit, and locked the sight onto the front left shoulder of the deer. Gates' thumb clicked the safety off, and his delicate index finger curled around the trigger and began squeezing, easy, just like he'd been told. But something was wrong. The harder he tried to squeeze, the less his finger wanted to react. He began hearing his own breathing—like somebody out of breath was standing real close—and his heart began to thump. The boy's wrist shook and rivulets of sweat broke out on his cold forehead, stinging his eyes, as the shaking spread from his right arm to engulf his entire body.

At some point, the deer looked up at the human in the tree, huffed once, and danced off into the woods, white tail flashing a mock surrender. Gates was left there shaking, unable to put the gun down, unable to do anything.

"You shouldn't have made fun of me like that," Gates told his father, but he was no longer up in a tree stand, looking down on dead, frost-covered leaves. Gates wasn't a ten-year-old anymore; he was an officer of the law, sworn to protect and serve. He was an important man.

"You better just shut up and pull the trigger 'fore you wet yourself." He heard his father's voice as if he was there; then his father laughed that awful, mocking laugh. "You sorry little sumbitch couldn't drop a deer, but you expect to take down a bear? You're a goddamn laugh riot, boy!"

Gates held the gun out toward the bear but couldn't quite steady the barrel. Sweat was dripping into his eyes, and he had to keep wiping them clear with his shoulder.

"Pull the trigger, you little fuckwad!"

"Shut up!" Gates screamed. On that cold morning in the woods, his father had walked up to him, laughing and pointing at his son, shivering in the tree stand, the deer long gone. The boy stood on the crooked pieces of timber, the muscles in his arms cramping, not yet able to lower the shotgun. His father laughed because he'd forgotten to pull up his pants when the buck walked past; he still had his little pecker out in the cold. It was just a coincidence that his father used the same path as the deer and stood in the line of fire. Gates remembered being tempted to try the shotgun trigger again.

"Put the gun down," Bagg said.

"Pull the trigger!" Officer Gates shouted, and it was somehow his father's voice. But his hands shook even harder, and the sweat poured into his eyes even worse.

"Pull the fucking trigger, you little fuckwad!" he screamed, but his finger refused to follow orders, and his arms and entire body quaked in a violent struggle between muscle and brain.

"It's wearing a tutu!" Bagg shouted into the cop's ear, shoving the torn piece of muddy pink material he'd removed from the screen door into the cop's face. *Pink*, Gates thought, the same color his father's white long johns had once turned when his mother tried to wash out spatters of deer blood. His father smacked her good and hard for that. He'd screamed that it looked like a fucking tutu and to throw them in the goddamn trash. "The bear is wearing a fucking tutu! It's some kind of pet!"

"I have to," Gates tried saying, but his jaw muscles were locked just as tightly as the rest of the muscles in his body. The lenses of his thick glasses had fogged over.

"Put the fucking gun down," Bagg screamed at Gates, who stood dripping sweat, the muscle cords in his neck twisted in a painful spasm as he fought the Glock's trigger and the mocking voice of his father.

"It's just trying to hide!" Bagg shouted directly into Gates' ear, but there was no change, just more tremors from the man's outstretched arms.

Officer Norman Gates had become a deadly statue, frozen somewhere between a humiliated ten-year-old boy in a frigid tree stand and a pathetic man unable to squeeze the last ounce of pressure needed to finish the job and stop the unrelenting voice in his head.

Gates sensed the sudden motion next to him but was helpless to react. There was a flash of black, a glint of light reflecting from the glass lens, and he recognized the object as the reporter's camera just as it struck him in the side of the head, stopping his father's jeering voice.

Chapter 17

Graceful Gracie woke up in a dark place and was at first relieved to be done with the terrible dream. But then she smelled the acrid cleansers and remembered she was hiding from the screaming cars that hunted her.

When she heard human voices behind her, Gracie cringed and closed her eyes. She tried to wiggle a little farther into her hiding place, but she was already in as far as she could go.

Even with the harsh-smelling cleansers, Gracie could clearly smell one of the men hunting for her now. The entire cabinet had been invaded by his odor. It was metal and oil, and full of heat. It was an electric smell that burned inside her nostrils. It was a heavy reek that cut through the air like a snake, looking for something to hurt. It was the bad, bad smell of the bad man who had trained her to dance.

"Help," Gracie murmured in her bear language. "Please help me."

At the sound of shouting and frightening commands, Gracie tried pushing even deeper into her hiding spot, her claws scrabbling against linoleum and wood. The awful reek became worse and then there was a heavy thump, followed by what sounded like someone falling hard onto the floor. Had one of the men turned on the other? Had they fought over who had the privilege of coming in for the kill? Gracie began to cry, weeping big bear tears as her nose became stuffy despite all the ammonia under the sink.

One man approached, taking short steps toward Gracie. She cringed, squeezing her eyes shut in anticipation of kicking or whipping, of the terrible beating to come. Instead, the man stroked her fur, fingers running gently across the old scars made by the man who had taught her to dance.

"It's okay, girl," the man cooed. His fingers found a good spot. "I'm not going to hurt you. You can come out of there if you promise not to eat me."

Gracie stopped crying but couldn't stop shaking. She wanted to be back in her cage more than anything in the whole world. She missed her smelly drunk man so bad it hurt. If Gracie had paid attention to what the roustabouts had been watching so intently on television one night last week, she'd have been trying to click her heels together three times, repeating the "no place like home" line over and over.

Gracie startled at the touch of this new man and tried to wedge herself deeper into the cabinet. But all the bark had gone out of his voice, which was now low and soothing. The man put his hand on her left leg, making long strokes along her trembling side and flank. But Gracie wasn't sure. What had happened to the other one? She thought she could still hear him breathing, but it sounded like he was making snoring sounds from down on her level. Gracie was confused, but the stroking was really nice and helping her to relax a little. Oh, god, being touched was good. She wanted to believe this new man wasn't going to hurt her if she came out. But if staying put made him keep rubbing her like this, maybe she'd never come out.

"C'mon, girl, c'mon outta there," the man said, still rubbing Gracie's quivering hind leg. "That cop is going to wake up soon and I don't think he's going to be in such a good mood. You have to help me, girl."

Having not elicited any sounds remotely menacing, the man moved forward on his knees and squeezed his arm farther into the cabinet to rub behind Gracie's head, gently coaxing her. "It's safe to come out, girl. C'mon."

Gracie decided to budge. The old bear tried to get a grip on the linoleum floor with her back paws, but they kept sliding. The man started pulling behind her left shoulder so that she was able to push away from the back of the cabinet with her front paws.

"That's a girl," the man encouraged in his human language. "Here we go!"

Gracie emerged from the acrid darkness in a sitting position. She looked down at her ruined tutu and the tears began to well up again. The stress had made her very emotional. But this man sitting next to her seemed to think everything was going to be okay.

"Everything's going to be okay, girl," he was saying to her.

Gracie looked beyond the man's shoulder to see the one who was sleeping. She eyed the gun still attached to his fingers. Gracie knew about guns. The bad man who trained her to dance had used one on her. It spit little steel balls at her that stung like bees. Human cubs also used them to pop the colored balloons to win stuffed animals. She didn't like the sound of guns or bursting balloons. There was nothing good about guns.

"I need to get you out of here." The man looked around the food prep room, maybe hoping for an answer to leap out at him.

The man showed his hands to Gracie the way she'd seen new people introduce themselves to the mutt circus dogs. Gracie leaned forward and sniffed, then licked the man's right palm. He let her lap his hand with her long, scratchy tongue. He reached around behind her ear for a gentle rub and Gracie melted forward into him, nuzzling and sniffing his armpit. "That's a girl," he told her. "You might be big, but you don't have any teeth, do you?"

From behind them came a single low groan.

The man pulled away from Gracie, keeping his left hand on her head, and struggled to his feet. "We have to go right now."

Gracie thought this new man tasted just fine and liked the sound of his voice. She let him lead her away from her hiding place. She was careful not to step on the gun or the sleeping human. She stopped to take a quick sniff at the spot on his head that leaked blood but decided it wasn't a bad wound. She had sniffed much worse.

Gracie followed the new man past where she'd scarfed down the yummy hotdogs, stopping to take a few quick licks of tasty grease she'd missed before. But this new man wanted her to keep moving and tugged her by the scruff of the neck just the way her good man did. She was a little nervous about going through the door where she'd heard the bad cars approaching, but it was all quiet now. She could hear birds jabbering away.

"Everything's going to be okay," the man said in human, tugging again at her scruff.

Gracie looked around at this outside world she hadn't had a chance to see much of before. The barking animals were gone except for their meaty scent. Two human faces looked out at her through windows in the back of a shiny, red and white truck. She'd seen those trucks come to the circus and take away hurt humans before. Those two faces were nothing to worry about. The bad car was there, but it was quiet and the flashing lights were dark.

The new man led her to a strange little truck and made a great sweeping motion with a zipper that opened up a back window. He swung open the back door and clicked a lever to get the backseats to lift forward, then patted a spot for her to climb up, just like when her good man wanted her to get inside her cage. Gracie knew this meant they were leaving, going someplace far away, and that made her very happy.

But Gracie's muscles were too sore from the swim and the escape from the barking animals. She got her two front paws up, but that was all she could manage.

"I can't," she said in bear to the man, looking over her shoulder apologetically. "I can't get up."

The man seemed to understand. He knelt down behind her and put his shoulder into her rear, pushing and grunting. There wasn't much room, but Gracie's big old body fit sideways as the man swung the back door closed.

The man rubbed Gracie's ears for a moment and she lunged at him with her long tongue, catching him across the lips when he started to pull away.

"It's going to be all right," the man told Gracie, and she tried to lick his face again. He stroked her head once more and then walked around to the driver's side door and hopped in. Adjusting the rearview mirror, the man started the car and drove, slowly at first, then sped up as he turned out onto the smooth road.

Gracie leaned out the back, craning her neck as far as she could around the side, hoping to catch the wind in her nose and flapping lips. She loved driving, and this truck was much faster than the big one that hauled her cage. It was very green here, and the sun flashed and flickered behind the tall trees. There were a million smells along this road, both old and newborn. She closed her eyes and huffed, pretending she was flying.

Chapter 18

Bagg and Gracie sat in the Jeep in a back corner of a McDonald's parking lot sharing a bag full of fish sandwiches and skinny French fries.

Gracie lounged over the folded down rear seat, drooling tartar sauce and bits of roll.

"You have a pretty big appetite for a ballerina." Bagg fed her a handful of warm, salty fries. "My little girl was a ballerina for a while."

Gracie gummed the fries and made mewing sounds for more.

"Then came soccer and she gave up her dancing career. She was about four when her mom and I called it quits."

Bagg pulled the lever on his seat and let it recline so he could give the bear a sip of vanilla milkshake.

"Her name is Morgan." Bagg tried to steady the cup as Gracie's tongue greedily lapped at the shake. "I haven't seen her in a really long time. It seems like forever."

Gracie nudged the shake cup away, eyeing the bag of fish sandwiches.

"Her mom and I had joint custody." Bagg unwrapped another sandwich for her. "I only got to see her every other weekend. That seemed like the worst thing in the world at the time. I kept having to say goodbye to her for twelve days, you know? I didn't think it could get worse than that. But it sure did."

Bagg fed Gracie the rest of his own sandwich.

"One Friday night, they just didn't show up. It was supposed to be six o'clock on the dot. That's how it was written in the court order. But then it was six fifteen, then six thirty. I kept waiting, but I think I knew right away she was never coming."

Bagg wiped his face with a napkin. As he went to toss it into the bag, Gracie plucked it from the air with her tongue and swallowed it.

"I don't know. Maybe if I'd called the township cops they'd have put out an APB, or something, and they'd have found them in line at the airport. Or maybe some cop would have shown up and told me to call my lawyer on Monday. What did I expect out of him? 'Your kid's with her mother and here I am wasting time writing up a report' was the attitude I got when I went to the station."

Gracie nodded for the milkshake again, and Bagg tried to steady the cup. White goo and drool dripped from his hand, a puddle forming on the back floor mat. He tried wiping the bear's mouth, but her tongue snared that one, too.

"They found her mother's car in the economy lot at the airport two weeks later. It's been over five years now. She was almost five, and now she's almost ten. Each year I try to figure out what a kid looks like at that age. How big they are, I mean. I know she's far away, but I'm always searching for her in crowds and things. Passing cars and grocery stores. Sometimes I think I see her, but I know better. She's a million miles away.

"She was my whole world." Bagg leaned back in the seat, and the bear arched forward and rested her chin on his right shoulder, foamy white lips making a warm wet spot on his shirt. Bagg absently rubbed her right ear. "I can't go into her bedroom. I had wanted to make it a second home for her, you know? We picked out cool posters and I bought a bunch of Christmas light strands and tacked them all across her ceiling."

"I put all those strands of lights up on a Friday afternoon, then picked her up and brought her back to our apartment. I told her I had a surprise, and she was all excited. I led her into her room, then snapped off her desk lamp and switched on the Christmas lights that lit up all over her ceiling." Bagg stopped. Tears were trickling down his cheeks as Gracie listened quietly. He saw her yellow eyes follow the crooked trail the little clear drops were taking over his stubbly whiskers.

"I heard her gasp, like she was looking at something magical," Bagg told the bear. "And that's just what she said, 'It's magic, Daddy. You made magic!'"

"But a couple of weeks later her mom took her away and the magic was gone."

Chapter 19

Jennifer, Morgan's mother, had put a lot of time and effort in planning the escape to their new lives. When she did things, she did them right, which was a stark contrast to her half-assed ex-husband and the half-assed life they'd had together. She just hoped she hadn't waited too long. It seemed like every time she turned around, Morgan became more and more like her father. Drifting through life, glassy-eyed and unmotivated, was loathsome and unacceptable. Lennon Bagg disgusted her, and she'd long ago come to wonder what it was about him that had originally caught her attention.

Jennifer cringed at the thought of her only child growing up an apathetic slug.

To this day, she relished the memory of Lennon's face when she announced she was leaving him. "You make my skin crawl," she'd hissed and had finally been rewarded with a reaction; the expression she caught on that normally dull, uninspired face before it turned away from her was crestfallen, humiliated.

But removing her daughter from her husband's daily influence had backfired. Morgan had come home from weekend visits more like her father than ever. She had been insolent and brooding, which made Jennifer hate the man even more. She had to do something drastic, beyond what the court was willing to do; she had to fix the problem herself.

Escaping from Lennon Bagg was as easy as buying a plane ticket. He hadn't bothered to hire a divorce attorney—not that he had any real assets to protect. They'd had maybe eleven thousand dollars in a money market fund, and it would be lucky if his 401k had another ten. With a kid, the house naturally went to her, with its modest equity. The idiot judge granted him joint custody and regular visitation, despite the fact that he'd be living in a shit-hole apartment. No, the problem wasn't getting Morgan away from her father, but the risk of making a mistake and getting caught was enormous. Jennifer took nothing for granted just because Lennon Bagg was an incompetent laggard.

Jennifer hatched her plan, paying careful attention to the smallest details. Her daughter was too old for Jennifer to change her first name, but most anyone would understand the confusion a small child had about a change of surname. Wasn't everyone divorced at least once? And borrowing the famous actor's name would make any sort of Internet search useless, lost among hits for *The Shawshank Redemption* and *Nurse Betty*.

Even more than five years and eight hundred miles of blue-green ocean hadn't done much to mitigate Lennon Bagg's influence. The girl obsessively drew pictures of birds instead of doing her homework. Her room was littered with them, and her teachers sent home warning notes regarding her erratic behavior and lack of attention.

❧ ❧ ❧

Morgan Freeman sat on her towel, alone on the beach except for the birds. At ten years old, the skinny little girl with pale skin and brown hair just touching her shoulders had already given up on a lot of things. Santa was the hardest to let go of, but there was also the Tooth Fairy, the Easter Bunny, and all that junk about crossing your fingers for good luck and not stepping on cracks. All were gone for the fourth grader, who had also given up on finding any real friends on this stupid island.

"Are you my dad?" Morgan halfheartedly asked a seagull. The question was strictly out of habit, since she'd seen him around enough to know better.

The gull had snuck up next to her towel in the pink sand, but without food, Morgan was apparently not all that interesting. It watched her for a minute or two, refused to answer any questions, and then flew back in the direction of its flock's usual dumpster hangout behind the church kitchen.

Morgan Bagg had been renamed Morgan Freeman, according to the passport and other documents her mother had spent several thousand dollars to have created.

"Oh, yes, little missus, like the famous actor!" the uniformed customs officer at Bermuda L.F. Wade International Airport had said, waving the two females on with a friendly smile.

Birds being dead people was a fact etched in stone; it was absolute truth and nonnegotiable. It was also the main reason other fourth graders called her Mental Morgan and Cuckoo Bird Girl.

"I don't care what names they call me," Morgan told a Sooty Shearwater that had hopped up to her, head cocked to one side to better eye the girl. "I know you, don't I? Have we met? You look really familiar."

The bird kept watching her from a safe distance. This big animal, it seemed to be thinking, wasn't making any sudden moves and maybe had something to eat in its pockets.

"I'm looking for my dad," Morgan told the curious, mud-colored bird. "My dad is a bird, too. His name is Lennon Bagg, and I miss him very much."

Back when Jennifer Bagg, now Freeman, had hustled her daughter through the Philadelphia airport, Morgan had kept asking about Daddy. She was supposed to see Daddy that night and spend the weekend. Where were they going? Was Daddy coming on the airplane, she had cried as her mother handed the tall lady in a dark blue skirt their tickets.

"I don't see Daddy anywhere, Mom." Morgan peered around her mother as they walked single file toward their seats.

"Daddy said we were going to make a real pizza tonight," Morgan told her mother. She refused to sit, blocking the aisle for the impatient, weary-looking passengers behind them.

Morgan had heard her mother and friend talking about an airplane and a place called Bermuda, whispering things about starting life over far away. Was this what all the secret talk had been about?

"Daddy's going to be really, really sad, Mommy." Morgan reluctantly scooted into her seat. "He can't make pizza without me. I have to put on the tomato sauce and cheese. He'll mess up."

"We're going to a very special place with beautiful beaches."

"Will Daddy be there?"

"No, sweetheart."

"Then I don't want to go! We have to get off the airplane right now!"

"Daddy can't come," Jennifer began, but she looked stuck to the little girl, like she was having a hard time telling the truth. It happened sometimes to Morgan when she broke something nice.

"If Daddy can't come, then I'm staying!" She was teetering on the edge of panic. "I don't care about beaches. Daddy can take me to the beach."

"Daddy can't come because he got very sick," Jennifer said to the little girl, who was suddenly quiet, her face frozen by the words. "He's very sick and you know how when people are sick they can be contagious? Do you understand what 'contagious' is?"

"You can make other people sick," Morgan whispered.

"Yes, Daddy is very, very sick and he's contagious."

Morgan looked past her mother, out at the runway lights. The stewardess began explaining the emergency procedures as Jennifer buckled them both in tightly. All the fight had gone out of Morgan as the plane backed up and headed away from the terminal. It revved its engines and then coasted out toward the runway.

Morgan sat quietly, worrying about her father. Had she made him sick?

As the plane raced down the runway, Morgan watched her mother peering out the little window. It seemed like her mother didn't care at all about Daddy. Why would they be flying away when Daddy was so sick, even if he was contagious?

"Is Daddy dead?" Morgan whispered to her mother, but Jennifer didn't answered, didn't even seem to hear the little girl's question. "Is he, Mommy?"

The tears on Jennifer Bagg's face seemed real as she turned and pulled her daughter into her arms as best she could with the seat belts still attached. "Yes, he is."

"What happens when you die, Mommy?" Morgan asked into her mother's silky, lightly perfumed blouse.

"You grow wings, Morgan. You grow wings and you fly up to Heaven."

The little girl rocked in her mother's arms, crying softly, thinking about the two boxes of pizza mix she and her dad had bought on their last trip to the grocery store.

"We'll make one giant pizza," Daddy had told her. "With anchovies!"

"Yuck!"

"With pickles!"

"Double yuck! I know you're just teasing."

Morgan fell asleep somewhere over the blackness of the Atlantic Ocean on her way to her new life. She dreamed about her father growing wings.

Chapter 20

The sun was an orange disc sliced in two by leftover jet engine contrails that were slowly breaking apart in the westerly breeze. The low sun always turned the sand a deeper shade of pink. Morgan had learned in science class that the pink color was due to the red skeletons of single-cell animals called Red Forams, tiny critters living beneath the coral reef. One of the boys from her class who boogie boarded on this beach had claimed it was whale blood from the great whale graveyards. Just like elephants, he had sworn, whales came to Bermuda to die.

"Look around." The boy grabbed up his board after they shared the same small wave and were swept onto the beach. "Everything comes here to die. Dead crabs, dead jelly fish."

"Even the seaweed comes here to die." He scooped a big handful of dripping seaweed, whipping it ahead of them into the surf.

When the other kids saw that the boy was talking to the creepy little girl who talked to birds, he raised his voice. "And stay off my waves, Cuckoo Bird."

Morgan hoisted her board by the coiled rubber leash and flopped down the beach in her swim fins. Most kids hated walking in flippers, but Morgan didn't mind at all. She felt very bird-like and figured it was good practice for when she died, especially if she became a pelican. There were about twenty kids on boogie boards, and Morgan made her way to the far end of the lineup before turning and stepping back into the surf. She lunged forward, splashing down like a Red-breasted Merganser, which was a silly looking duck whose head reminded her of the Roadrunner cartoon. She'd seen two Merganser drakes on this beach, neither of which were her father.

Morgan and her mom were living in the same rental as when they arrived five years earlier on Somerset Island. The island accounted for a large portion of Sandys Parish, which was the westernmost of nine Bermuda parishes. She was just finishing up the fourth grade at Sandys Primary School, where she was one lone student among two hundred kids, ages four to eleven.

The only good thing about school was art class, which was the one place where she wasn't given a hard time for drawing pictures of birds. Any hint of paint on her narrow bedroom walls was hidden by a gallery of her bird drawings, from the graceful Mute Swans—which really did talk—to a variety of black and white images of diving and darting Shearwaters.

Morgan's collection also included a Brown Boobie, which she sometimes imagined she'd become when she died. The boobies she watched on the rocks at the south end of her regular beach were amazing fliers, but lousy at taking off. They would stumble forward, almost falling over their big webbed feet, trying to get themselves airborne. Morgan could definitely sympathize. A boobie needed a good strong wind and a high perch for an easy takeoff. The coolest thing about these birds with small wings and long tails was how they fished from the air. They spotted a flash of silver below and went into dive bomb mode, plunging into the ocean at incredible speeds. It took her breath away each time. She sometimes thought she'd like to do that to the kids who were mean to her, just dive bomb them from above.

The little blue house she shared with her mom was on No Name Lane. It was just a few blocks from the west—facing windward beach, where Morgan went after school every day until the sun dropped into the ocean. Her school was a ten minute walk in the opposite direction, away from the beach and most of the interesting birds. The

114

whitewashed stone school was home to dozens of Laughing Gulls, obviously named for their high-pitched call that sounded like a person laughing. But it didn't sound like a good kind of laugh to Morgan. It sounded more like the mocking laughter of the kids who picked on her.

Morgan paddled her boogie board out through the small swells, aiming directly at the big orange sun. It was getting late, but she didn't want to go home yet. Here, far enough away from the other kids, she felt a little closer to her dad. Maybe he could find her better out here, away from the buildings and clutter. Morgan kicked in a slow circle with her swim fins, as she and her board lifted up and over the undulating sea. She was well beyond the place where you could catch even the outside breakers, but this was her favorite spot. And this was feeding time for the fish, so the littlest ones were jumping up out of the water to escape the bigger ones. Her mom didn't like her in the water this time of day, but one of Morgan's teachers had told them the only shark attacks happened on the eastern beaches, and those were very rare.

Morgan had seen a Galapagos shark once, but her teacher had already explained they were just bottom feeders that ate small fish and octopus. The shark's big dorsal fin had broken the surface ten feet away and scared the bejeebers out of her at first. It had circled her boogie board twice, probably just to check out the bobbing girl, finally sweeping under the water like a diving submarine.

Even though Morgan didn't want to be eaten by a shark, she wasn't afraid to die. She'd decided it wasn't going to be much different than her long afternoons and evenings out here beyond the breakers. Instead of wings, she had her swim fins. Instead of the breeze, she had the ocean to ride.

And anyway, she'd be able to find her dad much easier once she became a bird.

Chapter 21

Billy Wayne was on a mission as he sped up Great Bay Boulevard with Bill Cosby Jell-O Pudding commercials dancing in his head. He'd loved the television program about Cosby's family, the smart and funny mother and father. Mr. Cosby could tease and tease, but it was never hurtful. And all those children, with big white smiles and bright clean clothes, running around that expensive house. It hurt Billy Wayne when his mother called the family the nastiest word possible.

Billy Wayne didn't know what made the Haitian women outside the Laundromat so evil and menacing, even though he tried his best to ignore them, while the same color family on television were people he admired.

"Komon ou ye?" the women taunted, deep and guttural, each time he'd walk past on his way to the dollar store. They all spoke the words, one by one, some evil voodoo chant. Even if he'd known they were politely asking how he was, he wouldn't have felt any less intimidated. The tone of their voices was what scared him the most. And those glowering white eyes.

Maybe if you sold pudding in commercials you weren't capable of hurting people? Billy Wayne sensed that as a cult leader he should know these things, but his mother's hatefulness confirmed how he felt when the women spoke their evil language as he walked past. Billy Wayne had been warned about their voodoo and knew to keep moving.

Bill Cosby wouldn't believe in voodoo. No, sir, Bill understood what made the world a better place, so it was no surprise at all when Billy Wayne's book mentioned vanilla pudding.

Step number forty-one from *How to Become a Cult Leader in 50 Easy Steps*: "Keep plenty of vanilla pudding in the cupboards. Comfort foods are called just that for a very good reason. Vanilla pudding is easy to whip up and a delight for all ages. Just a small cup of vanilla pudding for each to share after a difficult and trying day will create a sense of fellowship among even your most skeptical followers."

Billy Wayne drove his Dart back to West Tuckerton, pulling right up to the same group of teenage boys who had previously sent him on the wild goose chase in search of the defunct sporting goods store. He hurried past them into the convenience store and scooped up every box of vanilla pudding they had. He dropped the armful on the counter and went back for a few boxes of chocolate. Billy Wayne decided chocolate was a clever touch and was proud of himself for going above and beyond what the good book said. He also just happened to prefer chocolate.

On Billy Wayne's return trip, he marveled at how fast the island had been transformed. From the top of the rickety bridge, he looked out over the two large main tents and the collection of smaller ones being staked down. Away from the shadows of the casinos, the tents seemed huge, and Billy Wayne's mind wandered to the wonderful and fiery speeches he'd give under the spotlights usually reserved for the ringmaster and performers. A nervous thrill ran through his body as he drove slowly down the gravel lane, careful not to spook the zonkey being pulled along behind the pretty young contortionist at the end of a thin nylon rope. The zonkey, as Billy Wayne had understood it, was the result of cross-breeding a zebra and a donkey. The resulting configuration was somehow easier to ride.

The contortionist, Amira Anne, stirred something deep inside Billy Wayne. He'd witnessed her act under the big tent back in the casino parking lot and found himself shamefully aroused. She was one of the performers who entertained the early ticket buyers. Billy Wayne had been perched in the second row of one of the three sets of bleachers when Amira had entered under a single spotlight to slow, sexy Middle Eastern music. She peeled off a full-length feather coat to reveal a glossy, skin-tight blue one-piece. Under the glaring light, Billy Wayne was able to see every curve and every niche of her wonderful body as she easily hoisted herself onto a platform in the middle of the ring.

Amira faced Billy Wayne as she lowered her chin to the wood base and stepped backwards over her own body, giving him and the small crowd a full-on view of her blue crotch. He adjusted his trousers to hide what his mother had called Satan's Little Pink Snout as the contortionist got to her feet and brought one leg all the way behind her head. Oh, God, Billy Wayne sighed as she leaned forward to grab the handle on top of the metal bar. The girl lifted herself by one hand and did a split over her head, rotating slowly.

Billy Wayne nearly exploded, tiny lines of sweat running from below each uneven sideburn, hands shaking. He wasn't able to look away from the girl and tried not to think about all the miserable chores and humiliation Momma had inflicted upon him after she'd caught him playing with Satan's Little Pink Snout as he sat on the toilet when he was twelve.

Billy Wayne smiled out the car window at the pretty blond girl leading the zonkey down the road and was startled when she smiled and waved back.

"We got a tent all set up for ya, boss," one of the ride mechanics told Billy Wayne, as he climbed out of his Dart with his two plastic bags full of pudding. "There's a pretty nice cot that used to belong to Enzo. It kinda smells like piss, but it's real comfy."

"Thank you," Billy Wayne said to the man whose hands and arms looked to have been stained black from years of grease and a lack of soap. "Oh, and would you please pass the word around that I'd like everyone to gather in the first main tent in an hour? I have a few things I'd like to say."

"Yeah, sure 'nuff, boss."

"Wait," he called to the mechanic who'd already turned to work on this new duty. "Please let everyone know there will be vanilla pudding."

Billy Wayne had now relegated a task and announced a magnanimous offering—the vanilla pudding—so he was feeling on top of the world as he went in search of the cook tent. There, he relegated another task, then went back to his new home, set up by the mechanic.

The round tent was red and yellow canvas, with twenty stakes around the perimeter, and a center pole that gave him a ceiling more than twice his height. At least four hay bales had been cut loose and spread around the mucky floor. The deep hay made it necessary to high step across to the cot, but he figured it would get trampled soon enough. With just the bed and one low wooden stool, the space seemed huge.

Billy Wayne hadn't been to church in more than a dozen years, ever since his mother had gotten too fat to leave the house. And even then, keeping her company was the only reason he had gone. To Billy Wayne, it all sounded like guilt and anger. It was fire and brimstone speeches from an old man in a white collar and a pressed black shirt. But his opinion was only based on little snippets from the Methodist minister. Billy Wayne had perfected the art of falling asleep with his eyes half open, and the dimwitted look it projected wasn't particularly unflattering to him; as a teenager and young adult, Billy Wayne spent most of his time appearing to be the imbecile son of the really fat woman. People tended to steer clear of the pair, and that was fine. Church went faster when you didn't stand around talking afterward.

But behind those half-closed, imbecile eyes, Billy Wayne was laying out a plot. Years before stumbling across his *How to Become a Cult Leader* book, he'd watched a dark documentary about a cult living somewhere off in a jungle.

The followers of this man were recruited through their faith in God but were then shown the real deal. That's just how the narrator put it: "The Reverend hooked them with scripture and then they were shown the real deal."

It gave Billy Wayne goose pimples.

The leader and his followers had committed mass suicide, so some of the details were sketchy and blanks had to be filled in. But the documentary producers had interviewed several people who had defected before things got out of hand. Suicide having been the ultimate fate of the cult leader distressed Billy Wayne when he first watched the show, but he knew in his heart of hearts it would never come to that with him. No matter how terrible and desperate things got, he was far and away too cowardly to kill himself. No way that was ever gonna happen.

The former members did their best to describe the cult leader's motivations, as they saw them. Billy Wayne struggled to understand what must be the important parts, where cults were being compared to communism. The members talked about how there were no social classes, with no repression and common ownership of all property and possessions. Decisions on governing policies were made democratically and everyone had an equal vote, including the cult leader.

And there was the tricky part, Billy Wayne thought then and struggled with now. It was a conundrum even his How To book didn't really have an easy answer for, and Billy Wayne craved easy answers. How could you be acknowledged as the leader in a society of equals? He suspected they must have covered it somewhere in the documentary, maybe during his trip to the toilet. He regretted not recording the show. He might have found the answer.

Billy Wayne had never led anything, not even the Pledge of Allegiance in homeroom, even though the teacher had all the kids take turns. Little Billy Wayne froze up each time he tried. Most of the class mocked him with giggling and cruel words, and the teacher finally let him off the hook and quietly skipped over his turns. The humiliation became one more reason Billy Wayne was more than happy to stop going to school and take care of his mother's needs full-time.

Billy Wayne also felt a connection to the cult leader profiled in the show. He, too, had been ridiculed as a boy. Neighbors of the leader's childhood home claimed he'd been caught starting fires and cutting the heads off cats. He then supposedly held elaborate backyard funerals, burying the little bodies in shallow graves. They'd called him a "weird little boy, bound for no good." Billy Wayne figured the neighbors could have made it all up for the television cameras. Billy Wayne had also been accused by his own neighbors of starting fires, as well as trying to kill their dog. And while he did go through a stage of lighting small fires—didn't every kid?—it was Billy Wayne's mother who had wanted the yapping neighbor's dog shut up once and for all. Billy Wayne truly believed he was just doing what his mom wanted when he fed the dog balled up pieces of hamburger with a bunch of fishhooks inside. The dog, though, just shit them out, which is how he ended up being accused. What kind of person pays that close attention to his dog's turds, anyway?

Retrieving the How To book and a yellow legal pad from his car, Billy Wayne settled in on the urine-scented cot to scribble out his first benediction, while the vanilla pudding was being prepared in the cook's tent. He was convinced his time had finally come. He and everyone around him were here for a purpose. Billy Wayne Hooduk's hand was not steady, but his number two pencil wrote with a flourish.

Chapter 22

Jesper Springs didn't give a flying rat's ass whether or not there was some sort of God either up there in the clouds or yappin' on some makeshift stage. Jesper's life was centered around either bolting together ride parts or tearing tickets in half while waiting for the parts to loosen enough to be retightened. And he was too damn busy to wash the grease off his hands and arms seein' they'd just grease right back up after drying off anyway.

After passing the word around about the boss wanting to give them a talkin' to, Jesper took his place on one of the hay bales in the main tent, as had the forty or so other remaining performers and roustabouts. Getting the tents raised had taken priority, and the bleachers and other chairs were still strapped down on one of the big trucks. The hay bales were convenient because they were going to be used for mud control and mucking the animal shit.

Jesper Springs drew the extra twenty dollars a week mechanics pay, but he often considered himself a magician. His one magic act was making himself disappear whenever he wanted to be invisible. Sitting right there on the hay bale, in plain sight as anyone else, Jesper slowed down his breathing and sat very still. The only moving parts were his eyeballs, and he even made them work in slow motion. Jesper could feel himself fading; light coming in from the big tent flap started flowing right through his sinewy, grease-stained body.

Invisible time was peaceful time, to Jesper. No worries about someone storming up from behind yelling to go clean this up, or go fix that goddamn thing he hadn't gotten around to fixing yesterday. Fact was, Jesper stopped hearing anything clearly when he went invisible. All the talking around him seemed far off, like his ear was pressed up in a tin can, or something. He didn't much care what people said, anyway. People were always yapping and yapping, believing everything they were saying without ever saying anything.

Invisibility ought to be a high paid performing act, but Jesper knew there wasn't much hope. How did you get even the dumbest of dumb, those people who slapped dollar bill after dollar bill on the counter to toss darts to win fifty cent toys, to pay *not* to see you? That was a tough one. Once he figured that one out, he'd start on his second great mystery, which was how to keep himself invisible inside the ladies shower at the YWCA.

Jesper's hay bale was off to the side of the contortionist's platform he and the other mechanic had set up for the Hooduk guy to use. Jesper eyed all the smudges he'd left on its nice white paint and then looked down at his hands, a little embarrassed. He'd stuck around for the vanilla pudding and hoped nobody saw all his fingerprints. Jesper sat even more still, made himself a little more invisible.

Out walked their new boss in a shirt and tie, looking like the cat's meow until he had to struggle his lardy ass up onto the platform. Jesper hadn't figured on maybe getting a step stool. That hot little contortionist broad sure didn't need any help getting up on that thing, no sir.

The new boss said something to the other mechanic standing next to the tent flap, who then fetched the first of three big trays of plastic cups filled up with vanilla pudding. Boxes of plastic spoons were also passed around, and everyone in the tent, including the boss, dug in.

Being invisible and on the far side of the tent, Jesper was the last to get his cup and spoon, but the wait was sure worth it. Vanilla pudding might just be the best thing in the world, he thought, scooping thick yellow spoonfuls into his piehole. He slowed down to savor the rich flavor and remembered back to when his ma and pa were still livin' back north of Chattanooga. His pa wasn't allowed to drink on Christmas, and his ma used to mix up a big pot of vanilla pudding to go with the corn fritters and baked opossum. Jesper got a little misty thinking about those good days when everybody's belly was full and pa wasn't piss drunk, just wantin' to slap you upside for nothin'.

Boss put his empty cup down and started talking about believing in only the things you could see. That wasn't nothin' hard to understand. Jesper had expected to be ignoring a lecture about not gettin' caught knockin' up any local girls. Or maybe he'd spout some of that fire and brimstone the travelin' tent preachers dished out back north of Chattanooga. The boss had, after all, said he was God for shootin' that homo's tiger. Shit, Jesper thought to himself, I musta shot me a hundred coon; does that make me Mother fuckin' Teresa?

"If you see me as your friend, then that's exactly who I am," Billy Wayne said. Jesper kind of liked that. The boss sure was nicer than those old Pisani pricks. Them cheap motherfuckers cheated him outta half his pay more than once for bein' drunk and fallin' asleep while running the tilt-a-whirl. Big fuckin' deal; the kids got some extra time on the ride. And it was Jesper who had to clean the seats they puked up on anyway.

"If you see me as your father, then that's exactly who I am," the Boss said, and Jesper figured that was a bad thing to be tellin' these people. Ain't no way you should want people thinkin' you're just some lowdown child whoopin' piece of shit. Jesper looked around the crowd of circus folk and felt sorry for the boss for sayin' that. The boss don't know circus folks.

"And if you see me as your God, then that's exactly who I am," Billy Wayne continued, and Jesper giggled. It weren't no fire and brimstone, but somebody callin' themselves God was a friggin' hoot. Hey, God, Jesper thought, how's 'bout you raise my Shelly Girl up from the dead? Send that truck driver who ran down my dog straight to Hell and bring her back all fixed up good as new. Ain't no real God looking down on this world who would allow a man's best friend run over like that. No way.

"We'll be more than performers and workers. We have a chance to be a family and fill our souls with love and kindness," Billy Wayne told his audience, but Jesper Springs had his head down in his greasy hands, sulking about his dead dog. He didn't pay any attention to the rest of what the boss had to say. He just sat there invisible.

Chapter 23

The bear cut loose an enormous fart in her sleep, vibrating the metal frame of the Jeep.

"Wow." Bagg turned the wheel out of the McDonald's parking lot, back onto Route Nine headed north, trying his best to breathe the good outside air.

Bagg had used his cell phone to track down the reporter from his paper working on the fatal tiger attack in Atlantic City. The runaway bear in a tattered pink tutu, showing up on a golf course no more than ten miles away, had to be connected.

"The two men who died from the mauling were the owners of the whole shebang," said the reporter, a veteran police beat reporter named Andy Cobb. He was now at his newsroom desk trying to gather background information on the circus and the deceased for a follow-up story. "Old guys named Pisani were brothers. Uh, Enzo and Donato, ages unknown, but they looked to be a hundred and twenty, maybe older. I haven't found out what town they're from, but all the plates are Sarasota County, Florida. The only name we have for the dead human cannonball so far is Enrique. The tiger was the other fatality."

"What killed the tiger?"

"Guy named William Wayne Hooduk, age thirty, from up in Asbury Park. He was a registered guest at the casino hotel that owned the parking lot. He popped the big cat with a .38 Special," Cobb said, the sounds of turning notebook pages in the background. "Pretty spectacular shot, if you ask me. One weird thing about the gun ..."

"What's that?"

"Hooduk claimed it was God's .38 Special."

"Hard to confirm that, I guess."

"Oh, yeah, you'd think," Cobb said. "But Hooduk also claims he is God."

"Does God have a criminal record?"

"Just bullshit stuff. God has a history of setting small fires," Cobb said. "Lots of probation and hand slapping. Looks like God mostly set garbage cans on fire."

"Where are they now?"

"They beat it out of town. Cops took statements and told them to hit the bricks. They packed up in a big hurry and got outta Dodge. Cops didn't say so, but I figure there's a stack of warrants coming back on them, you know? It's gotta be pretty typical for a traveling circus. Probably one of the reasons to run away and join the circus, am I right?"

"I suppose," Bagg said. "You know which direction they headed?"

"North on Route Nine. They pretty much cleaned out an all-night doughnut shop in Smithville. Something like fifteen circus trucks pulled up to the drive-thru window, scaring the shit out of the two Indian girls working the late shift."

"State Police looking for them?"

"Nah, not that I hear," Cobb answered. "Not unless any felony warrants came back. The Atlantic City guys were more than happy to have them out of their hair. Imagine the hassle of what to do with all the animals?"

"Yeah," Bagg said, and a big toothless yawn erupted over his shoulder as the bear squeezed herself down behind the back seat, seeming to settle into a deeper sleep. "You heard about the bear?"

"You went out on that, right? What happened?"

"I'm still working on it." Bagg thought about the cop he'd just knocked unconscious and the felony warrants that might be out on him right now. "There weren't any reports of a bear getting loose from the circus?"

"Nah. And the bear would've had to run down the Expressway to get anywhere near where they sent you. My guess is that it was probably a big black lab seen by someone who had just watched the circus story on the late news. Hey, you line anything up, yet? A new job, I mean."

"No, I have a bunch of résumés out." It was a lie. Bagg hadn't bothered looking for a new job.

"Yeah, I can't find shit, either. I don't know what the hell I'm gonna do. Hey, I gotta go. I got a call from Sarasota on the other line."

"Good luck. You're too good of a reporter not to get picked up by somebody."

"Yeah, well it's either that or I'm selling vacuums door to door," Cobb said. "And, hey, one more thing?"

"Yeah?"

"With all the shit going on with the paper, I know we all forgot what you're still dealing with. I'm sorry about your daughter. I'm real sorry. Don't give up hope."

"Thanks. I appreciate that." Bagg clicked his phone shut to cut off the call with his old friend.

Bagg listened to the snoring bear in the back of his Jeep for a while before twisting the key and heading north on Route Nine. He shifted gears gently, trying not to wake her. Their duo could travel a lot more incognito without a slobbering bear hanging out the back window.

"I could always run away and join the circus," Bagg told the sleeping bear. "That's what people do, right?"

                              ৡ   ৡ   ৡ

Back at the Absecon Golf and Country Club, Officer Gates finally came to, wobbling to his knees and gathering up his weapon, glasses, and baseball-style uniform cap. Dizzy and suffering a miserable headache, the young cop nervously checked his immediate surroundings for any sign of the beast. The last thing he remembered was taking aim as it prepared to attack, but then everything went black. Gates reached up and found a knot on the right side of his head. His fingertips came away dotted with small spots of coagulated blood, making his stomach roll and pitch and his head swim again. Christ, he hated blood. Lurching forward onto all fours, the young cop threw up his breakfast, then dry-heaved as tears squeezed through his clenched eyelids.

What would his father have to say about this little cluster fuck? Officer Gates moaned from the thought. "Norman! Norman!" he could almost hear the kids and their taunting chant. Who the fuck names their kid after a psychotic movie killer? And just when the joke was getting old, the goddamn movie studios released a sequel to start round two of the torment.

"The bear attacked me," Gates told the deserted snack shack. "I tried to fight it off, but it threw me down to the floor. I thought I was going to die."

Gates got hold of his breathing and replayed the lie in his head to see how it fit.

"I couldn't risk discharging my weapon," he explained. "The newspaper guy ..."

Gates hit a wall right there. He figured the bear took off, but where the hell was the reporter? And what about the girl and the goddamn EMT? Gates climbed to his feet as the dread began to spread through his body. He shakily made his way back through the front of the snack shack, his weapon again leading the way, his hat stuffed in his back pocket. He was half expecting to find a mangled reporter, and then a mangled waitress and EMT. They'd be all chewed to hell, having been torn from the back of the ambulance and partially eaten.

But the only things outside the small building were singing birds and his own Absecon police cruiser. The ambulance was gone, as was the reporter's Jeep. And not a single sign of a wild bear.

"Thin air," Officer Gates told the tweeting birds, holstering his gun and making his unsteady way toward his vehicle.

"Fore!" came a distant warning, and Gates understood it was shouted in his direction. He ducked and covered his already throbbing head with his arms, cringing as he waited for impact. His first reaction was relief as the shot came up a good fifteen yards shy of him. But the ball one-hopped the hard tenth hole tee area and smashed through the driver side window of his cruiser.

"Just fuck me." Gates stepped up to his car, not bothering to look at the golfers. Officer Gates had resigned himself to small things like golf balls shattering his windows. Those things were easy enough to explain and weren't something to worry about. He had the bear and the reporter and his father to think about right now.

Opening the cruiser door, Gates brushed a glittering pile of safety glass off the seat and climbed in. The radio on his hip crackled as the dispatcher sent one of the other officers to meet a subject to take a report on a stolen bicycle.

Officer Gates fingered the microphone talk button on his shoulder but didn't press it right away. The bear was gone and so was everyone else. If a phone call had gone into dispatch about an officer down, this place would look like Grand Central Station by now, and a bird outside his broken window tweeted to confirm it was not.

Officer Gates found himself at a crossroads as to what to do.

"Nothing," he whispered to himself, starting the cruiser. "None of this shit happened."

Gates slammed his foot on the gas pedal, spinning tires throwing divots of Kentucky bluegrass high in the air, as he raced past the approaching twosome.

Chapter 24

Slim Weatherwax woke up scared to death someone had up and buried him alive in the night again. His fourth and final wife, Missy Delilah, had conspired with her half brother to dig a hole out behind Slim's barn and then drag the drunken, passed-out Slim into the muddy grave. Missy Delilah and Slim had only met a few weeks prior, and the relationship had been of the whirlwind variety, to say the least.

It had been a marriage of convenience in so much as Slim needed a woman to cook his meals, while Missy Delilah had been looking for a semi-responsible, home-owning man who she could kill and take over his house, or so he would later come to understand.

Missy Delilah secretly hated to cook, which led to a few bumps in her scheme, as well as the end of their marriage. She quickly grew impatient, jumping the gun by trying to bury Slim before he was sufficiently soused to stay in the hole. Missy Delilah had been kind enough to fill Slim in on all her pent-up hate during their final night together out by what was supposed to be Slim's final resting place.

The plan might have also gone smoother if she'd waited for her half-brother to arrive at the scene of the crime, since he probably would have had done a better job of hitting Slim with the shovel as he climbed up the side of the muddy hole.

"What the hell you doin', Missy Delilah?" Slim asked, spitting out manure-tainted dirt, having regained consciousness during the burial process.

"You stay dead, Slim!" she shouted down at him. "I went to a whole lotta trouble."

"Help me outta here," Slim pleaded, clawing his way up the side of the four-foot deep hole that was pretty well lit by the floodlight he'd installed over the old barn's back door.

"You ain't goin' nowhere!" she hollered, giving up on shoveling to turn the long handled tool into a deadly weapon. Missy Delilah held the shovel high over her head, slamming it down with a whoosh and wet smack in the dirt next to Slim's head.

"You almost hit me!" The quart of whiskey he'd recently tossed back, along with his pants being loaded up with heavy dirt, made climbing a slippery business; he felt like a deer navigating a frozen pond.

"Hold still, Slim." She used her sweetest voice and took two shorter swings, both also near-misses.

Slim retreated from this whack-a-mole game with his crazy new wife. "I thought you loved me." He sat with his long legs crossed under him in the center of the hole, feeling a bit sad and defeated, despite having survived so far. He'd never gotten any sort of handle on the whole marriage thing.

All the dragging, shoveling, and whacking had taken its toll on the new bride, and she, too, needed a break. Missy Delilah slumped down on the hump of earth that had been removed to create the hole. From the way she handled the shovel, he could tell she had a hand coated in new blisters.

"Ain't nobody could love a man like you, Slim," she said down into the hole. "You didn't even bother to shower when we went to the preacher. You goes to work, then comes home drunk, only to park your boney carcass in front of the TV and start drinkin' some more. And you got a naked whore tattooed on your chest!"

"Sunshine," Slim said from the hole.

"What?"

"The tattoo is a picture of my first wife, Sunshine."

"I hate you, Slim Weatherwax!" Missy Delilah began balling her eyes out. The shovel dropped from her hand.

"It's okay," Slim said. "I mostly hate me, too."

In Atlantic City, Slim had slept through the noise of Enrique's cannon blast. He wasn't even stirred by all the screams and hollering as the ornery tiger tore apart the poor old Pisani brothers. Slim had never trusted big cats, what with how they sprayed piss everywhere and, well, had a tendency to go nuts and kill people. Not in a million years would his Gracie have hurt a flea—and she had plenty—let alone a human being.

Slim wished he hadn't also slept through the gunshot that blew a hole in the nasty cat, but he'd been sleeping like a baby when the shit hit the fan in the parking lot. A total whiskey, beer, and gin-sodden baby, that was.

Slim woke up confused as hell, pinned underneath several hundred pounds of tent canvas. It hadn't been laid out and rolled like it was supposed to be but instead had been hurriedly crammed in the back of the storage truck. The storage truck held the soft egg crate packaging, which made it a perfect spot to nestle in with a bottle or two and avoid any extra last-minute chores. The old saying of being out of sight, out of mind, was music to Slim's ears. The foam matting had also saved him from being crushed because it had allowed his long, thin body to sink down under the heavy weight of the canvas. He also couldn't budge an inch until a couple of the gofers started unloading the truck the next morning.

Slim climbed down the metal truck steps into a blazing sun, immediately regretting he hadn't saved a little hair of the dog. It got that way, though. As the years rolled on, you just drank until it was gone. Back in the good old days, you sometimes passed out with a little something left in the bottle.

Slim blew his nose on his sleeve and walked down toward the water to take a piss. His fifty-something-year-old body felt twice that, and he knew the ache in his neck was going to hang around for days. But there was nothing new about waking up not knowing where the Christ he was. Hell, since his fourth wife had kept his house in the divorce and turned him into a confirmed bachelor, Slim rarely knew or gave a crap where he woke up. And most days, he didn't even care if he woke up at all.

Shaking off the last of the piss, Slim stuffed his pecker back in the roost and went to check Gracie's cage on one of the big trucks. He felt bad not tucking her in, but she knew how to open the latch and mooch a drink from one of the dog bowls. A while back, Slim had unlocked her cage one night at the end of a week-long bender. He'd climbed inside and slept like a baby for two whole days and just never bothered with the lock again.

Everyone knew Gracie was gentle, but nobody was stupid enough—even when they were drunk—to screw around with a bear. Even a bear in a pink tutu.

It didn't take Slim long to find her cage empty, but he still wasn't all that worried. Hell, it took a load out of his workday not to be scooping out bear shit and changing the hay, since she'd started climbing out and finding a quiet place to do her business on her own. Not that Slim didn't catch hell when somebody took a load of garbage to the dumpster and slid on a pile of steaming bear shit, falling on their ass.

Catching crap from some garbage monkey or ride jockey was worth it, though. And Gracie always came right back. She scared pretty easy, and being a toothless bear takes away some of your advantage, should you come across something wanting to fight.

Gracie knew better.

But where the hell was she? Slim put a hand up to his forehead to shade his eyes, scanning the marshy flats, looking for some big, bent-over critter trying to squeeze one out. Slim took a walk around the outside perimeter of the trucks and all the busy setup work going on. His head hurt too badly to call for her, but the uneasy feeling starting to well up in his gut got his feet moving.

Not by the water, and not anywhere off the gravel road. Slim marched faster, realizing they were on some sort of island made by a salt water canal slicing in an arc from the ocean inlet to the east.

"Where's Pisani?" Slim asked the first clown he walked up to, whose old makeup stains etched a wide frown across the lower half of his face.

"Which one?"

"Enzo," Slim said impatiently. "Where's Enzo?"

"Dead," said the clown. "Tiger killed him last night."

"No shit?"

"Yeah, no shit, Slim."

"Well, where's Donato?"

"Dead. Tiger killed him, too."

"You seen Gracie?"

"Ain't seen her all mornin'," the clown said. "Maybe she's off takin' a dump."

"Yeah, I'm hopin' so." Slim went to find his old Ford pickup. He'd lost his license after his seventeenth DUI a few years back, and one of the Pisani brothers had told him he had to have one of the Mexican kids drive it. Who the hell was going to clean up after the bear if Slim got his ass thrown in jail?

If the door was left open, Gracie sometimes climbed up in the cab and slept on the soft vinyl bench seat. Her big old claws had torn the heck out of the seats, dirty yellow stuffing bulging out here and there. But the long seat was a perfect fit for her body, and there was usually a nice cross-breeze because both side windows had been broken out long ago.

Slim Weatherwax made his shaky legs do double-time across the mucky brown grass, prayin' to Jesus his Gracie was in his F-100 snoring away the morning.

Chapter 25

Bagg made his way north, checking both sides of the road for any sign of a traveling circus. The smaller two lane highway where the caravan was last seen joined up with the Garden State Parkway for a couple miles, then split off to head back toward the shore. Bagg figured that unless the convoy intended to make a break for New York, they'd stick close to the tourist spots along the Jersey Shore.

A conspicuous, slow-moving circus procession making its way through small towns could only get so far without being noticed by a gas attendant or a convenience store cashier. Bagg was confident he could quickly confirm whether or not they'd taken this route.

He pulled his Jeep into a convenience store parking lot in West Tuckerton, parking in the spot farthest from the building. The bear was hunkered down in the back, still snoring.

"How's it going?" Bagg asked the first boy who made eye contact with him outside the front door. The teenagers were lounging in the shade of the building's overhang, some sitting against the brick facade, while others had upended heavy plastic milk crates for chairs. All the boys seemed to have cigarettes dangling from their mouths. Bags of partially eaten junk food and soda cans were strewn about.

"Kay," said the boy. They all appeared equally bored.

"You guys happen to see a line of trucks come through here?"

"Yeah," said the boy. His friends all shook their heads in agreement. "A whole shitload of semis loaded up with bulldozers," the boy lied. "I think they headed down Great Bay toward the beach. Ain't that right, Marco?"

Marco shook his head in agreement and flicked his butt out into the parking lot to smolder.

"No, I'm looking for a different kind of trucks," Bagg said. "It's a circus. You haven't seen a circus come through here?"

"Oh, yeah," the first boy said again, cocking his head and making an aw-shucks motion with his shoulders. "They rolled through right after the bulldozer trucks, right Marco?"

"Yep, they sure did."

As a reporter, Bagg was naturally skeptical and caught on pretty quickly when bullshit was being directed his way. "And the circus followed the bulldozers down ... what road was it?"

"Great Bay Boulevard," Marco answered. "You make a left out of the lot, then take the second right and keep on goin'."

"It kinda takes you into the middle of nowhere," the first boy warned. "But that's where they were headed."

"To nowhere?" Bagg asked.

"Yeah, well, to the middle of nowhere," Marco answered and several of the boys stifled girlish-giggles.

"Look, guys, I have something that belongs to them and I really need to track them down."

"You a cop?" One of the boys now seemed a little more interested. "You don't look like no cop."

"I'm a reporter." From inside his shirt, Bagg pulled the press pass he still wore on a chain to show the boys.

A cop would have been much more interesting, appeared to be their reaction as they settled back down on their crates. Who gave a fuck about a reporter?

"You loan me five bucks?" another of the boys asked, and Bagg knew this conversion was going in the wrong direction.

"I got something I can show you," Bagg said, and several boys hooted.

"Hey, we got somethin' to show you!" several said in unison, laughing and grabbing at their crotches.

Just then, the bear let out a low roar from the far side of the lot, apparently to announce she was awake, hungry, and stuck in the back of a Jeep.

"What the hell you got in there, mister?" All the boys were suddenly on their feet.

"I told you, I have to find the circus. Bring that stuff." Bagg pointed down at the half eaten fruit pies and powdered doughnut packs and led the boys toward his Jeep.

The Jeep Wrangler was rocking on its springs from the great weight of its dark, hulking passenger. The boys slowed as they approached, keeping the weird reporter guy between them and whatever had let out the roar.

Bagg took the food scraps and walked to the open back window. Despite her rumbling tummy, the bear seemed to be hiding from the approaching humans and trying to keep quiet. But when she caught scent of the food, she pressed her nose right up against the door hinge where there was just enough space for odors to pass through. She made heavy chuffing noises, apparently pulling the scent toward her with deep, wet breaths. She sounded like a vacuum cleaner sucking up spilled water.

"Sounds like a giant snake," Marco whispered to the other boys.

"Sounds like an alligator," another said, as they started to crowd toward Bagg. The nearest boys in front tried to hold their ground.

"C'mon, sweetheart," Bagg crooned to the bear, reaching in to rub the big mound of fur barely visible above the top of the door. "I have something for you."

The bear pushed her way up in the tight quarters, lifting her chin over the edge of the door.

"Shit!" one of the boys said. "It's got rabies!"

"She's just drooling," Bagg laughed, as great gobs of bear spit ran down the back of his Jeep. The bear rested her chin on the door. Her yellow eyes darted from boy to boy and then zeroed in on the source of the smell. Bagg was holding a pie in one hand, and the bear sent her long tongue toward it, letting him know she was very interested. She let out a low, rolling moan as if to say "please."

"Whoa," one of the boys said, as Bagg cupped the fruit pie for the bear to slurp and gum. "It doesn't have any teeth." The boy looked as if he were imagining what it would be like to be eaten by a bear without teeth, all slurped and sucked down.

"I need to find her owner." Bagg took the rest of the doughnuts and other scraps to feed the big old bear. This bear was going to need a real meal and he figured to buy a bag of dog food from the convenience store. *Probably not gonna find anything that says bear food.*

"I heard 'em last night," came a small voice from the back of the group. "I heard the trucks come past my house before the sun came up. I thought it was the county truck with the sprayer in back, but the noise kept getting louder and bigger, you know?"

"Where were they headed?" Bagg felt the familiar old rush of getting to the real facts of a story. Politicians were really no better liars than a bunch of teenage boys hanging around outside a convenience store trying to make a little mischief.

"Like Marco and Chuck said. They went down Great Bay." The boy came forward, pushing the taller boys out of his way. "For real, though. You just keep headin' down the Boulevard until you come to the middle of nowhere. Plenty of room for a circus to set up down there."

Bagg wiped the bear spit onto his jeans and then peeled two ten dollar bills from the thin fold of bills in his front pocket. "Go grab me a bag of dog food, would you, please? You keep the change." The boy who'd heard the circus trucks sprinted back to the store and through the open door.

The boys were now surrounding the back of the Jeep, shoving each other for a chance to scratch the gentle old bear. She closed her eyes and pushed her big body as best she could up on the reclined back seats so the boys could get to the good spots near her belly.

"Here, mister." The out-of-breath boy who'd sprinted back with the twenty pound bag of dog food held it out.

"Thanks for your help, guys."

"Man, if I found a bear, I'd keep it," said one of the boys.

Bagg took the dog food from the boy and propped it on the passenger seat. He pulled the strings to tear it open and then wedged it between the backseat and the side window closest to the bear. She buried her head inside the bag and began to gum away at the food. Bagg made a mental note to look for some softer chow, maybe the canned wet stuff, if he didn't find her owner right away.

Bagg climbed behind the wheel and started the Jeep, as the boys slowly backed away.

"You make a left out of the lot, then the second right," the boy called Marco reminded Bagg.

"It kinda takes you to the middle of nowhere," Bagg finished for him, smiling. Bagg backed up the Jeep, then shifted gears and made a left into traffic and headed for nowhere.

Chapter 26

The bear popped her head out of the bag when the Jeep bumped out of the parking lot.

"Sorry," Bagg called back to her, but she went back to gobbling the dog food.

Bagg found the turn onto Great Bay Boulevard, a long straight road that headed south, directly toward the ocean. For the first mile or so, the road passed through typical shore area neighborhoods, then a marina on the left and a few more side streets with houses that backed up to canals. But then the developments gave way to wetlands, and the only trees were the ones that lined either side of the road. Beyond those trees were marsh grasses and muddy ponds as far as the eye could see.

A little farther and the trees were gone, replaced by a deep sandy berm, and then a wide expanse of dark water off to the left. Bagg had been to beaches above and below this area but didn't even know this middle ground existed. Bagg slowed the Jeep as the road became more and more covered with wind-blown sand. He glanced over his shoulder to see that the bear had eaten her way to the bottom of the bag and was now gumming the thick paper, slurping at the crumbs.

Bagg drove over a series of small bridges and came to what appeared to be an old ranger station off to the left. It was hard to be sure from this far away, but there appeared to be a uniformed man sleeping on the front step, baseball cap pulled down over his face, and a tall, skinny bottle next to him. By the angle he was splayed out, Bagg got the impression the man was passed-out drunk.

A little past the ranger station, the bear in the back of Bagg's Jeep let out a blood-curdling, right out of the deepest wilds of nature kind of thundering bellow. Bagg reflexively jerked the wheel, the Jeep's front wheels slipping and then catching again, as he nervously checked the rearview mirror. Something had definitely upset the bear, and all the stories coming over the wire he'd read about animal attacks came rushing back to him.

❧   ❧   ❧

"I smell home!" Gracie screamed out in bear language. "Home! Home! Home!"

"Easy, girl," the new man said to her, but she could smell the trucks and the other animals, and all the things she loved. Her good man was here, Gracie knew and tried to push herself up over the backseat to get a better look at where this little truck was going.

"Whoa!" the new man said, but Gracie was able to get her front end over the seat and could see the top of one of the big white tents.

"There it is!" Gracie mewed, pushing her way up between the front seats as the new man drove them up and over a little bridge. Gracie could see the trucks now, and all the smaller tents, too. Her hair stood on end and she was rocking the entire Jeep back and forth as they pulled up to the back of one of the smaller trucks.

"Good man!" Gracie called out in bear. She couldn't see him, yet, but thought she might smell him. Yes, his scent was mixed in here somewhere, as she held her nose up and breathed in all those good, familiar smells. "Good man!" she shouted again.

❧   ❧   ❧

Slim Weatherwax was miserable, twisting the greasy wrench to bolt together fencing as the mechanics unloaded the kiddy rides behind him. Neither his heart nor his throbbing head were in it, but this shit had to get done. The roustabouts were finishing off the last of the small tents, obscuring most of Slim's view of the marshes. Every couple of minutes, he'd struggle to his feet and shout Gracie's name between cupped hands. It sent a jolt of pain right through his forehead, but he called just the same. Gracie wasn't agile enough to climb up into truck wheel wells, wasn't skinny enough to duck down and hide in any of the grasses. Slim just couldn't understand, figured there must be something he was missing because his head was aching so badly from last night's booze. The bad feeling in his gut was all Gracie, though. Where that damn slobbering girl had gotten to was making him sick to death, but he was too proud to ask where they were, what state owned this stretch of stinking muck they were setting up in. Not that he'd get a good answer, since you weren't ever supposed to tell a drunk where he was. It was pretty much a law to screw with a drunk who sobered-up lost.

The sun beat down hard and Slim got to his feet to call Gracie's name again when a Jeep came up and over the rickety island bridge off beyond the little tents. Anybody else probably would have thought it was having some sort of engine troubles, but Slim knew better. He knew that wonderful and terrible noise—what a man might mistake for a bull getting its balls twisted something fierce—coming from the vehicle was a lost bear who'd found her way home. Slim dropped the big wrench and ran.

ॐ   ॐ   ॐ

Billy Wayne also took notice of the strange noises coming from the approaching vehicle, and reached into his open Samsonite and pulled out the Smith & Wesson .38 Special he'd only fired once before in his life.

"You took care of me once," Billy Wayne crooned to his loaded gun, making some very bear-like noises of his own, as he struggled to get up from the piss-smelling cot. Billy Wayne emerged from his tent in time to see a large black bear tearing across the grassy muck, its giant claws throwing mud up in its wake. The bear seemed to have zeroed in on one of his flock, one of the sulky ones who'd sat off by himself during Bill Wayne's vanilla pudding benediction.

Billy Wayne raised the gun like he had the night before, just as the bear began a last leap toward the helpless, cringing man. This was a much more difficult shot, being a moving target and all. He was one for one when it came to miraculous shots, as he gently squeezed the trigger, sighting down the barrel at the thirty-or-so yard target. With no more than a hair's worth of pressure left to go, the gun suddenly exploded out of his hands and stabbed itself into the ground, stubby barrel first.

"Ouch!" Billy Wayne cried out, both hands stinging equally. Trying to rub away the pain, Billy Wayne looked up to see the face of a strange man looming over him, breathing heavily.

"Why does everyone keep trying to shoot that bear?" Lennon Bagg asked.

Chapter 27

Billy Wayne imagined himself high up in one of the old biplanes trailing banners advertising Long Beach Island nightclubs and Coppertone suntan lotion. He'd look down on a true miracle, the birth of something he had led to this hallowed place. Fish Head Island had been nothing until he'd recognized its potential. It would look just like a beautiful flower opening its petals from up in those puffy clouds.

Billy Wayne barked orders he knew nobody really listened to. Not yet, anyway. But they would grow to trust him over time, and he had plenty of that to spare, so he didn't mind a bit of antipathy as long as they didn't show it to his face. He had called a meeting in his tent headquarters with the ride mechanics to go over a master plan for setting up. The two mechanics seemed to agree with Billy Wayne's input, shaking their heads while sometimes looking at each other, then went back outside to do what they'd all done a thousand times before. As long as the work got done and nobody made fun of him.

The two large main tents were erected at the center of the island, side by side. Their big flaps opened toward the clanking kiddy rides and the ocean inlet beyond. These rides included the mini-motorcycles, a merry-go-round, a small roller coaster that only managed to rise and fall about six feet, and a truck ride where toddlers could beep horns and pretend to steer. The spinning chain swing needed a new clutch, and without the Pisanis to place an order, the ride remained packed on a truck.

Fourteen smaller tents went up in a semi-circle around the two main structures. All their flaps opened toward the center, giving visitors a clear, circular pathway around the main tents, ending at the kiddy rides and the gaping mouths of the big tents.

Billy Wayne's red and yellow tent was at the near corner of the island from the bridge, directly behind the largest trucks. Only from above would anyone see the miniature town created by the trucks. The vehicles were parked in such a way as to leave a fifty by fifty foot square in the middle. The camper trucks with retractable awnings mostly lined this common area, and there were at least a dozen small pup tents already in place. This was their village, where the workers ate and slept, the new heartbeat of the island. Of Billy Wayne's island.

The main security system for this area was in how the vehicles were arranged. After years of practice, the trucks were situated so anyone entering would need to walk through a narrow, up-and-back maze walled off by hulking circus machinery. Somewhere near the halfway point of the maze was a menacing German Sheppard-mix staked on a thick chain, just short enough to allow passage with a little side-stepping.

It was low-tech security, but the mangy old mutt named Beelzebub had a hellish streak, having bitten nearly every one of the circus workers at one time or another. Even the recently deceased tiger had been wary of Beelzebub's lousy temper.

"Is that the thickest chain we have?" Billy Wayne had come within inches of having Beelzebub clamp down on his buttocks. Foaming spittle had splashed across the back of his pants.

"We've used it to tow the eighteen wheelers, boss." The ride mechanic eyed the heavy iron chain, probably regretting he'd had the dumb luck of being within earshot of the boss' cries for help.

Billy Wayne used a tissue to wipe his pants, trying to convince himself his screams hadn't made people think the damn dog had gotten hold of one of the little girls running around this place.

Visitor parking was delineated by orange cones poached from various road crew work areas on the countless highways the circus had passed through. Drivers would come over the low bridge onto the island and then be ushered immediately to the left. When that lot was full, cars were to be directed to a second and third lot to the right of the bridge. The old trick, Billy Wayne had been told, was to get people as far away from their cars as quickly as possible. Strand them with their wallets in hand, and decisions about whether to buy dinner were easier.

Although the circus owned two small generators, the ride mechanics had tapped into the pole-mounted transformer near the ranger shack. Large, relatively dangerous orange cords snaked through the marsh, humming with power.

"Anybody ever get hurt by rigging something like that?" Billy Wayne stood over the cord, which disappeared under the canvas wall of one of the main tents.

"Well, no, boss," the mechanic said, his greasy hand rubbing at the whiskers on his chin. "But we ain't never stayed no place long enough to borrow off a pole."

"But it works, right?"

"Long as it don't rain." The mechanic turned and stalked off, the first drops of an evening shower falling on their shoulders.

≈ ≈ ≈

Game Warden Clayton Flint's life changed in these first days of the new arrivals to Fish Head. He took to drinking himself unconscious indoors, instead of out on his insect free front steps. The first couple of times he'd reached that wonderful state of drunkenness—the place where there's still plenty left in your bottle and yet you can't seem to manage to get to your feet to pee—he'd been shaken something terrible by the sound of the lion. The big cat apparently suffered from emphysema and spent half-hour stints disengaging various wet chunks from its lungs.

Not totally unbearable in the middle of the day, but at three in the morning, just as you were entering the final stages of stupor, the effect was petrifying. So chilling was the deep, chuffing battle with its own fouled lungs when you were drunk and battling bed spins, even some of the old timers had been complaining, suggesting some strong cough medicine or that maybe it was time to put the sick old cat out of its misery.

Flint seemed to become more ambitious in his pest control tasks. He widened his spraying to include more than just the ranger shack parking lot. He made a slow lap around Fish Head Island every Thursday morning, once again happy to be killing bugs for a purpose, singing along to Bon Jovi songs blasting from his radio. The laps also gave him the opportunity to note which spots needed to be cleaned up. The preacher kid was good about sending someone right out with a trash pick-up stick and garbage bag. It amazed Flint how an entire circus left less trash than city people coming down for a day of crabbing, and he wasn't shy about giving the workers their due credit.

On just their second night on Fish Head, the circus opened for business, lights flashing and music rolling across the still marsh. Three dozen cars parked in the lot, mostly families and a few crammed loads of teenagers. A bottle of cheap vodka in one hand, Flint watched from the back step of the ranger station as not one person swatted the air around them.

~ ~ ~

Billy Wayne held vanilla pudding meetings at one o'clock each afternoon, about the time the last of the hardest drinkers had woken up, followed by private consultations.

"Boss, can I chew your ear 'bout somethin'?" was how it almost always began.

"It burns like that time I ate a whole bottle of chili peppers when I take a piss," was how it sometimes progressed.

Billy Wayne glowed with excitement every time his tent flap opened, though. Nothing was too trivial for this Messiah. In fact, the trivial stuff was easier to deal with. With the house share of the receipts, Billy Wayne found a goldmine of relief at the pharmacy in West Tuckerton.

Creams for jock itch and shampoos for head lice. An extra fifty bucks dispersed with the technicality involving prescriptions for infections, and the various sexually transmitted diseases being swapped back and forth among patrons and roustabouts. Billy Wayne's morbidly obese, hypochondriac mother had prepared him well for treating circus folk ills.

The psychological counseling was the most challenging and satisfying to Billy Wayne, especially when he seemed to get it right.

Step number twenty-nine from *How to Become a Cult Leader in 50 Easy Steps*: "People have a deep psychological need to keep their heads stuck firmly in a hole when confronted by emotional issues that could cause discomfort. If avoiding such confrontation is even the tiniest bit possible, widen the hole for them to get their shoulders in, too. Ever hear the saying about whistling past the cemetery? Teach your followers to whistle loudly and you'll be rewarded with peace and accord."

"I caught my Suzie screwin' Omar."

"Omar from the bed of nails act?"

"Yeah, I caught them screwin' on the bed of nails."

"Hmm." Billy Wayne would pause, flipping back through his good book's pages in his head for help. "Maybe they weren't having sex. Maybe they were trying some new act and didn't want to damage their clothes."

"She was moaning all hot and heavy. Then she came back to the trailer with little red nail marks on her knees."

"Jesus had nail marks," Bill Wayne said in a solemn voice.

"So you're sayin' that maybe they wasn't really screwing?"

"I have some pills for you." Bill Wayne would hand them over, explain when and how many to take.

The most unexpected addition to the circus was the new public relations department: a recently unemployed—and possibly wanted by the law—former reporter from the *Atlantic County Beacon* named Lennon Bagg.

Billy Wayne was not the quickest witted of human beings, but easily recognized what a disaster this Bagg fellow had averted by knocking the gun out of his hands. Shooting the trained bear would have undone every last ounce of faith he'd created by plugging the ferocious tiger. In fact, Billy Wayne probably would have been lashed to a cinderblock and sunk to the bottom of the inlet for the crabs to pick over.

Returning the bear to the circus had also earned the former reporter a tent of his own—albeit slightly smaller than Billy Wayne's—as well as his own piss-smelling cot. And retelling the story of the Absecon cop's savage attempt on Graceful Gracie's life also earned Bagg the protection and allegiance of the circus people.

"What kind of sick bastard would shoot a helpless old bear?" Slim Weatherwax had asked, while a large group had convened for beer and dogs at a fire pit in the center of the hidden common area. Billy Wayne, who had been lurking in the shadows, felt his stomach turn a little sideways at the close call.

The reporter guy had kept his mouth shut. Someone you could trust like that might come in handy for something around here.

Chapter 28

Cops could be trouble.

Aggravated assault on a police officer carried some serious jail time involving mandatory minimums, depending upon the degree. Lennon Bagg had been around cops enough to know any sort of crime against one of their members was inevitably ramped up to the most serious charge possible. In fact, a crime didn't even have to occur in the first place, if you happened to be in the wrong place at the wrong time. Bagg didn't have anything against cops in general and, in the course of his job as a journalist, had seen certain ones performing moderately heroic deeds every once in a while. But he also possessed a healthy bit of trepidation over what they were capable of doing to someone perfectly innocent.

On the suggestion of her lawyer, Bagg's ex-wife had gone to the police on a Friday night and claimed he'd threatened to kill her. It caused them to come knock on what was soon to become "her" front door and not "theirs."

"Mr. Lennon Bagg?" one of the two officers asked, and Bagg knew immediately that this wasn't going to be a pleasant visit. Bagg and his wife both loved and adored their four-year-old daughter, but their marriage was a car wreck.

The cops sent to gather up the scumbag, wife-beating lowlife could have been brothers, maybe twins. Both had short black hair, narrow builds and showed a disconcerting amount of teeth even when they weren't smiling.

"I'm Bagg," he admitted, backing away from the door as the officers pushed forward and asked him to turn around and put his hands behind his back, next to the kitchen table where the Bagg family sometimes ate dinner. They had explained the handcuffs were for everyone's protection.

"Did you threaten to kill your wife tonight, Mr. Bagg?"

"Not out loud," Bagg said.

"You think that's funny?"

"Well, I did think you two might have been a strip-o-gram," Bagg said. The cop tightened the cuffs.

"These feel real?" the cop hissed in his ear, breath hot and moist. Bagg was able to smell a mixture of cigarettes and Juicy Fruit gum.

"I didn't threaten to kill my wife."

"She told us a different story." One cop bent him over the table to rummage through his pants, while the other rummaged through the kitchen cabinets.

Bagg pictured Jennifer leading Morgan into the police station, having deviously prepared her for any questions by reminding her how Daddy sometimes yelled really loud and how frightening he could be. Jennifer would have planted terrible seeds by telling Morgan how bad Mommy felt when she made Daddy angry, and how she hoped Morgan had never overheard him hitting Mommy. Bagg could picture Morgan searching her memory for a time when something sounded like a slap from the next room. Bagg cringed, knowing for certain what Jennifer had done and how she'd done it. How easy it was to corrupt the mind of a little kid. Bagg knew he would hate Jennifer for the rest of his life. Whatever fucking around she'd done was irrelevant, and he couldn't have cared less. The initial pain of disloyalty faded quickly when you realized you didn't love someone. She'd kept it from him, so he assumed she'd also kept it from their daughter. But poisoning the thoughts of their little girl was beyond evil.

"Your daughter's in safe hands now that's she's away from you."

"You asshole." Bagg's cheek rested on the kitchen table, giving him a good view of the sugar Morgan had spilled during breakfast.

"Please don't put sugar on your cereal, honey." Bagg had slid the sugar bowl from her reach. Bagg didn't usually work Fridays, so he had been delivering Morgan to her morning pre-K.

"I didn't put it on my cereal, Daddy." Her tone indicated the thought would never have crossed her mind. She put her spoon down and carefully opened the little pink sweater pocket over her hip to display the two or three teaspoons worth of sugar she'd hoarded. Then, leaning with both elbows on the table, she said in a hushed voice, "It's for Pippy."

"Who's Pippy?" Bagg lowered his voice to match her whisper.

"I don't think you want to know, Daddy," Morgan whispered back.

"Why not? I like to know things."

"You said that stories about dragons give you nightmares." Morgan shook her head and reached a hand out to comfort her father with gentle pats. And it was true that he'd said it, although he'd only been intending to steer Morgan away from certain violent looking books on a visit to the library.

"Yes, dragons scare me, but what about the sugar?"

"It's my turn to feed Pippy," Morgan said. "Let's just not talk anymore about it, okay?"

"Okay." Bagg let her keep the pocket of sugar. Maybe sugar wasn't bad for dragons, he decided.

"You have the right to remain silent ..." one of the officers in dark blue began, as Bagg rolled his head on the hard table, tiny grains of precious dragon food sticking to his forehead.

Making the Friday night claim of abuse had become a popular tactic among New Jersey family law attorneys, according to a recent story in Bagg's own newspaper. The so-called victim would get the house and car keys, as well as the credit cards and access to the bank accounts on Saturday.

The soon-to-be ex-husband would get a weekend of cold McDonald's hamburgers and fries shoved through a narrow slot in the cell door and then get a first appearance in front of the judge sometime around noon on Monday. He'd emerge blinking at the sun with bloodshot eyes, hair all dirty and crazy, like a night-zombie caught out after sunrise. Some lawyers referred to it as the Friday Night Blitz Play, Bagg would later learn from the fathers' support group he attended on a single, depressing occasion.

The cops who hauled Bagg away hadn't particularly mistreated him. Bagg assumed it was routine to be made to strip naked and grab your ankles while a flashlight was shined up your ass. And if he hadn't had Morgan to think about, it probably would have been prudent to require Bagg to turn over his shoelaces. Had there been no little girl to worry about, hanging himself with his shoelaces might very well have become a reasonable option.

Was it any surprise how evil Jennifer Bagg could be? Bagg had thought about the real estate developer who had hired her small interior design firm to furnish a dozen or so model homes, part of a three thousand unit community under construction. They were also contracted for the interior design of the fitness center and property owners' association buildings. This meant big bucks for Jennifer's three person office. And it wasn't just the money now, but all the future jobs that would come with the new contacts they'd make, she explained.

To Bagg, Jennifer had never seemed happier. He noticed new dresses, and she left for evening meetings with impeccable makeup, reeking of a new perfume that smelled awful and expensive. Jennifer was a serious, driven woman. Thin and in her heels nearly as tall as Bagg, with hair pulled back to reveal the sharp features that would work well for a fifth grade school teacher sidled with an unruly classroom. One cold glare from Jennifer Bagg reached right into your soul and sucked the cheer right out of your most joyful moments.

This new Jennifer was sometimes giddy, and Bagg took advantage of her unusual playfulness at first. They'd had sex twice the previous month, and she'd even asked him to kiss her "down there." A good five minutes passed before she complained he was slobbering too much. Jennifer talked about getting away for a long vacation after the designs were finished—the designs she had to pore over with the developer on a more and more frequent basis.

One warm September night, Bagg was once again on his own, putting Morgan to bed. Their regular routine involved going potty, then a quick tubby with dozens of floating dolls and sea creatures. Morgan would turn herself into a unicorn with baby shampoo suds and stand still as he turned on the shower and rinsed her shiny little body. She had recently turned four, and most of the baby fat had given way to reveal a skinny physique, with a roadmap of tiny blue veins just under her pale skin. She was looking more and more like her mother, Bagg had thought, as he toweled her off.

"Mommy is on a date tonight," she said, as Bagg held out her underpants to slip one foot in.

"Mommy's working." In the steamy bathroom, an icy shudder passed through Bagg.

"No, Mommy has a boyfriend and she loves him, Daddy."

Bagg wanted to question his little girl, but there was still a tiny piece of him that didn't want to know.

Bagg helped Morgan into her princess pajamas and grabbed the brush from on top of the toilet.

"I heard Mommy say she loved him on the telephone, and that she couldn't wait to see him tonight."

"Tonight?"

And then Morgan reached up to her kneeling father's face and took his head in her hands, looking at him with the most sympathy she could muster. "Don't cry, Daddy. I love you with my whole heart and I promise I always will."

"I know, sweetheart." Bagg swept her in tight for a hug.

The little girl consoled her father, patting his back lightly. "And I promise I'll never, ever leave you alone."

But a couple of months later, Morgan's promise had been broken.

Chapter 29

Bagg decided a muddy island along the Jersey Shore was as good a place as any to lay low for a few days. It wouldn't take long before he'd know for sure what charges he was facing and whether he planned on facing them at all.

He laid back on his gamey-smelling cot, the tent flap closed, listening to the hustle and bustle of the circus being erected around him. His temporary home reminded him of a fortune teller's tent he and Morgan had strolled past at a carnival, what seemed like a hundred years ago.

"That's a gypsy lady," Morgan had informed him, pointing to the woman seated behind a crystal ball she was polishing. The Romani wore a long purple robe, with a wide bandana across her forehead, and gigantic jewelry dangling from her ears, arms and throat. "Elmo says they can predict the furniture."

"I think Elmo meant they can predict the future."

"I can predict the future." Morgan turned her face up at her father with a look that told him her legs were tired from walking and it was time for a ride.

"How's that, honey?" Bagg scooped her up, spinning her onto his shoulders.

"I predict I'm going to be a gypsy fortune teller for Halloween!"

"I thought this was an all Toy Story year. I already bought a six-shooter and cowboy hat. I'm gonna be Woody and you're gonna be Jessie."

"Mom didn't like when you said she could be Stinky Pete."

"I was just kidding."

Morgan leaned forward on her father's shoulders, cupping her hands to his right ear to tell a secret. "Mom didn't think it was funny, but I did."

That was what Bagg missed the most. Not really what was said, since most of the things shared were just silly bits you forgot in an hour or a day. The act of a little girl telling her father a secret. Of sharing something closely—the cupped hands to the ear, the warm breath, the immediacy and the emotion. Time seemed to stop when a little girl was sharing a secret with her father.

Bagg closed his eyes and lay back on the foul smelling cot. He worried what the cops would do when they broke into his apartment. Would they tear through the shrine that was once Morgan's room, looking for him in a place he hadn't dared set foot inside for years? Bagg imagined them pushing open the sliding door closet which he and Morgan had turned into her cozy hiding place, with layers of fluffy blankets and pillows and a reading light. There were four framed Disney posters along the back wall. Bagg knew they'd smash the light and picture frames, pulling out and stomping all over her delicate bedding. That's what cops did when you hurt one of their own.

"Stop it," Bagg said to the ceiling of his tent, and it seemed to work. He went back to concentrating on the sounds of the circus around him. At one point, he heard the Hooduk guy timidly ask someone to go run an errand if he wouldn't very much mind. Hooduk was apparently in charge, although Bagg noticed nobody really listened to anything he said. If Billy Wayne told someone to wash the pony crap off the bleacher seats, the person would eventually have a look for him or herself to see if it really needed to be done. At that point, the pony crap might get washed off, and it might not.

"This is my circus and these are my people," Billy Wayne had explained to Bagg, right after nearly putting a slug in the overly-excited and extremely affectionate bear.

And it was fine with Bagg, despite it only being mildly acceptable to the actual people of the circus. "They listen to me," Billy Wayne added.

It seemed to Bagg, who could clearly hear most of the confessions taking place in Hooduk's tent behind him, that Billy Wayne did most of the listening while these folks did all of the drinking and screwing around.

Bagg's other nearest neighbors included Pinhead, Veronica the Fat Lady, and Primo, who was billed as the World's Strongest Old Man. These people were touted as Freaks of Nature, although they would have barely stood out on the Atlantic City boardwalk. They occupied the tent directly to the left of Bagg's.

The tent to his right housed a more interesting pair, as far as Bagg was concerned. Very amiable guys named Pete Singe, aka Lightning Man, and Skip Kitt, aka Flat Man. Singe's job was showing and telling stories about his horrific burn scars from being repeatedly hit by lightning. He wore a robe over nylon running shorts and would display one terrific scar after the other. He'd show off the bright red zigzag beginning at the nape of his neck and running to his waist. He'd tell stories about the missing toes of his right foot, where one of the bolts of electricity had exited.

Singe spoke slowly of his injuries to anyone who'd listen, paying or not. He was just a storyteller unraveling good tales. He'd collected his injuries from above while employed as a commercial fisherman, park ranger, golf course groundskeeper, and lifeguard. He'd also spent ten dangerous years as a lineman for Florida Power and Light.

"Probably the worst hit was just a couple years back," Singe had told Bagg. "Rich guy I knew from the marina owned a big-time tuna boat, talked me into learnin' how to scuba dive. We went down to this spot in Honduras, lugging gear off the trucks, and headed down to these caves. Wouldn't you know what was comin' next? Storm rolls in and we're just about to climb down this ladder when a bolt comes zippin' out of the sky. Took the top off some hundred-year-old tree, ran along the wet ground, and shazzam!"

"That's incredible." Bagg had sat mesmerized.

"You know it. Imagine how hard that bolt of lightning had to search to find me in the middle of a jungle, just about to climb down into a cave?"

In all, Singe had claimed to have been struck twelve times, which would easily be a world record, although some of his burns couldn't be confirmed as lightning induced.

"It's all politics." Singe winked at Bagg. "And who am I to mess with the memory of that poor sap with the official record of seven strikes—may he finally rest in peace underground. He even got hit in the head twice and had his hair catch fire."

"Lightning killed him?"

"Nah, it was his own hand that killed him, not the lightning. Story has it, his woman ran off with another guy. Hard to hold on to a decent woman when you keep gettin' zapped by a hundred million volts. Makes everybody around you real nervous whenever it clouds up."

Singe's tent mate was the reason for installing the special flooring. Flat Man lived with a dire fear of gravity and the expectation of being slammed to Earth should he rise more than a few inches. He passed the time on glossy, snapped together laminate flooring. The smooth surface allowed Flat Man to display his debilitating phobia by performing mock household tasks. He'd dry dishes in a rack on the floor and use an old-fashioned feather duster on a picture frame and lamp. It was a pretty campy display, but the lamp also provided light for the hours and hours he passed the time reading.

"My job is nothing much more than acting like a museum painting," the barophobic named Kitt told Bagg. "People pay, then look at me for a couple minutes, then move along. I don't have any stories to tell. Not like Singe."

"And you can't get up?"

"No, but it ain't so bad. And look at all the crappy things that came raining down on this guy for spending so much of his life up on ladders?"

Singe gave a half-smile and shrugged in agreement. "He's pretty safe from lightning down there."

"Mind losin' the shoes?" Kitt slowly extended his arm along the floor to point toward a hand-painted sign above a rack asking all visitors to remove their shoes.

"Sorry." Bagg slipped off his North Face running shoes and placed them on the rack.

Kitt, dressed in old tan khakis and a Hawaiian shirt, closed the book he'd been reading and slowly spun around to make having a conversation with the newest circus resident a little easier. Bagg, not entirely sure of the proper etiquette in this situation, was tempted to lie down next to Kitt.

"It's better to just kneel," Lightning Man said, as if reading Bagg's thoughts.

"I wasn't always like this. I was an accountant at a regular desk and sat in a regular chair. I had a wife that was about average height."

"So what exactly is wrong?"

"Barophobia is the exaggerated or irrational fear of gravity. One day I was perfectly fine and then boom!"

"Boom," repeated Lightning Man, nodding his head sympathetically. He knew about booms.

"Yeah, boom." Kitt paused to stretch his neck muscles. "The circus came up not too far from our house in Wiscasset, Maine, three summers back."

"That's the north swing we used to do." Lightning Man sat forward in his terrycloth robe on a folding metal chair, absently rubbing his damaged right foot with a scarred hand.

Kitt nodded. "Wiscasset is up Route One, 'bout an hour up the coast from Portland. I figured that, it bein' a nice evening, I'd take Anne Marie—that was my wife—over to this broken-down circus that had rolled through our little town and plopped down in an empty field. Something to do, right?

"Not five minutes after we'd parked the car and walked toward the ticket booth, the barker starts callin' people over to this big blue and red cannon pointed up in the air. For some reason, my heart starts beatin' real fast and I'm breakin' out in a sweat, despite the temperature already dropping way off since the sun had gone over the hills."

"He thought he was having a heart attack," Lightning Man said.

"Yeah, well, I felt like something was really wrong. But Anne Marie was tugging at me, telling me to hurry up; she didn't want to miss this."

"The Human Cannonball," Bagg said.

"The one and only," Lightning Man said. "May he rest in peace."

"So, I let her pull me over to where 'bout forty people were standing to watch. Now, these were mostly people I knew and did business for. They were my neighbors and folks who owned the stores I shopped in every day. Some were saying 'Hey, Skip' and whatnot, but only half of me was recognizing them, while the other half was thinking they might just as well have been flesh eating zombies about to jump on me."

"Flesh eating zombies." Lightning Man repeated the phrase, nodding his head, apparently appreciating this part of the story.

"Yeah, so I'm all surrounded by these killer-monster deli and doughnut shop owners, with my heart slamming up against the inside of my ribcage at a million miles a minute, and my Anne Marie is all goofy and happy about a human cannonball act about to go off. Then the countdown begins, and I get it in my head that my heart is really going to blow up when the barker reaches zero."

"But it didn't." Lightning Man shook his head.

"By that time, all my zombie friends and neighbors are counting down, too. And everybody is yelling out zero and the cannon goes 'kaboom!' and I hit the ground."

"Hasn't been up since," Lightning Man added sympathetically.

"Didn't someone call an ambulance?" Bagg asked. "What did your wife do?"

"She was mortified," Lightning Man answered for him. "She just walked away and left him there."

"Wait a minute. You're telling me she left you there in a field being used by a traveling circus?"

"A marriage not meant to be," Lightning Man said, and Bagg, the ever diligent reporter, recognized he was probably being had. But these friendly, burned and broken men were as nice as could be, completely genuine or not.

"You got a wife, Bagg?" Kitt asked.

"No, but I have a little girl someplace." Bagg wasn't in the mood to go into details. He had several different versions of the same story, ranging from a quick mention of having a daughter all the way to the one he told when he was drunk. The one fueled by alcohol was much longer, especially drawn out because it was accompanied by shoulder-racking sobs, with the worst details repeated several times to hammer home how unfair life was.

Bagg always felt shame the next morning after confessing the entire story in such a manner. He was ashamed for losing control of his emotions, as well as losing control of his life after his daughter was stolen. It seemed as though he'd asked favors from every reporter he'd ever worked with. He had begged the cops, and he'd even tried begging his congressman. Everyone had seemed sympathetic, and even energetic at first. But, after all, Bagg had once been arrested for threatening to kill his wife. Maybe it hadn't been such a bad thing for the lady to vamoose with the girl.

The cops had dismissed his initial complaint by telling him to just give it a few days, that these things always turned out fine. But they changed their tune when other reporters started calling and asking questions on his behalf. Some actual police work was done on the Bagg girl's disappearance when it was pointed out to the police chief that his officers had purposely buried the father's initial report. That no follow-up had been done even after the ex-wife's car had been located at the Philly airport. Details like those made for bad press, especially in an election year.

And along the same lines of how the cops brought the hammer down on anyone even thought to have committed any sort of act against a brother in blue, newspapers had their own sense of protective justice. The chief of police had enough skeletons in his private closet to guard; he finally relented and managed to assign two detectives to track down the Bagg lady and the missing kid. It might have all made a good story, a solid exposé mixing unfairness and wrongdoing with a hint of corruption, but even though the newspaper had the goods, Bagg's managing editor didn't want to rock the boat quite that hard. Plus, with the girl still gone, there was no happy ending to neatly wrap things up.

Despite all the canvassing phone calls by the reporters and all the begrudging footwork by the cops, the trail simply went ice cold. Jennifer's friends claimed they didn't know a thing but wished they could be more helpful.

Weeks turned into months, and then one afternoon it was as if something began to die inside Bagg, as he sat in the newsroom in front of his blank computer screen.

"Hey, Bagg, you realize what today is?" one of the sportswriters, who Bagg sometimes hit a tennis ball around with, had asked while glancing up from his keyboard.

"What's today?"

"It was a year ago today your daughter went missing."

Bagg had closed his eyes, feeling the death going on inside.

An odd thing began to happen when it came to the measurement of time for Lennon Bagg. It sped up. He'd drag himself into the paper on a Monday morning, prepared for a long week of boring, routine interviews, only to hear people excited about the weekend. Milk seemed to go bad the moment he placed it in the refrigerator, and crazy amounts of mail would threaten to overflow his box. One day was often really three or four.

Sometimes entire weeks flashed by when he drifted off during a television commercial. Once, he found himself dreading the Christmas holidays, frightened by the depression surely to overcome him amidst everyone else's joy. But it was suddenly far too warm for December. The trees had grown dark, midsummer leaves overnight.

Some kind of insanity had settled over Bagg, but he had no will to fight. Perhaps the frenzied passing of time was a blessing, meant to bring a quicker end to his daily misery.

Somewhere out there in this world was a little stolen girl who was about to enter kindergarten, but had suddenly turned ten. Bagg wondered what his daughter looked like.

Chapter 30

Katherine Hepburn died, the Globe Theatre burned to the ground, the first appendectomy was performed, and Marvin Pipkin filed for a patent for the frosted electric light bulb. Yet an even more important event falling on a June twenty-ninth was the bell signaling the end of the school year and the emancipation of Morgan Freeman from Primary Four, at Sandys Primary School.

Most children transformed into screaming banshees, funneling from the whitewashed front archway, but Morgan only slumped forward at her homeroom desk, the overwhelming emotion, one of relief. Abatement from the deific clocks, a reprieve from the cold Pop-Tarts, final absolution for those contraband rolled sleeves, and, thank God, amnesty until September's heinous return.

Once Morgan sensed the building had regurgitated the last of her schoolmates, she sat back and carefully removed an ancient cigar box from her lift-top desk. She set the object on the desk she'd carved dozens of bird figures into with the sharp end of a protractor. One last furtive glance at the open door, and Morgan lifted the box lid just enough to confirm that the contents were still intact. Satisfied, she zipped it safely inside her backpack.

Morgan had loved Mrs. Jones during the first weeks of school. Maybe it was the kind smile and soft voice so unlike her mother's. Morgan stayed after school to talk to Mrs. Jones back then, so very long ago. Mrs. Jones confided in Morgan how she, too, had come from far away, another island called Australia. Mrs. Jones said she knew Morgan's father had passed away from a sudden illness, as had her own father. And Morgan bought right into it. She was the first person who might have understood Morgan's search for

166

her father. The funny, strong, handsome man who had thrown her up into the air a thousand giggling times and told her the bear becoming a magic butterfly bedtime story every time she'd asked. Morgan shared and shared, telling every memory she had coveted for such a long part of her short years.

"I'm trying to find him," Morgan told Mrs. Jones.

"What do you mean?"

Morgan's voice was low, sharing her secret for the first time. "My father's a bird and I've been trying to find him."

"You mean a bird that flies?"

"Yes!" Morgan had nearly shouted. Of course this gentle teacher could understand. The kids had teased her for talking to the birds, had ostracized her so boldly it had come to the faculty's attention early on. Birdbrain, Daffy Duck, and Looney Bird were just a few of the nicknames she'd accumulated.

But Morgan experienced her first bitter taste of genuine betrayal late that afternoon. She had hugged Mrs. Jones and nearly skipped all the way home, planning to spend time in her room with her drawings, rather than deal with the kids on the beach. Morgan's mood was too good to have it spoiled by the nasty kids who taunted her mercilessly while she bobbed beyond the small breakers, out by the various ducks and gulls. Out by the birds who either left her alone, or took time to listen if she needed to talk.

The phone had rung near dinnertime and she had crept to the door crack to listen.

"Hello, Mrs. Jones," her mother said in her most pretend-nice voice, reserved for people who her mom either wanted to impress or wanted something from. "She told you what?"

And Morgan's heart broke again.

"I see. Yes, I understand ... right ... I completely agree."

No, she had not seen and she had not understood! Mrs. Jones had listened and understood! *How could she do this to me?*

Morgan ran to her covers and buried herself, wishing she was dead and that she could fly away from that place where grownups were liars, only pretending to like you in order to hurt you. She expected her door to open, the springs of her bed creaking as her mother came to sit with her. The phone conversation was over, but Morgan heard nothing. No squeak of her door, no footsteps, only the tick of the clock on her bed stand and an occasional slow-moving car passing her window.

It was hot under the blankets, but Morgan held her ground, waiting for whatever trouble she was in to come to her. She was uncomfortable in the tangle of her school uniform, the navy blue skirt and blouse with the stiff collar that always poked her neck. The passing minutes turned into an hour, and Morgan heard the click of the living room television and then bits and pieces of a newscast.

Night eventually arrived outside of her pile of blankets, and at some point her mother popped her head into her room. "Brush your teeth," Morgan's mom said and left just as quickly. There was no, "I'm disgusted by this obsession." Not this time.

"Therapy" was another word Morgan's mom had floated out there, but Morgan knew it was an empty threat. No way would her mother risk having anyone finding out her child was in therapy. Talk about crazy. People might look at Jennifer Freeman as if she were the cause of her daughter's problems.

The next morning, Morgan saw Mrs. Jones in a whole new light, and everything was different. She had obviously mistaken her kind smile, since it now didn't look the least bit welcoming, more like a grimace. And there was something sour about her voice. Something to make you cringe, like watching someone bite into a lemon.

Morgan cringed when her teacher said, "Good morning, dear."

"How could you?" Morgan wanted to say.

And Mrs. Jones smiled that same smile each time she came by Morgan's desk to snatch away the small pencil-on-paper drawings she'd worked on so diligently. They were drawings of gadwalls, grebes, herons, kites, sandpipers, and egrets; drawings of kestrels and a Bald Eagle. Maybe even a drawing of her father.

The drawings were relinquished back to Morgan on the final day of school, and she secreted them away in the special cigar box. The box had once resided on her father's dresser before their home was broken. It was in the background of photos, somehow left behind by him, and then packed away and shipped on to Bermuda. If her mom had recognized it as her father's she would have stomped on it, or burned it in the fireplace like so many of the pictures Morgan had wanted to keep. It was the box where she kept a pink flamingo feather she'd discovered along the road to school and hoped to someday transform into a quill pen. The box was a piece of her father, even though she couldn't imagine him ever smoking a cigar. Was he a secret cigar smoker? Had he found the box? Had it been his father's? Morgan cherished every possibility, made up stories for each.

June twenty-ninth was a hot day, and her backpack was heavy with spiral notebooks and art class drawings she rescued before the janitors came through to scrub the school clean of any remnants of the year. She made her way down busy Broome Street, to Long Bay, and then cut through backyards to No Name Lane. She unclipped the front door key to their little blue bungalow from the main zipper on her backpack. Her mother wouldn't be home for at least an hour, and this was Morgan's time to pour a bowl of Cocoa Puffs, pee, and then throw on her one-piece swimsuit.

Energized by the sugar and thoughts of no school for two entire months, Morgan grabbed a towel, her swim fins, and her boogie board. Sticking the house key in her sneaker, she slammed out the back door. The best waves were over at Dunkley's and Hungry Bay and on down to the south shore beaches, but Morgan didn't really care if there were waves or not. If the swells kicked up over on the East Coast, the boys who usually hung out at Margaret's Bay would climb on the bus and leave her with rolling swells that gently splashed the pink sand. Morgan also loved the times that the low pressure systems steamed by off the western horizon, close enough to churn up waist-high or better waves, but far enough out that the wind didn't chop the waves apart. Riding big waves was like flying and it was good practice for later on.

The storms would also populate the bay with every bird imaginable. Although they had found refuge, they were also nervous and short-tempered from being in a strange environment. Morgan was entertained by the birds' interactions; they were territorial and oddly aggressive. Various species, unused to such close proximity, were just like people from different countries who suddenly found themselves huddled together during a disaster.

The water was dead calm this hot June day, and only a small group of kids huddled in a shady spot at the very north end of the beach. Morgan could smell the cigarette and marijuana smoke as it drifted ever so slowly down on the light breeze. She buried her house key as usual, putting her towel over the spot, and weighed it down with her sneakers. There was nothing worse than when one of the old farts with a metal detector came by and scooped up your house key, which they were known to regularly do.

Grabbing her boogie board and fins, she padded down to the center of the long beach, wading into the warm water while tightening her board's wrist strap. Twenty yards out, she rinsed the sand from her fins, slipped them onto her feet, and remounted her board. Morgan rested on her elbows, holding the board tightly, slowly kicking her way due west.

The first fifty yards was shallow water over sand, and then she reached the coral reef that ran parallel to this section of Sandys Island. She kicked her way through a line of gulls who begrudgingly made way for the little girl on the boogie board.

"Are you being rude or are just too lazy to move?" she asked them, and one answered in its seagull language. "Thank you," Morgan said, as the gulls closed ranks after letting her pass.

She kept kicking, despite entering a place much farther out than her mom would have ever permitted. The water deepened beyond the reef, with fast-moving boats and possibly some large biting fish. Morgan's destination was a circular reef, thirty yards in diameter, about five hundred yards from the beach. From back on land, it would seem as if the little girl had disappeared among the light chop stirred by the steadier breeze that blew this far from shore. As if she'd vanished into thin air.

Morgan kicked and kicked, finally reaching the distant reef and finding the friend she knew liked to hang out here. The brown pelican bobbed in the shallow water over the center of the reef, cocking its head to eye the girl.

"Hello, Gus," Morgan said.

"Hello, Morgan," she heard him say in return.

"How's the fishing?"

"I have a belly full. You're done with school for the summer?"

"Yes, finally." Morgan paddled in a wide slow circle around the bird, which had a long beak that looked like a weird smile. The reddish brown mane of hair on its head looked a little like the Mohawk-style some of the tough boys in Hamilton sported. But Morgan knew Gus was anything but tough. The old bird had once been a much-loved primary school art teacher in Hamilton, according to stories he'd told.

"Any good plans for the summer?" His attention was no longer fully on the girl. A shimmer of white fish bellies had caught the pelican's eye, and he couldn't help watching the tasty treats darting unwittingly about, directly beneath his predatory gaze.

"No plans, really. Just gonna keep looking for my dad."

"Did you see that?" Gus asked the girl suddenly. The school of fish had been joined by another, much larger group, and the roiling mass had bumped the large, floundering pads of the bird, teasing his senses.

"It tickled." Gus's head now tilted completely to one side to eye the water beneath him. "There must be a million of them down there."

"I thought your belly was full."

"But they look so good." Gus was tantalized by the glimmering flashes, oh so close. "Maybe just one more?"

"Can you catch one from up high?"

"You called me a showoff last time."

"You know I was only kidding," Morgan said. "I think it's wonderful. Please?"

Gus stretched his wings, then beat them down to gain lift, and rose in an awkward, almost impossible manner. The enormous school of small fish scattered in all directions away from Morgan's board before rejoining at the edge of the reef, swirling and rolling like a huge, shiny torpedo just beneath the surface.

"From way up high!" Morgan called to the pelican, whose initial clumsiness was replaced by a muscular, slow grace. Gus climbed to about a hundred feet and began easy clockwise laps around the reef and girl, head again tilted to search out the goggle-eyed scads that had shifted to the west.

"They're getting away!" Morgan teased, but Gus had already apparently zeroed in on his target, ignoring the girl. As if a switch was snapped, Gus's forward progress halted and he dropped like an anchor from an airplane. Unlike some dive-bombing birds, his wings remained outstretched, his neck still arched. Gus slammed through the surface of the ocean, hitting the water hard. The impact would by no means have impressed an Olympic diving judge, for he sent a splash of salty water five feet into the air behind him.

Morgan marveled at the show, nearly tumbling from her board as she clapped and screamed at the bird's mighty descent. Gus broke back through the surface, shaking water from his Mohawk, a shiny, foot-long fish sideways in his beak, twitching weakly.

"That was amazing." Morgan paddled toward her friend, who tilted back his head to gobble down the scad.

"Thank you. Oh, there's something I almost forgot to tell you."

"What?" Morgan asked, as the pair paddled back toward the safe spot at the center of the reef. The deep water always felt a little creepy to Morgan, especially this time of day, when the sun was getting lower.

"I heard a rumor from a passing flock of mallards." Gus trailed off as column of scad wandered back across the reef to rejoin the school scuttled about by the plunging pelican.

"What rumor, Gus?"

"Well, you know I've been sure to mention the little girl from the big island who has been looking for her dead father for many years."

"And?"

"And just last week, I spoke to a duck who claimed to have spoken to a bird, of which species I don't recall." Gus paused, perhaps trying to recall the species, but having no luck.

"Yes? What did the bird say?"

"It was a bird who was once a man with a daughter your age. And, most curiously, she had your name. Quite a coincidence, don't you think?"

Morgan's heart began to race. "What did he say, Gus? He met my father?"

But Gus only stared at the girl, bobbing in rhythm a few yards away. "Gus, please, what did he say about the bird?"

Still silence. "Gus!" Morgan shouted, and the bird rose up and flapped its wings, backing away from the commotion. "Gus, please tell me!"

Morgan gave up pleading and just bobbed on her boogie board, waiting to see if the pelican would resume his story. But the evening wind had picked up, and the hot day had turned chilly out on the open water. The standoff lasted another ten minutes before the large bird turned away from the girl, flapped its heavy wings, and performed its awkward takeoff again. This time, the bird headed low over the ocean to the north, leaving the little girl alone.

"Please," Morgan said, but there was nobody to hear her. No answer, only the rocking sound of her board on the choppy sea. Morgan turned her back on the low orange sun and kicked her swim fins in steady strokes. It was a very long way back home.

Chapter 31

It was the Fourth of July on Fish Head Island and the money flowed in like high tide during a full moon.

Two hundred thirty-some years of independence from the Kingdom of Great Britain was reason enough to pay for the privilege of witnessing swords being swallowed, fire being eaten, and death being defied in various hair-raising manners. Illegal fireworks exploded over the inlet, mirrored in the murky water.

Business was booming, despite the cannon having been abandoned in the hurried exodus from the Atlantic City parking lot. With a half-dozen workers assigned to garbage duty, even Warden Flint was apt to be found in a fair mood, straddling one of the hay bales lining the gravel road along the inlet coastline, sipping from a tall bottle of Russian vodka. A wry smile cracked his ruddy face when a couple strolling by mentioned how nice it was there were no bugs.

"You're welcome," Flint drunkenly mumbled, tipping the bottle in a toast, as he watched that reporter guy down at the far end of the inlet. He was hunting around the mud flats like a hungry bird, stooping over and gathering up small bits of something from the edge of the still water. His pants were rolled to just below the knees, and his bare feet were black from the warm mud.

The ranger also noticed the crazy old Rooney broad hovering behind the reporter, arms folded across her chest, but he had no way of knowing if any words were actually coming out of her flapping gums. The woman was always fuming about something, and her mouth never stopped running, even if no words were being spouted.

Flint had the displeasure of a brief encounter a few days back, as he passed her in his truck, sticking his hand out the window with a friendly wave. Rooney had been strolling along the gravel near the bridge to the entrance of the island and looked up with a genial-enough expression.

"Go fuck yourself," Rooney told the ranger with a cordial wave of her hand, as he rolled slowly by in his truck. Flint was watching her in his side view mirror, brow furrowed, trying to figure out what the hell that was about. Not paying attention to the road, he had to slam on his brakes, stones crunching, when the clown he nearly ran over screeched.

Now, Flint watched the old bat skulking about behind the reporter, thinking he wouldn't be a bit surprised to see her walk up and kick the guy in the ass.

≈ ≈ ≈

Lennon Bagg squared his shoulder to the water. He took a deep, relaxing breath, adjusting his bare feet in the warm, shallow surf. He cradled the flat, round stone, tumbled smooth by a thousand years of waves, between index finger and thumb, preparing for another toss. Reaching back his right throwing arm, elbow level to the water, Bagg snapped his wrist forward, sending the stone skimming past the tiny shore breakers to the glassy water beyond.

He counted, "One ... two ... three ... four ... five-six-seven-eight ..." before the front spinning edge dug into the water and jammed its progress to a splashing halt.

"You dumb fudgepacker!" The voice from over his left shoulder startled Bagg enough to make him spill the collection of stones he'd been cradling in his shirt. "My husband could skip a rock better than you and he's been dead and rotting for ten years. Asshole!"

"Afternoon, Mrs. Rooney." Bagg didn't look up at the old woman. Making eye contact invited more insults that lasted longer. He set about retrieving all his good stones before the tide pulled them into the deeper water.

"Get a haircut, Bagg," she called to him from the gravel road. "Your hair makes you look like some kind of hippie shithead."

Belinda Rooney, who the kids and some of the adults called Cruella, was the owner of the sharp, energetic voice heard echoing around the game stands.

"Hey, Peckerhead, I bet you *wish* you threw like a girl," was a regular taunt. "Hey, lard-ass, wanna work a few calories off throwin' a dart?"

Whether Rooney had developed the art over years or had always been so caustic, nobody remembered. The Pisanis had tried to tone down her insults—at least cut some of the profanity—but once she was on a roll, she was on a roll. On the bright side, she seemed to get real enjoyment from her job and her game tills were always overflowing.

Rooney paused for a reaction, then gave Bagg a disgusted look as though she knew he was busy jackin' off in the water, probably just lurking there for some ten-year-old boy to wander by so he could whip out his little dick. People are for shit, Rooney constantly reminded those around her.

"Fucking hippie." Mrs. Rooney looked depressed, as if needing some other fuckwad faggot on which to bestow a little rage. Finally she stalked off, her blue housedress flapping indignantly in the light breeze.

Bagg took another deep, relaxing breath, momentarily contemplating hurling a handful of wave-smoothed stones at the old loon, before refocusing on the calm waters out beyond the break.

Calling Bagg a hippie was a jab Mrs. Rooney likely imagined would get under his skin. And even though she was infamous for her evil tongue, her ability to call on small pieces of information to personalize her attacks was often effective.

Bagg had talked about his parents while drinking beer and roasting marshmallows in the community fire pit. His folks had been honest-to-God hippie folk, right down to living on a commune, eating what they grew. The Summer Farm flourished during the late sixties and early seventies in New York's Catskill Mountains as an anarchist retreat for seventy or so souls who had rejected the establishment. It was hectic and disorganized on purpose, since any sort of organization was shunned. There were no established meal times or any real codes of conduct, and transients were always welcome and immediately given equal say in whatever needed deciding. The main drawback was all the fist fights due to the unbending demand for anarchy.

"I bet they had their own still," one of the mechanics jealously lamented, having to spend his hard earned money on store-bought booze.

"I don't remember a still," Bagg said.

"I bet they grew their own pot," another man said, who had then taken a deep drag off a joint filled with crappy Mexican dirt weed that smelled like a wet dog set on fire.

Bagg's father had been an admirer of Russian Communist leader Vladimir Lenin for his hand's on style of revolution. His father sported the same Lenin-style goatee, and had gone so far as to suggest naming his son after the Bolshevik, although the two tabs of microdot acid he'd swallowed turned the spelling into the English music legend's version. The young commune couple had let it be, so to speak.

The commune where Bagg was born was unofficially founded on April 16, 1967, the day after an anti-Vietnam war protest in New York City, where Martin Luther King, Stokely Carmichael, and Dr. Benjamin Spock were all headliners.

Honey and Dylon Bagg were among the four hundred thousand marchers gathered in and around Central Park for a peace fair, on an unseasonably cold and dreary day. Dark clouds spit on and off icy drizzle and fat snowflakes. The mass of people then headed down Fifth Avenue and made their way east to Dag Hammarskjold Plaza at the UN.

The city officials had braced for violence and mayhem, sending out thousands of New York City's finest to keep the rabble-rousers at bay, but only five arrests were made, despite numerous reports of police provocations. The five arrests were actually people belonging to a group opposed to the march.

As speeches wound down, the marchers made their way back up to their tents in Central Park. They hoped to warm up and sing a few songs accompanied by the hundred or so acoustic guitars slung from various shoulders. Politics over, it was time for a peaceful party.

But late that night, when the television crews and newspaper photographers had made their deadlines and gone home, four dozen busses on loan from Rikers Island, Sing Sing, and even all the way up from the Attica Correctional Facility, groaned to a halt along East Drive in the park. Out marched hundreds of cops in full riot gear, where they proceeded to round up as many of the trouble-making hippies along the Central Park Zoo fencing and on the shore of The Pond as they could grab.

In all, the raid netted some seven hundred peaceful demonstrators, who were likely the most stoned and therefore the least able to run away.

Dylon and the recently impregnated Honey were shoved into a black bus with Sing Sing Penitentiary written in bold white letters down each side. Their tent and sleeping bags were rolled up with those of their fellow dirtbag hippies and strapped to the long rack on top of the prison bus.

Four bumpy hours later, three of the buses pulled to the side of a dark country road. The cops riding in the front seats barked for everyone to get off. The camping gear was tossed from the roofs, and a scraggly group of peace marchers found themselves stranded in darkness and utter silence. They were left shivering from the cold and numb from the drugs, which had mostly worn off.

"We need to make camp," Dylon Bagg suggested, setting the hippies into motion. A single small flashlight was found among their belongings and everyone picked up a fair share of gear. A single file of about seventy people, including ten children, followed the small light away from the road and down to a clearing next to a stream.

"Home sweet home," someone said, and none of these people had any idea how prophetic those three words would become. The New York City Police Department had cleaned up Central Park and restored some of the normalcy for its upstanding and tax-paying citizens. A bunch of dirty, troublemaking hippies had been properly and quietly expunged.

The newly pregnant Honey Bagg was credited with naming the planet's newest commune The Summer Farm, after using a bottle of nail polish to paint the words on a white bandana and flying it from a stick over their tent.

"It sounds warm," Honey said.

On Fish Head Island, those first nights spent around the fire pit, safely surrounded by the carefully arranged maze of trucks, were something of a homecoming for Lennon Bagg. These people were familiar. Sitting next to him, the old woman with leather for skin, not a tooth left in her head, might have been pointed to by mothers as a warning for who would come snatch Johnny away if he didn't keep his room clean. In fact, there were plenty of Boogie Men for mothers to point to among the forty or so remaining workers. From the obvious Freaks of Nature to the boy with one leg shorter than the other.

Bagg had lived his adult life surrounded by people with health plans and money for deductable payments. He had lived among people with an expectation of at least trying to fix things that went wrong with you or your children.

But that hadn't always been the case.

Bagg had witnessed the form of dentistry practiced at The Summer Farm. The whiskey pain killers and the pliers used for rough extractions. As a little boy, he'd seen a broken arm set with wooden splints, no thought for an x-ray. Bad cuts had been splashed with soapy water and stitched like a torn house dress.

People hadn't intended to lose their teeth. Their babies hadn't been born with treatable conditions on purpose. The people who raised Lennon Bagg simply lived with whatever damaged them. As a little boy, he'd never been told there was a Tooth Fairy, probably because you never stopped losing teeth until they were all gone.

The leathery woman now gumming a bottle of warm Old Milwaukee might have been the same woman who had come running into the woods toward the screaming boy when Bagg was just five or six. Bagg had been exploring a deer path in the woods up on the hill above the Summer Farm. He was either naked or wearing torn old underpants when he tripped on a cable-like vine, falling forward into an innocuous looking pile of brush. When he went to push himself back up, a fiery burst of unimaginable pain raced up from his right hand, a pain so terrible, the first screams caught in his throat and no sound came out.

The boy again tried to pull away from whatever had him, but the same electric pain gripped his entire body. Reaching with his left hand to clear away the sticks and leaves, Bagg discovered that he'd been impaled squarely through the middle of his hand by a section of broken root. A bloody, half-inch-wide piece of wood had entered his palm and exited the dorsum. It looked like an angry finger pointing toward his face.

Little Bagg found his voice, shrieking so loud and long that he blacked out from lack of oxygen. Passing out had saved young Bagg the excruciating sight of the root being removed, an act he later found out was left to the toothless old woman who had reached him first.

Even back in 1973, most anywhere in America, an ambulance would have been called and emergency medical technicians led jogging into the woods to perform such extractions. But among circus folk and commune dwellers alike, when something was broken, you fixed it yourself. And scars were the lines that etched the events of your life.

Bagg's eyes fluttered open to the sight of the old woman's straw-like white hair and the mass of wrinkled skin that was her neck. Her filthy dress had come unbuttoned and a flabby mound of warm flesh pressed against his cheek, a coarse nipple rubbed as if offering to be suckled. Another child waking to such a sight would have been convinced they were being abducted by an awful monster, some sort of wicked and perverse witch. Bagg's eyes drifted beyond the old woman to the trees and flickering sun behind. The rhythmic bouncing of the downhill walk, combined with what was now a dull throbbing from his wound, made all the color run out of Bagg's world.

"It hurts bad."

"We're gonna get you all fixed up." She smiled down an impossibly wide, camel-like grin that stretched from ear to ear. "You boys always gettin' into somethin'."

"I fell down."

"Yeah, everybody falls down." She struggled for breath as the deer path leveled off. "The trick is to keep gettin' up, boy."

The old woman delivered Bagg, white as a ghost from pain and blood loss, to the small cabin his parents shared with another family of three. She slipped away for a few minutes and then returned with a squeeze bottle of dish soap, some rags, and her sewing kit.

On Fish Head Island, the people around the fire pit had been dirty because people who worked hard got dirty. And if you didn't have good showers, you stayed mostly dirty. One or two had cancer, which would shorten their lives considerably.

The man on Bagg's left tapped his shoulder and passed him a grease-smeared bottle. Bagg held it up to the yellow, licking flames and caught a glimpse of the scar on the back of his right hand. The first small sip from the dirty bottle carried the aroma of paint thinner but wasn't so bad going down. He took one more sip and passed it on.

Bagg sat in the light of the fire, now absently rubbing both sides of his scarred hand, feeling a bit of comfort from the storm.

Chapter 32

Sir William, the barker who had been in charge of riling up the early arrivals and igniting Enrique's cannon fuse, was assigned the task of sending volleys of fireworks out over the inlet every evening to announce that the show was about to go on. Sir William was an anomaly among most circus folk, since he was nearly sixty and looked no more than forty. He was handsome—as long as you didn't get too close—with most of his thick head of blond hair hidden under a U.S. Calvary hat he was never seen without.

Sir William had bolted metal pipes to stakes, loose enough to adjust firing height with a quick turn of the wrist. Six pipes were permanently set up near the water, giving him a clear shot at any low flying aircraft and passing boats. To anyone within a few hundred yards at dusk, it was obvious that something was taking place on the patch of ground along the inlet, especially when colorful flaming balls skimmed across your deck and you spied a smiling and waving man in an odd hat standing next to smoking launchers in the distance.

Strands of lights were switched on as the sun dropped behind the marsh. The music was cranked loud, competing with the metallic clack of the mini-coaster and truck ride. The main event was a forty minute show of non-stop action. Sir William gave the first clown the go-ahead signal when the last customers were settled into the bleachers. The lights went down for a ten count then came up with two spotlights trained on a sad face clown in the center of the ring. Sneaking up from behind was a smiling clown, who stole the other clown's big red nose and took off running. The sad clown tried chasing after the other, but his enormous feet kept tangling and he would fall hard again and again. He resorted to throwing buckets of silver confetti and firing a marshmallow gun, always missing, hitting surprised adults and laughing children. The clown chase continued under the bleachers and down the narrow aisles, and bumping across spectator's knees. It raised the energy level for the entrance of the zonkey-riding dog and some noisy chainsaw juggling. The slightly arthritic lion taming was followed by the bear act.

Graceful Gracie entered from the shadows and danced in wide circles, her pink tutu bright and shiny under the lights. She would then drop to all fours, stopping to beg a taste of cotton candy by rolling over and playing dead in front of the bleachers, sometimes catching peanuts in her mouth. Slim often joined her for a dance, doing the tango or the box step, depending on how much he'd had to drink.

Sir William signaled to the roustabout at the light controls to drop the blue gel over the spotlight and then jogged out to the center of the ring. "Ladies and gentlemen of all ages, I present to you a beautiful, mysterious and titillating talent from lands far away. The alluring gyrations of Miss Amira Anne!" Exotic music washed over the crowd as camera flashes worked a strobe-like effect on her delicate contorting. Men craned forward in their seats, and women seemed unsure whether to hate the tiny spectacle or be envious.

The chasing clowns returned with their frantic pursuit, as tiny Amira bowed and exited. Rising from the middle of one bleacher was a man in a police costume, oversized gold star pinned to his chest, who drew a sword from the sheath on his hip and bounded down to restrain the clowns. Cowering under the glare of the shining blade, the smiling clown returned the red nose to its rightful owner and the hero cop celebrated the justice he'd delivered by tilting up his chin and swallowing the long narrow sword. After withdrawing it slowly, he bowed to the cheering crowd and skipped out of the spotlight.

All of the performers returned for two laps around the center ring, including most of the Freaks of Nature who'd come to join the procession from their own tents. Graceful Gracie was usually the last to exit the encore, scouring the dirt floor for any remaining peanuts.

~ ~ ~

The summer rolled on. When Gracie wasn't performing, she was usually off doing surprisingly cub-like things. The old bear chased the noisy gulls and sometimes snuck up on workers napping in shady spots, pouncing and play-growling, gumming their soft spots in pretend death-grips.

When Gracie tired of digging up agonizingly delicious smells buried deep in the muck and had suffered enough pinches from the tasty crabs scooped out of the canal, her attention turned to the snoring prey huddled among partially repaired machines.

And there was nothing quite like the surprise attack of a snarling black bear, even one missing all forty-two teeth, to urge a person back to work. Waking up with several hundred mud-encrusted, reeking pounds on top of you—your neck suffering a hickey of epic proportions—pushed the limits on what was tolerable.

"Slim, get yer friggin' mutt bear offa me!"

Gracie knew this was human speak for "I give up!" She'd let go of whatever soft spot she'd latched onto and give the ex-prey an affectionate kiss from chin to forehead, lest there be any hard feelings. And, heck, they were probably going to play the same game again tomorrow.

Gracie watched the cars rumble over the Fish Head Island bridge every afternoon but knew to keep her distance. Her good man had warned her that the people in those cars were not to be played with unless she was on a leash or it was during a show. Soon after the cars began arriving, the music from the kiddy rides was switched on and Gracie couldn't help but dance wherever she had been exploring. The tent flaps for the noisy games and the Freaks of Nature were tied up shortly after. Gracie danced in two main event shows on some days and two extras on nights when the lots were overflowing with cars. She could sense how much people loved her circus, the happy screams and all the wonderful laughter.

And it was nice to stroll along the bay in the evening without all the usual biting insects, for sure.

Gracie and the other animals were in better spirits than they'd been in years. Instead of being packed up in their cages every week or so and jostled across steaming highways with choking exhaust and no chance to stretch their legs, they enjoyed the softness of the marsh grass and all the room to roam—more than any place they'd ever known. Sleep was easy and deep, because their rest wasn't disturbed by car horns and piercing sirens. It was a quiet place, with salty smells from the edge of the earth.

Here on Fish Head, the lion still hacked, but not quite as much. The temperamental zonkey hadn't bucked off a trained dog—or even the clown who sometimes worked her into his act—in weeks. Even Beelzebub, the ill-tempered guard dog, seemed to have found an inner peace, for days went by when he didn't try to bite a single person.

❧   ❧   ❧

Billy Wayne Hooduk, of course, took full credit, as instructed by his book.

Step number forty-seven from *How to Become a Cult Leader in 50 Easy Steps*: "When things go wrong, be fast and unwavering in assigning blame. When things go right, be equally prompt in accepting praise and basking in the glory and good will you deserve."

Billy Wayne was also going to rely on the advice of step number forty-eight: "Give people the impression they have a clear choice, making certain the decision you want them to select is unquestionably the only reasonable option."

Over small cups of vanilla pudding, Billy Wayne looked out at the bleachers and counted fifty-three people, which was a few more than when they'd landed on the island. Splashing around down at the edge of the bay were another eight or nine filthy kids, plus there was Flat Man, who needed his pudding delivered. Billy Wayne knew he'd have to be careful with his remarks this afternoon, since money could do funny things to people, especially those who weren't used to having much of it. He certainly wasn't used to being around the stacks of cash being emptied from the various tills.

Billy Wayne had assumed the role of therapist, mentor, decision maker, and accountant since leading the troupe to Fish Head Island, despite never performing any of these jobs in his life. But even with a complete lack of understanding when it came to balancing a checkbook, Billy Wayne recognized that the Pisani brothers had been cooking the books by simply erasing a couple of zeros here and there, calling each season a marginal loss.

Not showing a profit and therefore not being able to raise wages was surely the motive of the two old brothers. Billy Wayne assumed it was a circus trick as old as tight rope walking and human cannonballing.

The eight major performers were paid two hundred dollars a week each, plus two percent of the Big Top ticket sales. The ten Freaks of Nature each made a hundred fifty, while the three dozen other workers made a hundred a piece. Adding in food for the people and animals, as well as other minor expenses, the cost of running the circus was about eight thousand dollars a week. Counting Big Top ticket sales, ride tickets, concessions, game booths, and Freaks of Nature tickets, the Pisani Brothers Circus was clearing more than thirteen thousand dollars a week.

Billy Wayne had a tall wood stool in front of him as he stood on the contortionist's platform. People lounged in the bleachers across from him, scooping the last of their vanilla pudding. The midday sun had heated up the tent, and even with both flaps drawn open, the smell of hot manure was powerful.

"Good afternoon." Bill Wayne began each daily speech the same way. "I'm not going to talk about garbage, although we do need to watch the canal up on the north end, since the wind has been blowing papers into those weeds and it's getting pretty bad."

Billy Wayne wanted to address his recent discovery that the ten port-o-potties were being emptied into an old water truck and then driven in extremely illegal pre-dawn missions to the neighborhoods off Great Bay Boulevard to be dumped. Instead, he decided to keep this meeting entirely positive.

"No, I'm here with important news." Billy Wayne wished he hadn't worn his suit jacket, since it had gotten hot as heck in here and smelled like zonkey shit. Sweat was running down his back and he had to keep wiping his forehead on his sleeves. Billy Wayne reached down and hoisted a sturdy steel toolbox onto the stool in front of him. He took a small key from his jacket pocket, twisted it in the lock, and lifted open the lid as it faced him. "In just a little more than one month," he scooped up rubber banded thousand dollar stacks of mostly five and ten dollar bills, "We have profited more than twenty thousand dollars."

There were hoots and mummers and holy-shits from nearly all the workers.

"I'll take my share now!" someone called out.

"Hey, I want mine, too!"

"And it will be yours." Billy Wayne pointed to someone in the front row who hadn't said anything. "And yours and yours and yours, too. But if we divided the dollar bills among everyone, it would be just an extra couple weeks of salary, and then where would you be?"

Billy Wayne could almost see the rusty machinery grinding inside the heads of the people who were looking up at him. He knew some were imagining the endless bottles of middle-shelf booze, while others had already undressed the real hookers they were going to be able to score.

"You dumb fuckers will blow it all on booze and whores," Mrs. Rooney glumly added.

Billy Wayne paused to draw upon step number forty-eight. Ensure the decision you want them to make is the only reasonable conclusion.

"We can split this money up, or we can put it toward making this place our permanent home. Sure, we could spend it on repairing the trucks." Billy Wayne gestured toward one of the mechanics who responded with a nod. "The big trucks have a lot of miles on them and need more work than they're worth. Good money after bad."

"The one Peterbilt needs a new Allison, and the Freightliner's goddamn differential's all fucked to hell. And that don't ..."

"Thank you!" Bill Wayne called to the mechanic, who looked around, embarrassed.

"Lotta things broke," the mechanic quietly added.

"So I bring a very important decision to you." Billy Wayne placed the toolbox next to his feet and then formed the stacks of bills into a pyramid. "Do we fix the trucks and split up any remaining money, or do we dig in and build a home?"

Billy Wayne's own rusty machinery had been grinding away, imagining the beautiful air conditioned building where he would minister to his flock. He pictured a pulpit of sorts, with a large portrait of himself on the wall behind. There would be a kitchen, with an oversized refrigerator stuffed with ice cold sodas and big tubs of chilled pudding. There would be a real bedroom, with a downy bed that didn't reek of piss, where he could surely convince the contortionist, his lovely and exotic Amira, to come visit. Billy

Wayne stood behind the stool stacked with cash, shifting his legs to conceal the beginnings of another erection. The lack of a lockable door, or any door for that matter, had made Billy Wayne's masturbation ritual an often interrupted affair. More times than not, he was left to relieve himself while on his side, late at night, facing away from the tent flap, which never properly closed. His new bedroom would have a solid door with an excellent lock, Billy Wayne dreamed.

It was the sulky reporter who spoke up first. "I grew up in a place kind of like this." Bagg addressed the people surrounding him in the bleachers. "We also started out with tents and built some basic shelters that were good enough to keep us warm all winter. You people with campers just need kerosene, right?"

"I'm tired of all the packin' up," someone in the back shouted.

"The animals sure like it here," said another.

"I'm not sure I have a vote," Bagg said. "But I'd vote to give this place a chance."

Billy Wayne made a mental note to thank the reporter later, then waited a couple of minutes for the idea to completely settle with the roustabouts. He watched the resignation come across the faces of the men who'd already mentally spent their windfall on imaginary high-class hookers. Or maybe even on the forty dollar variety.

"We'll put the matter to vote." And Billy Wayne raised his own right hand. "Raise your hand to vote in favor of staying."

One after another, hands were raised. A few people who had been suffering intolerable hangovers had to be elbowed in the ribs, but the motion carried almost unanimously. Billy Wayne stood behind the pyramid of cash that he now saw as a down payment on a dream he couldn't have begun to imagine when he first swiped *How to Become a Cult Leader in 50 Easy Steps* from the library.

Triumphantly, Billy Wayne scanned the crowd of jabbering circus people, finally catching the eye of Amira Anne. She was sitting next to the reporter, dressed in frumpy gray sweats, her hair pulled back in a ponytail. What a perfect wife she would make, Billy Wayne thought. His heart ached at the simple beauty of this woman. A woman who could twist and stretch in so many heavenly manners. When my cathedral is complete, I'll ask her to marry me, Billy Wayne fancied, not noticing that, hidden behind the hulking body of the fat lady in the bleachers, Amira's tiny and delicate hand was firmly clasped in the reporter's.

"Then the last order of today's business is to decide on a new name to christen our island. I think we could come up with something more adventurous, more inviting to the magic of our home than Fish Head Island, don't you think?"

There were no offers. Billy Wayne prodded some more, while in the back of his mind hoping perhaps the reporter would suggest Hooduk Island, in honor of the man who had made this all such a success. "Maybe something which describes the family that we've become?"

"Save your breath, douche bag, and just call it Fuck Head Island." Mrs. Rooney rose from the third row of bleacher seats with a flourish, pushing people out of her way as she stomped down the metal stairs and stormed out the mouth of the tent. She made a quick u-turn and popped her head back in to add, "It smells like zonkey shit in here, you assholes."

Billy Wayne lifted the toolbox back onto the stool and began replacing the cash. "We'll work on the name." People began to file out into the sun.

Chapter 33

All the hammering wasn't doing Warden Flint's throbbing head a bit of good. From a couple hundred yards it wasn't particularly loud, but the monotonous beat went on and on, sinking an imaginary nail deeper and deeper into his left temple.

Flint took full responsibility for his current condition, which had him laying face down underneath his pickup truck, naked except for one work boot on his right foot. Thank Christ for all the poison, or he'd have been eaten alive spending a warm August night in the middle of a marsh, within spittin' distance of the Atlantic Ocean.

Flint reached down to adjust his testicles and scratch his ass.

That dopey little Hooduk had been bringing by those convenient plastic bottles of vodka that didn't break when you fell down a flight of stairs, or whatever, but last evening had been Christmas if there ever was one.

Flint was sitting on the front steps of the ranger shack when Hooduk pulled in and began wrestling a big box out of his trunk. His eyesight had been crap for years, but Flint could read the red letters on the white box, even before Hooduk freed it from the back of the Dodge.

"Stolichnaya," Flint read, but his initial excitement was tempered with the thought that it was probably just a used box from the liquor store. No way had the little turd dropped three hundred bills on the good stuff. But Hooduk lugged the sealed case up the steps and gently placed the box next to the game warden.

"You're a good man." Flint actually meant it. In fact, the little fart of a preacher had kept his word when it came to ridin' his people to pick up their trash, and makin' sure the port-o-potties were cleaned out regularly.

"Well, I'm a fair man, at least." Hooduk took a seat on the top step, the case of vodka between them. "I wanted to let you know we're stayin' on a bit."

"I figured as much when I seen the lumber roll by. You just keep them people on a short leash. I see them kids pluggin' gulls with pellet rifles again and I swear to God."

"It won't happen again."

A little investigating by Flint had uncovered that a pair of boys had dismounted and unchained what was actually one of the dollar-a-try automatic bb guns from the target shooting game. If a player was able to completely annihilate the red star at the center of the target with a hundred pellets, they won a stuffed prize. The boys had swiped the rifle, hooked it up to a bottle of helium they'd come across in one of the storage trucks, then headed down to the edge of the inlet for some live target shooting.

Mrs. Rooney had not been a happy barker when she discovered the weapon missing from one of her more profitable attractions. It didn't take her long to locate the two piece-of-shit boys using the long, birdshot-filled tubes to load the rifles, blasting away at the dumb birds. The boys had either maimed or killed four seagulls and had just finished another reload.

"You little sons-of-bitches!" Mrs. Rooney snatched away the freshly loaded weapon. The boys were kneeling in the wet sand, laughing and having a good old time taking turns, but now they cowered below the nasty old witch. And the nasty old witch was pointing a loaded automatic pellet gun at them.

"You nutless little cretins got any last words?" She took aim at one of their foreheads.

"Run!" one of the boys shouted, and they did just that. First scrambling to their feet, old sneakers sliding and not getting an immediate grip, the two boys made their cartoonish getaway back toward the circus tents. Mrs. Rooney picked up the helium tank and began pursuit, her blue housedress flapping in the wind, her mass of gray hair bouncing all around her head. A group of circus folks, Billy Wayne included, had gathered watching from next to the kiddy coaster, as the two boys ran for their lives.

❧   ❧   ❧

Warden Flint had discovered the dead birds later that afternoon, and he wasn't the least bit happy. It wasn't just a matter of a few dead seagulls. Hell, there were little balls of dead gulls all over the place. So many, that you started not even seeing them after a while. They were along the highway, washed up on shore, and here and there out in the marshes. Seagulls were probably the least endangered bird on the planet, and the world could certainly do with about a billion less of them. But once one showed up dead from birdshot, the proverbial shit was headed straight for the fan. You could drive over a flock of them with a goddamn Sherman tank and the State wouldn't blink an eye or bother to lend a shovel to scrape them up. But shoot even one of the mangy fuckers and you had a full-fledged federal case on your sorry hands.

Flint went back to his truck to grab the shovel out of the bed and very quickly buried the birds before tracking down Hooduk.

The expensive case of vodka went a long way toward smoothing things over, but it would only take one little fuckup to kick the legs out from under an arrangement that currently suited everybody just fine.

"It's all of our asses on the line," Flint told Billy Wayne. He ran a long, dirty thumbnail down the top of the case, cutting through the tape seal and removing a bottle. The warden cracked the screw top and took a hard sniff of the clear, faintly-scented alcohol. "Like water." He tilted the bottle up and drained a third of it.

Everything after that was just bits and pieces of grainy images. Flint had a vague recollection of trying to take a punch at Hooduk, but also had some memory of hugging him really hard, telling him he loved him, maybe even kissing him on the mouth. There was also something about his truck keys and having a hardy need to run his poison-mister around the marsh. Something about being bitten on the ass had sent him into a rage. Alcohol was a wonder drug, but it sure could fuck you up something fierce. It got to the point—after years of practicing the art—that as long as you didn't wake up in the slammer, then all was fine in the world. Feeling like an asshole about what you did when you were under the influence was a waste of time and easily cured by cracking open a fresh bottle.

Waking up under the truck, Flint's first sensation was that of feeling the need to adjust his balls, and something was making his ass itch. The head-thumping pain rushed at him when he shifted his body to scratch. Where his clothes had gotten to was a mystery to be solved later, but he figured he'd at some point taken refuge under the truck to get out of the sun.

If only they'd quit that friggin' hammering.

Chapter 34

The hammering that was so evil to Warden Flint's throbbing head was music to Billy Wayne Hooduk's sunburned ears.

Step number forty-five in *How to Become a Cult Leader in 50 Easy Steps*: "Make your cult a home away from home. Whether it means splurging on the good toilet paper or hanging pretty flowered curtains, a successful leader must recognize that the failure to provide the small touches of home can lead to mutiny, or at the very least, to unpleasant griping. A subscription to *Better Homes and Gardens* is highly recommended for lasting happiness."

Walls were framed out, while concrete pilings were poured. Pilings to support my temple, Billy Wayne thought, giddy with joy, a stark contrast to the dark nights of uncertainty and dread he often sweated through.

Billy Wayne's desperate search for approval had left certain pages of his stolen cult leader guide book dog-eared and smudged. He was a man raised on shortcuts, general malaise, and an easy willingness to allow others the spoils of their own hard work.

Billy Wayne had clung to the glimmer of hope shining from late night television infomercials. His past efforts to follow each guaranteed guide telling how to go from rags to riches had not failed due to some inability on his part, but rather due to flaws in the programs. Billy Wayne was certain of this.

Once, for ninety-nine dollars, Billy Wayne had received two VHS tapes and a thick packet of literature on how to buy foreclosed houses and resell them for astronomical profits. The fine print mentioned things like mowing the lawn and a coat of paint as part of the secret to success. Paint and a lawn mower? Curb appeal? Before they had your money, they told you over and over how simple it was to get rich. Then, you started reading things about how the amount of effort increased the amount of return. Weren't they just describing some sort of job?

And each program was remarkably similar once you started watching the tapes, even though the actors were changed around, and what you were expected to sell was different.

As Billy Wayne drifted off to sleep in his bed at home one night, he experienced one of the few epiphanies to ever streak across his semiconscious mind. Billy Wayne got the idea to star in his own infomercial, in which some Joe Six-Pack became rich enough to own a mansion in Florida and park a Ferrari out front. The idea was shear genius, Billy Wayne thought. He would have taken notes about it if he had a pencil and paper on his nightstand, instead of all the way across on his dresser. It was a perfect, totally foolproof idea and he couldn't for the life of him imagine how he'd never thought of it before. It made selling foreclosed houses and collections of yard sale junk seem like the dumbest ideas ever.

Billy Wayne's thoughts turned philanthropic. When the money from the infomercial started rolling in, he'd hand-deliver a check to the church, showing those spiteful people how he was someone to look up to. Wearing his Sunday best, he'd rise from the pew, smiling down at all his neighbors who had talked all nasty about his momma, and stroll right up to the Pollack minister. He'd pull the fat check out of his inside pocket and hold it out to show the congregation. Billy Wayne could picture how they'd stand up, cheering and clapping, saying bless you over and over. Little kids would tug on their mothers' skirts, asking who that man was.

"That's Mister Hooduk," the mothers would say.

Mister Hooduk, Billy Wayne thought, smiling. Everyone would know his name in a good way, instead of as "the fat woman Hooduk's kid."

The Pollack minister would take the check, telling him what a generous man he was, shaking his hand and not letting go.

But then Billy Wayne drifted off to sleep. Whatever brilliant, sure-fire concept he'd realized, discovered, or invented never saw fruition, and he forgot about it completely. Maybe just a brief, hazy glimpse passed by him while he sat sulking over his morning bowl of chocolate puff cereal the next morning, but it was gone forever.

The failure Billy Wayne experienced from trying to follow every infomercial program was perfect and complete. If it was during the day and his mood was good, he could almost laugh at the perverse perfection he'd clearly mastered, his absolute incompetence at everything. He was successfully batting zero. But late at night, the utter failure closed in on him. He became a befuddled little boy, bereft of hope or purpose.

In those lonely hours, Billy Wayne lost what little feeling of control he sometimes managed during his good days. Even as an aspiring cult leader and circus shepherd, he would feel fear and loneliness sweep over him and assume a fetal position—as much as his fat stomach would permit. And just as he had as a child, he would stifle the sobs that racked his body, worried that someone would hear his pathetic sniveling.

"I don't know what I'm doing, Momma," Billy Wayne sometimes whispered to the side of his tent, tears and snot making a wet circle on his filthy pillow.

Billy Wayne's main comfort was the sound of the lion's struggle for breath, its painful, emphysema-induced hacking that copycatted the sounds from his own tent. Billy Wayne knew the pain the lion felt. Not from whatever diseases the old animal suffered, but from being stripped of its dignity.

What has life for a mighty lion become when respect is replaced by pity? The thought made Billy Wayne's melancholy even worse, but at least something else understood this kind of suffering. Perhaps it was best that he didn't know the lion was born in a five-by-six foot cage in Pontocola, Mississippi, the product of an illegal exotic animal breeder.

Billy Wayne had heard the teasing his entire life. The kids had been ruthless right up until he stopped going to school. He did his best to run his mother's constant errands while school was in session, when it was less likely for Mister Fatty McLard Pants, or just plain old Queer Boy, to be spotted and chased, have his ears flicked, and titty twisters administered.

Billy Wayne had memorized a passage from page sixty-six of his cult leader book. He whispered it under his breath over and over, like a prayer, or a nervous tick: "It is only their weakness that makes them sour. Your calling is to the wretched for a higher purpose. Remember that Jesus had a really thick skin."

At thirty years of age, Billy Wayne was a newly emancipated man and de facto leader of a traveling circus that had recently grown roots. Despite his importance, he still heard the snarky remarks. He did his best to be deaf to them, dismissing each as a stern teacher would a challenge from an undisciplined child. It was the difficult art of turning the other cheek, patiently waiting for a better teaching moment. There were opportunities in each of these hurtful instances, and Billy Wayne took solace in the knowledge that he was developing as both a man and a leader.

Billy Wayne Hooduk was learning to solve problems by artfully dodging any real advice or decisions, despite the nonstop counseling sessions he held each evening with half-drunk followers. He was learning that life had a way of working out however life was meant to work out. Trying to change things was nothing more than interfering with an inevitable force, as his book confirmed.

"You can nudge an elephant all you want. You can get right up behind it and put your shoulder to its flanks. You can push with all your might. But unless that elephant suddenly feels compelled to move, it is just as likely to lift its tail and shit all over your head," Billy Wayne's book warned.

Late at night, done masturbating to the images of Amira Anne's steamy, twisting, spandex-clad body, Billy Wayne often grew morose over the countless episodes of failure in his relationship with his mother. He might be sleeping on a cot reeking of an old man's urine, in a tent out in some dark mud flats, but had Jesus' path been any rosier? His mother would have to understand his journey, just as Billy Wayne now recognized what he could have done better for the woman he'd come to see only as oppressive and demanding.

In the morning, a paper plate filled with scrambled eggs blunted the edge of the night-suffering. The rising sun glimmering over the inlet really did signal a new day. There was a cathedral, Billy Wayne's cathedral, being hammered together by the roustabouts who had eaten during first shift. The ragtag group of men were lustfully swinging hammers not for some temple, Billy Wayne knew, but for the idea of indoor plumbing. And for a real kitchen and a chance to take turns standing in front of an air conditioner turned up to full blast. Motives, like building permits, didn't really matter to Billy Wayne, as long as he got what he wanted. He gobbled the last of his eggs and wandered out to watch the progress, careful not to get too close; someone might offer him a hammer or something.

Truth be told, circus workers were not all that used to constructing permanent structures, and the building plans scribbled up by the two mechanics looked like they might result in a rather complicated tree fort. Instead of something pegged down or strung up, Billy Wayne's permanent cathedral was to have a large meeting room, a kitchen, two bathrooms, and an office big enough to double as a bedroom for Billy Wayne.

"It's gotta sit on pilings," one of the mechanics had said.

"What if it don't?" asked the other.

"It'll sink under the mud or wash out into the ocean."

"So we should go with the pilings?"

The concrete pilings were hardening while walls were being framed out. None of it made sense to Billy Wayne. It was like one of his mother's giant jigsaw puzzles she spread out on the kitchen table before she got so fat. Billy Wayne had wandered by as she plucked a piece from here and there, some fitting, some not. Billy Wayne tried to help but never once had he gotten two pieces to snap together. He quickly grew impatient, and with the television free, he clicked on cartoons and flopped onto the couch with a bag of chips.

As Billy Wayne watched, four of the circus trucks arrived, stuffed and overflowing with building materials. Plywood, two-by-fours, big pieces of wood that must be for holding up the floors or the roof, a small mountain of shingle bags, coils of wire, and rolls of pink insulation that looked like cotton candy. The fact that he hadn't signed off on more than five hundred dollars didn't raise any red flags for him. He had no clue what these materials cost, so it was easy for him to pretend they hadn't been stolen. He also ignored the fact that his men were returning before any stores were open. Perhaps it was a case of an "immaculate" transaction, a little like the "immaculate conception," which meant Jesus's Mother Mary had somehow gotten pregnant without sinning. Billy Wayne was also fine with pretending not to hear the wagers on who would get what first, as well as the whispers about such and such construction sites they'd recently driven past.

"Comin' along just fine." The lead mechanic startled Billy Wayne enough that he sloshed hot coffee on his wrist.

Billy Wayne had learned the man's name was Happy, or just Hap, because of his general good disposition. He'd learned it from a routine the two mechanics went through each time there was cause for an introduction. The other mechanic's name was Dick and claimed to be named for his genitals, or just because he acted like one. Billy Wayne hadn't really been able to follow the joke through to the punch line, but he now knew that one was Happy, the other, Dick.

"It's going to be a fine building." Billy Wayne didn't bother to mask his outright joy, despite the new burn on his wrist he was licking and blowing on. He wanted to use words like temple and cathedral to describe it but knew he shouldn't get carried away. Each time he pictured the word "shrine," the corners of his pudgy mouth curled up, and his eyes drifted far away. He'd also had the words "pantheon" and "tabernacle" reach the tip of his tongue, but he wasn't certain what exactly they were, just that they also sounded formidable, worthy of this project. They were words his Pollack minister had used in his preaching.

"I never seen these boys work so hard," Happy said, as the current crew was joined by those from the second breakfast shift. There were now more than two dozen pairs of hands setting huge pieces of wood on the pilings, which one of the mechanics decided had set enough, using those things with bubbles in them to make sure everything was level. "Especially not this early in the mornin'."

"I imagine it's the sense of community that has them so motivated. Like an Amish barn raising, you know?"

"Yeah, could be the Irish, or maybe just most of them boys really lookin' forward to usin' an indoor shitter." Happy took a long pull off a can of Old Milwaukee. Billy Wayne noticed he also had a can in each front pocket of his jeans. "Them port-o-potties get mighty hot, and we ran outta chemicals years back. They didn't used to smell so bad."

The two men stood in the shade of one of the main tents, Hap with one foot up on a stake, while Billy Wayne leaned one arm against the angled rope it was anchoring. Billy Wayne turned back toward the New Jersey mainland. Squinting into the morning mist, he could make out one of the pickup trucks with the Pisani Brothers Circus name painted on the driver side door. It was coming fast and hard toward the Fish Head bridge. Several men stood in the truck bed, whooping and laughing, holding on with one hand, beer cans in the other.

"Looks like them boys found a goodie." Happy followed Billy Wayne's gaze as the truck went up and over the bridge too fast, nearly launching the men and whatever cargo was in back. "I heard they got twenty bucks riding on the first ones to come up with a hot water tank. That's a case of beer and change back."

The truck threw up a rooster tail of dust as it barreled down the gravel road, the driver eventually jamming his brakes and sliding sideways in the wetter muck near the construction site. The commotion had even interrupted Gracie's morning frolic through the marshes, as the old bear lumbered home to investigate what had gotten the humans all excited. The bear shuffled up to where Hap and Billy Wayne stood staring, leaned back on her haunches and shook mightily. Neither seemed to care about the flecks of muck they now wore.

Billy Wayne held his ground alongside the mechanic, as they watched the figures dismount and begin to taunt the men who'd returned earlier with what were apparently lesser finds. Those men now peered over the sides of the pickup, shaking their heads in what might have been jealousy or respect, as the tailgate was dropped and a large object wrapped in heavy plastic was carefully slid out.

"What in the hell can that be?" Happy wondered aloud.

But once the object was set in the mud correctly, a rush of adrenaline coursed through Billy Wayne's body like the night he'd first watched Amira Anne's heated undulations in blue spandex. Billy Wayne licked his lips, his heart beginning to race, as he watched the men cut and then slowly unwrap the heavy plastic, exposing the first signs of beautiful, deep wood grain.

The shape was unmistakable. There was no doubt what this precious object was.

Billy Wayne was unashamed of the tear that rolled down his pink, freshly shaven cheek. Didn't care who saw his shaking hands, which were barely able to hold his now lukewarm cup of coffee. With each twist of the plastic, more of the object was unveiled. Billy Wayne felt the power of this Holy Grail delivered by such humble and ignorant people. They might as well be unwrapping the helm from Noah's ark, or an especially beloved Moai Head direct from Easter Island.

With the last bit of plastic tossed aside, Billy Wayne could read the words on the beautiful lectern, recently unscrewed from its pulpit and absconded away to its new home on Fish Head Island: "Welcome to the Church of Jesus Christ of Latter-Day Saints."

Bless the sinners, Billy Wayne thought. Bless each and every one of these magnificent, whore-mongering sinners.

Chapter 35

The clouds slowly tumbling across the dreary sky were as dark as ever. It seemed like a mistake that the rain had stopped. Something was wrong, as though a steady drumbeat lasting for days had quit for no reason, or a car on a highway had stalled with a half tank of gas left. Perhaps if the sun had broken through to return some of the color to the world, the circus folks would have been quicker to venture out from their damp, hollow spaces. Even a traveling circus growing roots was vulnerable to wretched weather.

Two bad fights had broken out during the rainy spell. A combined twenty-six stitches were knitted into the faces of four men and two women. Three teeth could not be salvaged. All would make up once the weather turned nice and the money started flowing again. It had happened before and would happen again.

Billy Wayne's nervous energy matched the swirling skies above. He paced back and forth in the muck, rubber boots stamping their imprint in the mud. The footprints lasted for a few seconds, then water seeped from below to flood the impression.

"I just can't believe it." Billy Wayne paused directly in front of the finished building. Hap stood cowering in what would be his shadow, if the sun were out.

"I know what you mean, boss," he said, mostly under his breath.

"They really did it." Billy Wayne stood staring, eyes wide as they could be.

"Well, ya ever see postcard pictures of that building in Europe? Whatcha call that place?" Happy scrunched his face to search his memory, great lines erupting across his eyes and forehead. "Mother of Christ if I can't see it clear as day."

"Vatican City?" Billy Wayne tried, as the pair stood side by side facing the first building ever constructed on the marshy shores of Fish Head Island.

"Nah, it's close to Italy, or maybe inside Italy." Happy tilted his head to get a proper perspective on the canted structure. "But it's got something to do with pizza."

Billy Wayne realized what was on the tip of Happy's tongue. The mechanic was trying to come up with the Leaning Tower of Pisa, but Billy Wayne didn't care to give him the satisfaction. The tilt of his marvelous new cathedral was a technicality. Would you turn your back on the love of your life over a third nipple? Or a couple of webbed toes?

Billy Wayne saw perfection. He half expected the clouds to part at any moment. A marvelous ray of light would stream down to highlight this creation, just like in the pictures in the Pollack minister's Bible. How could anyone not see it?

The tilt was merely an act of God, Billy Wayne knew.

Globally speaking, that August was one of the hottest months in recorded history, and there was no exception on Fish Head Island. But sandwiched in between strings of ninety-plus degree days was a week of torrential rains over the course of which more than five inches fell.

The nearly intolerable heat had sent the roustabouts into a case of the doldrums, while Billy Wayne mostly lay in his muggy tent dreaming about air-conditioning, counting the painfully slow pounding of shingle nails. What had previously sounded like the rapid fire of a Tommy Gun had fallen off to uneven and intermittent sniper fire. When the rains came, the exterior work was declared complete and the installation of the two likely-stolen toilets and all the pilfered kitchen appliances began.

Billy Wayne preferred not to know how seemingly brand new items kept showing up on the island, yellow energy saver tags still attached, instruction booklets tucked away someplace inside. But the afternoon hit-and-miss thunderstorms and seasonable heat of July had given way to one intolerable weather pattern after the next, and the cash flow had dried up as fast as the rain fell. The pile of surplus cash had taken a hit, as there really was no good way around feeding man and beast. Sure, the rice, beans, and bulk hot dogs could be supplemented with the big bags of chicken necks sold as crab bait, but the soup it made tended to taste like crab bait.

The scavenger hunt was secretly welcomed. Billy Wayne considered his quiet consent the equivalent to turning the other cheek.

"Swear to God, somebody just left it right on the curb. Just imagine how rich you gotta be to throw away a perfectly good refrigerator like that? Be a crime to let it just be hauled to the dump."

The pilings on one side of the building had sunk another six inches, but it surely couldn't rain forever. Maybe the weight would eventually level them off? Three of the eight windows had been hung upside down, and there had been quite a bit of creative carpentry involved after they had discovered the walls ranged from eight to nine feet high at various spots around the six-hundred-square-foot kitchen, toilet, and temple. But with a coat of white paint, the one-story building was to be a fine foundation for Billy Wayne and his people. So what if the peas were going to roll to one side of the plate? And a slight uphill walk to the toilet never killed anyone.

"Appears some of them windows are hung upside down." Happy's voice was filled with sympathy. "Could very well pinch off your fingers trying to get some air."

The low spots on the road to Fish Head Island were covered in water, especially at high tide, and the big circus trucks themselves had turned into islands. The circus spent the long days in a kind of lockdown, with no customers and no performances. The only occasional flourish of activity took place when an especially heavy gust of wind pulled up a stake and put one of the smaller tents in peril of being lost at sea.

There was a lot of drinking, but not much more than during the average week. When the rains finally let up, Happy had fetched Billy Wayne to come have a look.

"They shoulda knowed to dig deeper to get down to bedrock with them pilings," Happy said, as the two stood with their backs to the mainland, the cockeyed building between them and the inlet. Some of the braver seagulls had come out from where they'd huddled in crevasses, battling the swirling wind to search for bits of food.

"My momma had a book with pictures like this." Billy Wayne gestured to his new cathedral with both hands.

"A lopsided house book?"

"What? No," Billy Wayne said. "There was a famous painter who had gone to school to be a draftsman, some sort of architect, you know? His name was Salvador Dali, and he liked to paint these really crazy things."

"I heard of him. The guy from India that got killed for having a hunger strike. Terrible way to go."

"Dali painted wonderful images, like pictures of melting clocks, and there was one where a fish is trying to swallow up a big tiger, while another tiger is about to pounce on a naked woman."

"He paint her bush?" Happy jabbed a pointy elbow into Billy Wayne's soft side.

"I don't remember. But I'm saying that for all its flaws, it's still a piece of art." Billy Wayne stood admiring his crooked temple, hoping air conditioners could still be installed in the screwed up windows.

"Long as it don't sink down all the way and fall over in the mud."

"Sometimes, you just need faith," Billy Wayne said.

"Or maybe two-by-fours to prop it up with."

Chapter 36

The August heat also settled over Bermuda, as Morgan watched the white object take wing on a southerly wind, rising from the top of one of the prehistoric-looking palmetto trees standing guard at the edge of St. Margaret's Bay. It soared bird-like at first, before a sudden updraft lifted it a hundred feet in the early evening sky, directly over her regular spot on the beach.

The wind went still, and the large rectangle of paper floated toward her, rocked back and forth by friction, coming to rest at her sand-covered feet. The week-old front page of *The Royal Gazette* was filled with color photos, including an image she was very familiar with and had drawn at least a dozen times.

The Bermuda Petrel, or "Pterodroma cahow," was Bermuda's national bird. Known locally as the cahow, it was thought to be extinct for three centuries, before its rediscovery in the early twentieth century. The cahow was credited with single-handedly fending off the Spanish conquistadores with its shrill nocturnal cries, which absolutely terrorized the superstitious Spaniards. But the much less skittish and more practical British colonists in the seventeenth century killed them for food and brought rats, dogs, and cats from Europe to destroy their breeding habitat.

The cahow was the saddest of birds, in Morgan's world. Morgan could remember the hurricane, when she was six years old, that had wiped out most of the cahows' nesting burrows. She and her mom spent two days stowed away in a big concrete hotel, where her mother had to keep warning her away from the windows.

During the worst storm to hit Bermuda in fifty years, the winds topped a hundred twenty miles per hour, tearing off roofs and knocking down trees. Morgan was drawn to the thick hotel windows. The worst of the winds came in the afternoon, and she held her hands up to the huge piece of glass and pressed her cheek against it, feeling the incredible power just inches away. The little girl couldn't fathom what it was like to be a bird caught in this storm with nowhere to hide. She had seen fifty gallon metal drums tumbled and flung like toys. The gas station overhang across the highway had been lifted up and tossed away like a stray umbrella.

Morgan's tears smudged the glass as she willed the wind to stop. But hour after hour it pummeled the island, and she just knew the birds were all dying as she, her mom, and all the other evacuees waited inside.

Morgan fell asleep in her mother's arms and dreamed she had run outside as the eye of the storm passed directly over the hotel. She ran from bush to bush and tree to tree, searching for birds to save. She found little clumps of feathers here and there, but as the back side of the eye wall approached, there were no live birds to rescue. Just as she'd feared, all the birds had been blown away. She knew they'd died while she'd been hiding away in the big hotel, dry and safe.

The photo on the front page of the *Gazette* showed a cahow soaring low over the ocean, the way Morgan preferred to draw them. The cahows were excellent fliers and spent the first five years of their adult lives over the open ocean, before returning to their original nesting place to breed. They contributed to their own fragile existence by laying only a single egg each breeding season.

Born and then set free for five years to circle the ocean, Morgan thought. How big that ocean must seem at first. Whether you were forced by natural instinct or the hands of your own human mother, being away from home—away from everything you loved and knew—was hard and unfair.

Morgan had spent countless evenings watching the sun disappear out across the bay with the cool breeze and darkness enveloping her, feeling small and pointless. She was just a puny speck on a sandy rock out in the ocean. Maybe her mom was worrying about her, but probably not. Morgan sometimes heard the cahow bobbing out in the water. The Spanish explorers had been scared off by its eerie cries in the night, but maybe the birds were just lonely. Morgan knew what it was like to be alone, crying at night on the beach. For her, it was a pretty regular gig.

In the dying light, Morgan scooped up the newspaper and squinted to read the story about the cahows and other birds. Some man was donating money and land for a nature reserve and bird sanctuary, and Morgan tilted the paper toward the last of the orange glow to read the small print.

"Bermuda is an amazing and critical place for bird lovers," Michael Dupont, the man donating the money, was quoted as saying. "There are three hundred and seventy-five species of birds on this tiny nation and seven are globally threatened. And it is an important stopping point for migration between North and South America."

Morgan knew this from school and had drawn most all of them.

The story described the new sanctuary, a series of three islands inside the inlet of Castle Harbor, where the ground was high enough to protect newly constructed artificial cahow burrows from storm surges. There would also be breeding grounds for longtails and terns, as well as the thirty or so species that used the area as a pit stop during long migrations.

There would be an official dedication and grand opening of the reserve, with a picnic lunch and bands from two high schools. Governor Vereker would accept Dupont's generous endowment for future care of the preserve on behalf of Queen Elizabeth II. The ceremony would be held on Saturday, September 15, according to the story, at the

Tucker's Town main dock. The VIPs would then board boats and tour the new sanctuaries at a respectful distance.

"I'm delighted this project has gone so smoothly," Dupont said in the article. "With the heart of the hurricane season upon us, it's been a goal to have all the work complete. For anyone who doesn't see the point in what we are doing, I urge them to get out into nature and close their eyes, to experience and see with their ears. Listen to the songs of the birds. These songs are the links to our past, and man's footprint has caused terrible disruption in migratory paths and fragile breeding grounds. But it is not irreversible, and it is not too late if we recognize the work that still must be done."

Castle Harbor was the largest bay, maybe three miles at its widest, at the far end of Bermuda from Morgan's spot on the beach. Still, it was only a little more than ten miles from their home as the crow flies. Morgan's mom had taken them to visit some of the old stone fortresses built on tiny islands, which had provided protection for the harbor from various marauders. But they rarely went beyond Hamilton anymore, except to meet her mother's travel agent friend at the airport every couple of months. The airport made up the entire northern boundary of Castle Harbor.

The newspaper described Dupont as a video game designer from Charleston, South Carolina. He'd become interested in setting aside natural reserves for birds after visiting habitats destroyed by hurricanes. He'd spent more than fourteen million dollars purchasing coastal marshlands from South Carolina to Maine. Most of his projects involved nothing more than keeping the land free from high-rise hotels and trophy homes, leaving the land in pristine condition.

There was a head shot of Michael Dupont, smaller than the one of the soaring cahow, and he looked awfully young to be so rich, Morgan thought. His face was long and skinny, too pale for a birdwatcher's. Wouldn't a birdwatcher be outside all the time? His wire glasses made him look smart, and his spiked hair was kind of cool. He also wore a geeky blue shirt, buttoned all the way to the top. Morgan supposed Michael Dupont knew all about being teased in school.

According to the paper, the Bermuda project was of a much grander scale, beyond just setting aside land otherwise doomed to development. "Here, we're involved with protecting endangered species, as well as overseeing the mid-point on the migratory highway."

Morgan reread the last sentence several times, by what was now moonlight. "Migratory highway," Morgan said to herself, looking out at the black water, wondering where Gus—the teacher turned pelican—would be spending the night. A carpet of stars had layered the sky and the moon had risen over her left shoulder. She should have been home an hour ago, but it had been so peaceful ... None of the kids had come down to boogie board the flat water today. Time had gotten away from her, slipping by as it always did when she wasn't walled-up inside her school.

Mr. Dupont could hear the birds talking, but Morgan bet he couldn't talk back to them. Morgan knew she possessed a special gift, an ability most people found impossible to believe. People like her mom and her teacher, Mrs. Jones. It was perfectly fine to make kids believe in Santa Claus and the Easter Bunny, but wanting to find your own father made you worse than a bank robber. Some fairy fluttering into your bedroom to buy your old teeth was fine. Leprechauns sleeping under mushrooms and tending pots of gold at the end of rainbows were reasonable. How many of those freaking shamrocks had she been forced to cut out of green construction paper in her life?

"I have to stop crying," Morgan told the dark, empty beach. She creased and folded the newspaper into smaller and smaller squares, then tucked it away in one sneaker before slipping both shoes onto her sandy feet. "And I'm not crazy."

Standing up, Morgan shook out her towel and resolved to run away from home two weeks from tomorrow. A man as smart and rich as Mr. Dupont would surely see what a valuable asset a girl who could talk to birds would be.

And she knew he would help find her father.

Chapter 37

Being a lifelong alcoholic had its truly bad points. Each of Warden Flint's attempts to quit drinking was greeted with agonizing hallucinations, both visual and tactile. His delirium tremens were not of the congenial pink elephant or miniature men variety. Possibly because of his vocation, Flint's excruciating bouts were marred by mutant insect larvae, which invariably crawled and squirmed toward his mouth, nostrils, and ears. It was the acute sense of them "wanting inside" that drove Flint back to the bottle.

As a bug exterminator at heart, Flint was never free from his nemesis, drunk or sober. The sudden appearance of the crazy Hooduk woman's kid in his life lifted his nightmares to a new level. He'd been able to deal with the creepy crawlers, but guilt was a surprisingly powerful emotion Flint wasn't used to.

The empty bottle slipped from Flint's fingers, falling over onto the wood floor with a hollow clink then slowly rolling a few feet toward the front door. He heard the sound of glass on wood, followed by a wet sloshing noise, like a fish at the bottom of the bait bucket trying to show it still had life in it. Somehow, he was standing behind the front door of the ranger shack, listening to the damp, wriggling sounds getting closer, growing in volume and intensity. The old floorboards hummed, and when he looked down at his feet, he noticed wetness spreading under the threshold, turning the bleached wood dark. The wetness inched toward his work boots.

Flint reached a shaky hand toward the doorknob, twisting the cold brass, pulling the door toward him. The sky was moving with dark, cloud-like swarms of mosquitoes, and the ground was a pulsating mass of larvae, undulating toward the shack and its wooden steps like a deep, angry ocean.

"March!" It was a woman's voice from behind Flint, and he craned his neck to see that it belonged to that Hooduk woman he'd knocked up years back, the mother of the fat little preacher boy.

"March on out of here!" the woman demanded, and Clayton Flint looked back at the pulsating mass of baby mosquitoes that seemed ready to devour him.

"Please." Flint was powerless to change the course of this dream, and he knew it. It was what his daddy had called a "foregone conclusion," as in, "Son, you busted out my Buick window with this baseball, so the fact that I'm gonna whoop your ass with this here belt is a foregone conclusion."

Allison Hooduk stood firm in the middle of the messy ranger shack, arms crossed like a dour schoolmarm's. "Get out of here, now!"

Flint's first step onto the front porch was like stepping in a pile of dog turds, as the mass of larvae gave way around his boot. They were now on the cuffs of his pants, squirming upward—wanting and needing—and Flint took another step out into this sea of twisting little creatures. He moved forward to where the top step should have been, the mostly brown larvae moving in waves, maybe four feet deep as far as the eye could see. The buzzing black clouds above him seemed to egg him on, taunting him to become part of them.

"Please, no," Flint muttered to the clouds of black mosquitoes that shifted and dipped and made Flint's stomach sick with vertigo.

Flint heard heavy footsteps from behind, as the Hooduk woman charged across the shack toward him, screaming. "You killed my baby!" The impact knocked the breath out of Flint, snapping his head back, sending his body airborne from the top step in an awkward belly flop dive. The warden landed face down in the swarm of mosquito larvae, which immediately filled his mouth and nose, making him cough and gag, as he pawed at his face. They also crawled into his ears.

Clayton Flint was spitting and sneezing phantom larvae as he woke from his dream, face down on the floor next to the ranger shack couch that doubled as his bed.

Flint checked to make sure he had all his clothes on, then searched the immediate area around the couch for last night's bottle of vodka. Two gulps later, his head felt a little better, a little less full of those frigging mosquito larvae, for sure. His knees popped and his back groaned, as he got to his feet, then headed out the back door to piss off the deck.

Warden Flint sent a pale arc of urine out into the marsh. They were out there, he knew, billions of them, growing and squirming, turning over with little flicks of their twitching bodies. The rains did that. It filled every goddamn piece of garbage with a watery nest for them to grow and flourish. Flint zipped up, tucked in his shirt, and prepared for the war ahead of him. He could deal with half-witted, inbred circus folk, dopey bears in skirts running wild, and creepy little preachers with kooky mothers, but he would not tolerate insects of any sort disturbing his peaceful existence. His skin crawled at the thought.

As if to taunt him more, a small white butterfly, no bigger than a dime, rose up out of the marsh behind the shack and flitted every which way, designing crazy patterns in front of the gray sky. Before these damn rains, not even the most hardened of cockroaches could have survived thirty seconds in those toxic grasses. Hell, any snake eating a cockroach out there would have keeled over and died a jerking, painful death.

One more slug of Stoli vodka for the road and Warden Clayton Flint found his keys and headed into battle.

Chapter 38

It was like holding a little girl's hand and the feeling was bittersweet.

Everything about the contortionist was miniaturized, from the overall size of her body, to her airy, child-like voice. Amira Anne was by no means dwarf-like, nor did she have the baby fat of a child. Amira's narrow, four and a half foot frame was simply a tiny, more petite version of an average-size woman. That she must weigh no more than seventy pounds and walked with the light touch of a ballerina, made her appearance all the more wispy and ethereal. When Bagg watched her performance under the glaring spotlight, he didn't get the same sexual thoughts as he saw on other mens' faces, Billy Wayne's included; Bagg thought a lot of it looked gymnastic, if not painful.

Bagg and Amira Anne sat on a thin white blanket in the soft grass at the far corner of the island. Off in the distance was the noisy hum of the game warden's pesticide mist blower; the crazed Flint was making looping passes around the island, sometimes veering into the marsh and getting stuck. He'd throw open the door, shouting curses and then somehow managing to get himself unstuck. Bagg could see the glint of a long, slim bottle being tilted over the steering wheel.

"Something's wrong." Amira Anne spoke in such a small voice, and Bagg assumed she meant the game warden, since that was the direction they were both looking.

"He's just drunk." Bagg watched Flint's truck disappear back over the island's bridge. Bagg and Amira hadn't spoken more than a few dozen words over the months, but she sometimes appeared next to the towering Bagg and he'd look down to notice a tiny white hand in his own. It made him smile.

"I meant there's something wrong inside of you." Amira looked up at him with almond-shaped eyes that were almost Asian. Her dark hair was swept back in a ponytail. "You're the saddest person I've ever met. And working in this business, I've been surrounded by some pretty sad people."

"I miss my little girl." Bagg felt too tired to recount the history of his troubles, the loss of his daughter. By this time, Bagg's newspaper would have officially shut its doors, its presses and office materials appraised for auction. He'd tried to reach his friend Andy Cobb—the reporter who had covered the tiger attack—but it had been too late. His number at the paper was an out-of-service message, as were Cobb's home and cell numbers. Like people who ran off and joined the circus, disappearing into thin air was a trick newspaper staff members seemed to be learning. With a history that went back over three hundred years in America, newspapers were sick and dying even in their Boston birthplace. Reporters, photographers, and editors charged with being the watchdogs were now out of work, suddenly stripped of the ebbing power they'd so desperately clung to, folded back into the world of regular people. A press pass made you a little special. Not much, and sometimes not at all, but it was always there to help you at least try to get through some blocked door, past some gatekeeper. Then it was over. Like an unanswered question asked at the end of a press conference, the words just awkwardly hung in the air. The reporter was sometimes angry, and sometimes embarrassed.

Bagg had gone through his phone's list of numbers before reaching a lifestyle writer who had landed a spot at the *Philadelphia Inquirer*, itself in dire financial trouble. But she had no news for Bagg on any charges being filed against him. Lilly Epstein's desk had always been stacked with a hodgepodge of arts and crafts, fashion magazines, and local restaurant menus. Bagg had teased her that her job description seemed an awful lot like someone trying to burn through an expense account. She had been the newsroom's consummate schmoozer, with a direct line to all the latest gossip.

"What happened to you?" Lilly's voice crackled over the poor cell connection. "People said you'd run away and joined the circus."

"What?" Bagg wasn't certain he'd heard correctly. Did they know where he was?

"You disappeared. You left your desk a mess and somebody eventually stuck all your things in a box. People figured you said the hell with coming in. Is that what happened?"

"No cops came looking for me?"

"Why would cops be looking for you?" Lilly sounded more interested, as if there might be some good tidbits to be had. "What did you do?"

"Nothing on purpose. Listen, I had this run-in with a crazy cop and I wasn't sure if I was in trouble. It was really nothing, but I figured there also wasn't much reason to come back to the paper. I should have packed up my things, though."

"What are you doing? I mean, where are you?"

"I guess I did run off and join the circus." Bagg thought of the posters he'd helped Hooduk design, as well as a handful of press releases he'd written and delivered to the penny savers and weekly tourist rags, especially after the rains had dried up the customers. He'd also filled out the tightly creased emergency check he kept in his wallet for the remaining account balance and had mailed it to his landlord from a box out near the Parkway. Did he have until October before his belongings were boxed-up or thrown away? Would the security deposit give him until November?

"You haven't found anything?" Lilly probably meaning a new reporting job.

"Not yet." Bagg thought again of his daughter, knowing she meant a job.

"Well, I hope that works out for you. Hey, deadline's coming up and I gotta run."

People kept asking Bagg what was wrong with him. Amira's observation wasn't the least bit new. After Jennifer disappeared with Morgan, he'd been consumed by the emptiness. He'd learned what a doubled-edged sword hope was. Sure, it gave you something to cling to, something to live for. But it also seemed to turn everything into disappointment. Where there was hope in every late night ringing phone, there was also the utter disappointment when the caller was a wrong number, or someone wanting you to cover a shift for them.

Dreams were torture in this way, as well. Bagg would wake up in the early morning hours, Morgan calling for her daddy from the other room. Bagg would throw off his blanket, stretch his back, and then head for the door to get his little girl a fresh cup of water from the bathroom faucet. But somewhere between his bed and the bathroom, Bagg would remember there was no little girl anymore. He would remember he was alone and that it was just a voice from some dark place in his mind sent to remind him, sent to torment him. And there was the agonizing guilt from those recurring dreams. Or were they nightmares? Guilt because Bagg would wake up annoyed at Morgan, a perfectly reasonable mild anger at being disturbed from a deep sleep. But after collapsing back in bed, he'd fall asleep ashamed, hating himself. He swore he'd do anything in the world to see his daughter again, if only for a moment, but here he was getting pissed off about being woken up, even if it was by some sort of ghost.

Hope had settled in that little dark place in his mind, exposing itself every once in a while despite Bagg's best efforts. Hope was cruel and Bagg didn't have it in him to explain to the pretty little contortionist sitting across from him near the inlet water exactly what it had done to him.

"I miss my little girl. She's with her mother someplace."

"Well, why don't you go see her? You do want to see her?"

"I don't know where she is." Bagg couldn't talk about this. He'd been too close to the edge, had teetered away from it, and knew how easy it was to fall back into that hole. "I can't talk about what happened." A new idea swept over Bagg as he looked beyond her, out toward the ocean, not really seeing anything but a fading image of Morgan's face. There wasn't just one hole you fell into. When you lost your child, there was always another ledge to fall off. You had some good days, but you really weren't going anywhere. You were always about to trip, to plunge into a worse place.

It wasn't that long ago when Bagg had smashed half the plates in his apartment because he couldn't remember on which side of her nose that little freckle was. He'd cut both hands falling into that particular hole.

He swore to himself he wouldn't break down in front of this woman. His clothes were dirty, his hair was greasy, and he was living in a tent. His life had been reduced to very little worth and he tried desperately to hang on to what he could. Even saving the bear had really only been about trying to salvage something for himself.

But then they came. The ridiculous tears that robbed his pride and sliced through his dignity poured out, and he hated himself for every single one. Showing how pathetic he was sank his spirit to a new place, a new spot in a deeper hole.

"You don't have to tell me anything." Her feathery touch on the sides of his head was so much like Morgan's. It was the same touch his little girl had used when he'd been sick, or when she'd woken him out of one of his bad dreams the nights she'd been allowed to fall asleep in his bed. Amira leaned forward onto her knees facing him, her large brown eyes probing his. "But you have to find her. This is no way to live. You have a kind soul and I've watched you look at these people." Amira made a sweeping gesture with one skinny arm back toward the tents.

In his misery, Bagg was confused, thought perhaps she was accusing him of something, of looking down on them. He wanted to tell her these were the same people who had raised him, who he'd grown up with. "I mean you look at them like you understand the troubles that brought a lot of them to work for a traveling circus. It's like you've given up and become one of them, wallowing in your own loss. Is that any way to live?"

"I tried to find her."

"And then you quit," Amira said flatly.

"And then I quit."

"You'll get your own freak show spot. They can call you Hollow Man."

"That's mean," Bagg smiled.

"Sometimes the truth is plain old mean. She was stolen from you? A wife? A girlfriend?"

"Yes, my ex-wife."

"So at least she's safe," Amira said carefully.

"I hope so." There was that word hope again. "It's been a long time. I tried to find her, but it was as if both of them disappeared into thin air."

"This circus has been a lot of places. A lot of places that might as well be thin air."

There was a time in his life where he would have kissed her, back when his heart wasn't so mangled and his life so screwed up. Her body was all angles, her limbs moved in deliberate motions. She took his right hand in hers, petting the top of it with delicate strokes. Bagg wasn't sure of the last time he'd been touched like that. It was the way a child sometimes tried to comfort an adult. Grown-ups sometimes forgot the power of gentle touching.

"So I should start checking the thin air?" he asked.

"Of course you should." Amira leaned close and kissed Bagg very softly on his unshaven cheek. "If all that's left is thin air, then that's definitely where she is."

Chapter 39

Tommy Bonjovi was an outlaw, livin' life large behind the wheel of a '95 Chrysler LeBaron convertible he'd hot-wired in a pancake house parking lot in Ship Bottom. With the AC cranked and the wind whippin' his long hair, Tommy popped out the car lighter and sparked a fat spliff, the joint catching evenly with one long, even pull. The fucking rain had left him antsy; his cabin fever had turned to full-blown swine flu. Tommy was feelin' the need for an adrenaline jump start, as the sun had come back shinin' bright and hard.

The pot was courtesy of his old man, a lazy, fat-ass cop. He kept a secret box in his closet stuffed full of all sorts of good shit he'd collected by shakin' down the kids he nabbed dealin' or buyin'. Pussies who didn't have balls enough to stand up to that piece of shit deserved to get ripped off. Still, it was a wonder none of 'em ever snuck up and popped the prick in the back of his sweaty, bald head. It made a big enough target, for sure.

Having an asshole cop for a father did have its advantages when it came to slippin' out of his own squeezes with the law. His old man wasn't trying to do him any favors, though. He just didn't want the embarrassment of a son sent to juvie for criminal mischief, whatever the fuck that meant. Criminal mischief? Like he was some sort of fuckin' mischief-makin' elf! And then there was the burglary, the vandalism, and the garage he accidentally set on fire. Whatever. Shit happened, then you got old and died.

"This is one great day, you little bastards!" Tommy shouted at a group of small children splashin' around in a backyard kiddy pool, making a left turn for the sake of makin' a left turn. The road was still steaming off the last of

226

the rain, and the LeBaron's ass-end tried to pry loose. Accidentally spinning out and killing a group of preschoolers in a plastic pool too close to the fucking road would make him a legend. Especially in a jacked ride, oh boy! Tommy was tempted to make a u-turn but remembered the Rollins Band cassette in the inside pocket of his leather jacket on the passenger seat. Time for some tunes. He drove with one hand and slammed the tape into the car's player and cranked the knob.

"Ha, I knew swipin' a ninety-five was for a motherfuckin' good goddamn reason!" A car with a cassette player might have been dumb luck for your average criminal, but everything was shittin' gold nuggets for the badass behind the wheel of this ride.

The voice of Henry Rollins began preaching out of four speakers. Henry Rollins was the God of all gods, the toughest of all punks. There was heavy metal, and there was hardcore industrial grunge. And then there was Henry Fucking Rollins, far and away the toughest mo-fo to ever live. Rollins told gruesome stories and could cave any motherfucker's skull with one punch. Tommy had every Black Flag and Rollins Band tape made, including all the pirated versions he could get his hands on.

Tommy was gonna get the same SEARCH & DESTROY tattoo across his shoulders, which was the coolest ink on the face of the planet, once he got out of the fat fuck's house. For now, Tommy mouthed the words to "Liar," because that's exactly what he was. The song was a story, split up by blastin' riffs and intense motherfucking vocals.

"I'm a liar; yeah, I'm a liar!" Tommy shouted to the music, pounding the steering wheel to the throbbing beat. It was an epic song, the blow by blow of Tommy's own screwed up life. The music and lyrics bounded from fast to slow, then back to fast, and Tommy totally understood the pace, the frustration, the need to be fucking heard.

"Anybody around better know that everything I say and all the nice friendly smiles, were all just lies to burn up their wussy souls." Tommy spoke these words slowly, mixing in some of his own. He could do it because the song belonged to him, too. He personalized it like a dog pissin' right on top of some other dog's piss. "Yeah, I'm a nice fellow, a sweet talker. I let you feel good and warm inside, until it's time to cause hurt and some really bad fucking pain."

"'Cause I'm a liar!" Tommy shouted along with Rollins, swerving the LeBaron to almost hit a rabbit darting out onto the narrow road, which was smooth as silk under his hot rubber. "Nobody gets in Tommy's way, 'cause I'm a liar, baby! A liar!"

Tommy took another hit off the joint, choked on the smoke, then popped the burnin' roach into his mouth and chewed it up. Amped on the tunes and buzzed from the pot, he stomped the accelerator to the floor on a road that was as straight and long as a freakin' runway. The LeBaron's engine thundered as the white arm of the speedometer slid across the one hundred ten mark.

Scraggly trees skimmed past like a picket fence, and even the music became lost to the howling wind. Tommy's hands were clamped to the wheel in a death grip, arms straight out, head tilted back for some serious speed. Stealin' a quick glance, he just about had the needle pinned at one hundred thirty miles per hour when something large and black came lumbering up out of the marsh grass from the right side of the road. It was the biggest fucking dog he'd ever seen and he didn't have time to even consider moving his right foot from the accelerator to the brake. Instead, to avoid a head-on collision, Tommy shifted the wheel ever so slightly, clippin' the ass-end of the monstrously big dog and what appeared to be some sort of pink dress covering its hairy ass.

"What kind of asshole puts a dress on a dog?" Tommy asked, as the wind surged under the car, lifting both right-side wheels up in the air. A tornadic gust snatched Tommy's leather jacket and it took off like a startled bat, while the horizon assumed an entirely different perspective. It was one insane, fucked-up instant, but Tommy had enough time to imagine he was up at Six Flags riding the Nitro. Man, that was one sick ride, Tommy thought, as the road was now over his head, still rushing by at an impossible speed.

In the next seconds, there was a whole lot of crunching metal and breaking glass, as the LeBaron slid along Great Bay Boulevard upside down, finally coming to a dripping and ticking halt, one tire still spinning like crazy.

Had Tommy Bonjovi survived the impact, he might have heard the whimpering circus bear.

Chapter 40

The smells were sweet and sour and everything in between. The sun was warm and the mud was deep and squishy. The marsh over in this spot was filled with big bugs clinging to the tops of grass blades, and when you got close, their wings spread out and they took flight, whirring crazily. The vibrating air tantalizing, Gracie imagined these playthings must taste delicious, although she couldn't quite seem to get hold of one.

Gracie's small brain actually came close to making the connection between the truck that spread that awful tasting water and the lack of bugs, and how the marshes farther away from her good man's nest were alive and buzzing. But awareness came and went, and there was all the chasing to do.

Gracie ran across the marsh to see what all the commotion was with the big white birds who were huddled up, barking at one another in bird language. As usual, the birds scattered when they saw her coming, abandoning an especially large and prehistoric looking horseshoe crab they'd been snacking on.

Waste not want not, thought Gracie, who gummed away at the dead crab's belly, the jealous seagulls skulking around at a safe distance, not the least bit happy with this development.

That's when Gracie first noticed the most beautiful bug she'd ever seen in her bear life. This bug flew like a bird but danced like a bear. It even wore a beautiful orange dress, as it fluttered high and low. Gracie was hypnotized by the elegant magic its wings created. The bug came to visit Gracie, seemed set to land on her nose, but changed its mind at the last second. Instead, it flittered here and flickered there, and the entranced old bear left the remaining crab for the cranky gulls in order to follow the delightful bug.

Gracie rose up, stirred into her own dance, as the butterfly wobbled and wiggled ahead of her. The bear had been a little worried about her new pink tutu, which her good man had been too drunk to help her take off, but his oversight had turned into a wonderful bit of luck. Gracie strutted for the bug, managed a pirouette of her own, showing off her own pretty outfit. She pawed at the air in her least menacing way and tried to mimic the graceful moves on display above her.

Gracie marveled at the bug, who was sometimes caught in gusts of wind, occasionally toppled in the crazy turbulence. But there was no need to panic when you had such fine wings. The breeze was blowing the exquisite orange butterfly across the marsh and Gracie did her best to keep up. Imagine being able to dance and fly at the same time?

Gracie was nearly swooning from happiness when she followed the mesmerizing creature up out of the marsh and onto the hot pavement, where another movement caught her eye.

The old bear might have screamed if she'd had more time, but what she really wanted to do was say goodbye to the butterfly, who had risen way up high in the air, away from the sudden danger down below. Gracie was wistful and sad she didn't know the bug's language. But surely the butterfly, who had witnessed Gracie's graceful dance, must know her thoughts, the spirits of these two dancers bridging any barrier of mere language.

Gracie's last words, right before being struck dead by the Chrysler LeBaron, were, alas, spoken with gratefulness and hope in her own bear language.

"Goodbye, little friend, and thank you for the dance."

Chapter 41

Some ran and some walked, but every last person made their way back over the Fish Head Island bridge on foot to investigate the terrible sounding crash. The screeching metal against unforgiving pavement was a shrill summons.

A few had made daily trips into the town at the end of the road, while others had only been on the rushed scavenger hunt sorties. The Laundromat business in West Tuckerton was booming, its owner raking in buckets of quarters from the muddy circus people. But for some, like bear trainer Slim Weatherwax, this was the first time off the island since the procession of tired circus trucks had arrived, himself pinned under the hurriedly stowed canvas tents.

Slim hadn't seen Gracie since she'd wandered out into the marsh to do her early morning business, which almost always included rechecking a hundred of the same snake and groundhog holes as the day before, pooping, sniffing the tide line for new smells, then going back to see if there were any snakes or groundhogs to interrogate. The routine had mostly kept Gracie out of Slim's hair so he could drink in peace, and she wasn't pouncing on napping roustabouts as often, so they left him alone, too. With all the cottontail rabbits darting here and there, often tantalizingly close, hunting down a snoring human was only fun when she was feeling lazy and only up for some easy prey.

Slim's gut was telling him something bad as he walked up and over the bridge, where they all got their first clear view of the single car crash that was smoking and steaming, a few hundred yards up the road. By the look of the wreck, they were gonna need a big spatula to remove whomever was ridin' in that mess of metal and glass. It barely even looked like a car. Heck, if they'd been walking on a runway, the wreck could have been a plane. In a junkyard, it could have been mistaken for a tangle of appliances.

But what tore at Slim's gut was what had caused the crash in the first place. There were no trees along here to slam into. There were no second cars, no train tracks, and there were sure as hell no icy spots on this slab of hot top.

"Maybe the sand." Slim ambled closer, looking out into the marsh for his Graceful Gracie. "Maybe them tires lost it in the sand."

From beyond the pile of metal, people crowded around what must have been the driver or passenger, farther up the road. There were the sounds of sirens carried on the wind, along with a horn that whined like an air raid siren. Slim looked up in the sky for enemy aircraft, but there was just one old biplane off to the south. It pulled along a flapping sign for some brand of suntan lotion, or a beer special at one of the crazy dance clubs up on Long Beach Island.

"Slim!" someone called back to him from the group of people who'd run and jogged up ahead of the rest. About a dozen were standing or kneeling down, all worried and upset.

"Why the hell you callin' my name," Slim said, low to himself. "I sure as hell ain't no doctor."

But Slim knew.

Fact was, when you lived your whole life in a traveling circus, you came to expect the worst damn things to happen. Bad things. You started feelin' good and comfortable, and they'd come right up outta wherever the hell those things slinked around in. They yanked you right down. They'd get you by the ankle or right by the head. Sometimes they'd pull you down by your heart.

Slim knew it was his heart up there in the road.

Slim Weatherwax walked past the mangled car without more than a glance and was thirty feet or so from the circle of folks. His feet stopped moving as they all turned their heads to him, every eye boring into him like he was one of them freaks passing off a tumor as a horn, or something.

"Why the hell you lookin' at me?" Slim said, barely loud enough for them to hear over the sirens wailing in the distance. Slim stood his ground, knowing if he didn't get any closer, just maybe things would stay like this. Knowin', but not knowin'. Slim looked away from the group of people, some of them crying like babies. He looked out at the marshes on the side of the highway. Right then and there, he swore to God he'd give his entire life to see his Gracie still runnin' free like the dumb old bear she was.

Slim stood in the middle of the hot highway, with the smell of burning rubber all around, and the sirens getting closer and closer. That stupid bear was like a magnet for ticks, Slim thought, looking out over the grasses where the little bloodsuckers lived. Slim would spend hours pickin' the damn things off her as she lay back, showin' her fat belly to him. Gracie would have nosed at the kerosene filled peanut butter jar to let him know she was ready, get all in his face with her hot, stinky breath until he did what she wanted. It wasn't the worst job in the world. He'd also scratch her favorite spots under her armpits and rub up under her ears. If a man didn't have a dog, he'd do well to have himself a big old bear. Least a bear didn't have barkin' fits and chase its tail like the other mutts around this place. And Gracie could bite you all day, leavin' just a purple smudge and some spit.

"Slim?"

But Slim didn't want to answer. No, he was just going to stand there in the middle of this goddamn road for a while. He'd already had his share of hurt. Hell, he'd had enough shares of hurt for two people and then some.

"I don't need no more hurt," Slim said, but nobody could hear him as the ambulance slowly passed the group of people surrounding the dead bear. Slim tilted his weathered face to the sky, eyes closed. A half-smile crossed his sharp features as he could almost feel Gracie's rough tongue giving him slobbering thank you kisses for the belly rubs.

The ambulance rolled by the tall, skinny man in the middle of the road. If Slim's eyes had been open, he might have seen a butterfly flitting high overhead, nudged here and there by the salty sea breeze.

Chapter 42

Sheriff Jaroslaw's name meant fierce and glorious back in Poland. A good name for a cop walking the beat in Warsaw maybe, but in Ocean County, New Jersey, it just seemed to evoke endless dumb Pollack jokes. The sheriff's father and grandfather had been policemen in Gdansk, a city of a half-million people on the Baltic Sea, which was perhaps why Jakub Jaroslaw had been drawn to the coast here in New Jersey, thirty years earlier.

Sheriff Jaroslaw, neither fierce nor glorious, had survived his three decades as a peace officer by adopting a credo he'd picked up from American movies, from which he'd also learned the language and a healthy respect for how things could blow up in your face when you least expected it. He repeated this philosophy whenever he pulled up on a call, or even when he went to deposit his paycheck in the bank. He'd even said it while walking up the front steps of a strange woman's house, flowers in hand, on his first and only attempt at a video date.

He said this: "I don't want any trouble."

The sheriff looked down at the envelope he'd been sent to deliver to the so-called offending characters who'd taken up residence at the end of Great Bay Boulevard. The cease and desist letter was from an attorney hired by that damn cop who'd had that damn kid, who'd gotten himself killed in that damn stolen car. These things usually smelled like a lawsuit, but Jaroslaw figured the cop just wanted to cause whatever trouble he could for these people. Didn't matter that the kid stole some family's car and then went racing down a highway at a hundred miles per hour, plowing into a circus bear, killing it and his own stupid ass self. One more good reason for Sheriff Jaroslaw to be thankful no women had been inclined toward a second date and possibly burdening him with a kid of his own. Kids brought more trouble than anything.

Jaroslaw had even allowed the letter to sit right there on his front seat for two whole days before making this drive. He had every intention of giving the traveling circus ample time to pull up stakes and hightail it out of his county. After all, he didn't want any trouble, thank you very much.

But as the sheriff slowly pulled up and over the bridge to Fish Head Island, he was dismayed to see nobody had gone anywhere. He'd more than half-hoped they'd pulled up stakes on their own, figuring trouble must be on its way. In all his years, he'd been down to this end of the boulevard maybe a half dozen times, and most of those calls were checking for runaway kids. This was, after all, a good place to make yourself seem lost for a while.

Jaroslaw parked his sheriff's department car next to a lopsided building that seemed to be sinking into the mud on one side; somebody had screwed up setting the pilings. It stood precariously between two large tents, an air conditioner poking from one side window. There sure as hell wasn't supposed to be a building down on these mud flats, Jaroslaw knew. He wondered what these people had been up to, then immediately erased the concern as best he could. The sheriff grabbed his hat and the letter and slid his large body out of the car and into the oppressive heat. He was aware of all the people barely outside of his view, back in the shadows of tent flaps.

"I don't want any trouble," the sheriff whispered and then climbed the two steps to the front door of the crooked building.

"Afternoon, officer." Billy Wayne Hooduk greeted the sheriff, cool air rushing out from behind him, as the sheriff held out the letter. "What's this?"

"You in charge?"

"You could say that."

Jaroslaw let go of the envelope, which was the moment of serving papers that always made him feel like he'd taken the lid off of a bottle of something that stank.

"I'm sorry." Sheriff Jaroslaw turned his back on the pudgy little man who stood staring at the envelope in his hands. The sheriff would be just fine if the guy waited until he was miles away before reading the bad news.

The sheriff dropped his heavy frame back into his car, which rocked on its springs, placed his hat next to him on the seat, and began to back away from the building. More than ever, Jaroslaw felt eyes on him, but now he didn't feel threatened. What he was getting from this place was the sense of sorrow, of the tragedy that had recently gone on around here. Probably the accident, Jaroslaw figured. Now they're getting their asses shut down, like it or not. And if they weren't gone in seven days, Jaroslaw would have to trudge back down here with whatever court order the lawyers for the dead kid's father managed to get signed. Maybe even a criminal complaint, a big pain in his fat Pollack ass.

Getting the car turned around, the sheriff headed back toward the bridge, noticing the mound of fresh earth at the base of the short span for the first time. There was a cross made from whitewashed wood planted at one end, some wild flowers strewn loosely over the sun-baked mud.

Sometimes trouble comes and finds you, Sheriff Jaroslaw thought, watching the traveling circus getting smaller in his rearview mirror.

Chapter 43

"Morgan flew away." Jennifer Freeman read the simple caption at the bottom of the picture, while sitting on her daughter's bed, the sheet of white paper with a drawing and message resting on her lap.

Jennifer didn't at first recognize it as something Morgan could have made. The fine strokes of the pencil drawing included intricate details much further beyond what Jennifer imagined her daughter capable of producing. She at first mistook it for a photograph of a small bird trailing below and behind a large flock, perhaps trying to catch up. The large flock was unusual, even a little crazy, because each bird appeared to be a different species.

Morgan's mother studied the picture as if trying to find Waldo, or some clue. But there were no apparent patterns, except for one thing: there was one bird at the front of the large flock that appeared to be the same kind of bird as the one giving chase.

"Morgan flew away." Jennifer reread the caption and then pulled her eyes away from the elaborate piece of artwork. Something was wrong in this room, she thought. Something was different.

"I can see the paint." Morgan had wallpapered every square inch of her room with her nutty bird drawings, in some spots three layers deep, but now there were blank spaces of light blue paint among the dizzying array. And just as her eyes had searched the drawing on her lap for clues, she now tried to make some sense of the missing artwork from the walls.

Morgan had read the story about Michael Dupont to her mother over a hurried breakfast the morning after the newspaper landed at her feet. The man was described as the great benefactor behind the bird sanctuary project being dedicated this coming Saturday. But Jennifer hadn't listened to her daughter. It was all just more of her obsession, her nonsense, and she was tired of telling her to stop. Jennifer had tuned it all out, concentrating instead on buttering her waffles and trying to decide whether she should finish off an old project or get started on the new client's designs.

It got worse and worse with this kid. Each day, Morgan became more and more like her ridiculous father. Being married to Lennon had been torture, a punishment for being young, stupid, and careless with her diaphragm. Jennifer had rebelled against her own father, a driven salesman who had provided every opportunity for her and her brother and sister, and she'd made some bad choices. She'd let her guard down and fallen for the tall, frumpy journalism major. She'd paid for the mistake for too long. Stupid. Dumb. And she'd thrown away six critical years of her life and was left with a kid who brooded like her father and was just as embarrassing half the time.

Jennifer had turned her back on her father, only to be welcomed into the clan of the wretched, backwoods hippies who were Lennon's parents. It was no wonder her ex-husband had no ambition, having been raised like an animal by potheads. Jennifer had turned up pregnant and too blinded by stupid love to do the right thing and end the pregnancy.

Not that she regretted having Morgan. Jennifer looked back down at the meticulously drawn birds on the sheet of paper. It was perfectly clear to her that this was completely her ex-husband's fault. She loved Morgan with all her heart, but there was no doubt of the genetic influence of her father. And, of course, his disgusting parents who had shoveled a path to an icy cold outhouse behind their log home. An outhouse!

It was on that first and only visit to the Catskills home of Lennon's parents that she'd probably been impregnated.

She'd left her diaphragm back at her apartment, and the relationship was still new enough that she let him have intercourse with her just about every night. Jennifer's skin crawled at the memory of the tiny room, with cheap wood paneling and bed springs so creaky she kept trying to make him slow down, stop making it bounce so noisily. But for whatever reason, she found him loveable at the time, a stray mutt in the rain. She wanted to please him, so she tolerated the bad smells and the dirty sheets. Back at his own cluttered apartment, she tried to be nice to his roommate, another journalism major with an equally bleak future.

"The mistakes we make." Jennifer scanned the walls decorated by her befuddling daughter. "She talks to birds and they talk back to her."

Every one of these drawings was going in the trash. First thing tomorrow, she was making an appointment with a full-blown psychiatrist. This baloney was going to end once and for all, Jennifer decided. That's it. You may think it's cool to grow up acting like a strange little outsider, getting picked on by those horrible, nasty kids, but I have news for you. Your days acting like a loner drama queen are over. Done. Your time for brooding about your worthless father is over. Period.

Jennifer once again looked down at the drawing, and it made her furious. She crumpled the paper with an angry sigh, balling it as tightly as it would go, then rose from the bed and stalked out of the ungrateful brat's room. On her way to the kitchen trash, she paused at the phone hung from the wall next to the refrigerator, briefly contemplating calling the police to report her missing daughter.

"Morgan flew away." Jennifer opened the lid of the trash can and tossed in the wadded-up picture.

Chapter 44

Pete Singe was used to things flying out of nowhere, hitting him like a freight train. Being left gasping for breath and near death. Heck, the seventh time he'd been struck by lightning there wasn't even a cloud in the sky, or at least any that he remembered. One second he was running his push mower across his tiny backyard, the next second he was laying right down in the grass clippings, eye to eye with the nozzle of his garden hose, his hair all crackling and smoldering. Luckily, he'd had the presence of mind to reach for the nozzle and put himself out.

Five men sat at the card table in the center of the new building, watching Lennon Bagg's yellow pencil slowly begin to roll toward the edge, while trying to come up with at least one good idea on how to save their circus.

"The big rigs are in mighty bad shape, Billy Wayne," Happy the mechanic said, as ten eyes watched the pencil drop off the side, bounce surprisingly high off its eraser, then begin rolling again toward the window with the air conditioner. "The salt air is a killer, you know. A real killer."

The three-page cease-and-desist letter made very little sense to the men. It was written by a lawyer with bullshit, mumbo jumbo jargon that didn't mean shit in the first place, Singe had decided. Criminal negligence for possessing protected wildlife? Did it mean the zonkey? Or the lion that'd been trying to cough up the same lung for two years? Maybe the toothless bear the shithead kid had run down?

"We're a goddamn circus," Singe told the other four. "This is just their way of showin' us the door."

"We can fight it," Bagg said. "Hire a lawyer, right?"

"Building code violations," Warden Flint said. "Health code violations. Which of you boys happened to get a building permit for this fine leanin' tower of shitstorm?"

"What if it's a house of worship?" Bill Wayne was exasperated and already near defeat.

"You sayin' maybe Jesus H. Christ went up to the court house with his building plans and twenty seven dollars?" Flint was hungover and his mood was as dark as it ever really got. "If that's the case, then all this mopin' around is for nuthin', praise the Lord. Hell, Moses himself gave that hacking lion its rabies shot, am I right? Nothing to fucking worry about, no sir. You left your balls hanging out and some asshole grabbed hold."

"He was just asking," Bagg said. "You have any ideas?"

"Well, I have an idea," said Flint. "I have an idea that I'm about to get shit-canned along with the rest of you sorry bastards."

"Who owns the island?" Singe asked. "Is it state property?"

"State property ends back on the other side of the bridge," Flint said.

"You pulled me out of the canal the day we met," Billy Wayne said.

"Don't mean I ain't responsible for patrolling down here, and the waterways are all my responsibility."

"How do we find the owner?" Singe asked.

"How the fuck do I know?" Flint rubbed his temples with sharp knuckles.

"It's public record," said Bagg.

"What are you thinkin', Bagg?" Singe watched Bagg stoop to retrieve his pencil and then rush for the door. "Bagg?"

෧෧ ෧෧ ෧෧

"Lilly?" Bagg barked into his cell phone. "Lilly, I need your help with a property deed and any information you can get on a property owner."

Lilly's voice was far away, almost lost in the crackle and sizzle of the poor cell connection; barely one out of five bars showed on the small screen indicator.

"Bagg, I'm a style writer, what do I know about deeds?"

"Lilly, it's life or death. It's a couple of phone calls from the press, is all. Then search the database for news items."

"Who do you want me to call?"

"Start with the Ocean County Courthouse, in Toms River. Then the assessor, or maybe the clerk's office. Try asking for the registrar of deeds. I'm not sure, Lilly, but we need to know the owner of Fish Head Island, which is at the end of Great Bay Boulevard."

"Fish Head Island? Life or death? I have a deadline coming up."

"It's my life." And Bagg really meant it. He had walked with the phone toward his tent, his home for over a month now. "And if you can get a name, please just run it through Google as well as the Associated Press for any recent news hits."

"You'll be at this number if I find anything?"

"Yes. Thanks. I'll be waiting to hear."

"Oh, and Bagg?"

"Yeah?"

"I'm sorry about your daughter."

"I know, Lilly." Bagg snapped the phone shut.

Chapter 45

"He's some sort of big time bird freak." Lilly began giving the rundown to Bagg over the phone, about an hour later. "Got a pencil?"

"Yeah, go ahead." Bagg cradled the phone with his shoulder and dug out his reporter's notebook and pencil. He sat down on the front step of the new building, the four men behind the door waiting on the news in the chill of the air-conditioning. "Tell me everything."

"Okay, so his name's Michael Dupont, twenty-nine, from Charleston, South Carolina. Made a boatload of money designing video games, then sold his company to Sony for the tidy little sum of fifty-eight million dollars in January of nineteen ninety-eight."

"Wait, that would have made him twenty?"

"Um, no, looks like he was still a teenager when he deposited the check." Bagg could hear Lilly's fingernails clicking away at her keyboard.

"And the birds?"

"Oh, yeah, there are a whole bunch of Google hits on him for buying up land along the East coast. Mostly wetlands, and all are empty spaces."

"For the birds? He's some sort of conservationist?"

"He's given big checks to the Audubon Society, the Save the Migratory Birds Society, Project Puffin, and about three dozen other groups."

"The other groups all involve birds?" Bagg pictured the slaughtered seagulls the boys with the stolen pellet guns had left for Flint to secretly bury.

"Hold on." There was more clicking. "There's a group called the Out of Africa Project that might be something else.

And there's a couple names of what sound like small town zoos. That any help?"

"Yeah, Lilly." Bagg was a little hopeful, weighing the possibility of whether a sick lion and exotic zonkey would merit much sympathy from a philanthropic bird lover.

"He's been buying the land to set aside as bird sanctuaries."

"Fish Head Island is a bird sanctuary." It wasn't a question. The guy bought this muddy stretch of land to set aside for the birds.

"I suppose, but it's just a speck on the map, and there were no press releases. It's only listed in the tax office as a property transfer. I found ten or eleven just like it without looking too hard. Guy must have a couple of realtors keeping an eye on properties, snapping them up when they hit the market."

"You have a current home address for him?"

"Yes, but he's probably not home. There's an AP wire story saying that this Saturday he's at a ribbon-cutting for a bird sanctuary he funded in Bermuda. Says the Governor will be accepting a generous endowment for future care on behalf of Queen Elizabeth II, in someplace called Tucker's Town."

"You're sure it's this Saturday?"

"That's what it says."

"How far from the airport?"

"Hold on." There was more rapid-fire, fingernail on keyboard clicking. "Quick cab ride."

"One more favor?"

"You want me to book you a plane ticket?"

"Two, Lilly, make it two tickets."

Chapter 46

"You understand the risk involved in traveling to the Bermuda Triangle seated next to a man who is one bolt shy of being struck by lightning thirteen times?" Pete Singe asked Bagg. The stewardess was finishing her preflight safety speech, as a video version also concluded on the small screen on the back of each headrest.

"I'm not big on flying." Bagg pulled the nylon seat belt as tightly as it would go, triple-checking that his tray was as upright as it could possibly be and making sure his cell phone was not going to ring and cause the plane to explode.

"I read that on average a plane like this gets hit by lightning once a year," Singe added. After a couple of years living and working so close to a guy with a mortal fear of lifting his head three inches off the ground, Singe apparently didn't see any problem needling his friend with a simple case of aviatophobia. People with a fear of flying had it easy, he told Bagg, what with all the buses and trains. Bagg's phobia was a little like complaining about your hiccups to someone who'd just fallen into a shark tank.

"And you only get hit about once every four years?" Bagg twisted the knob for air but accidentally pressed the button for the stewardess.

"Yeah, give or take. I suppose it means I'm about due." Singe looked around the cabin roof as if deciding where the lightning would come from, as the captain released the brakes and backed the plane up.

"I don't feel so good."

"Yeah, last time I was on a plane was the trip back from the Honduras cave." Singe removed his baseball and tilted the top of his head to show Bagg the scar. "It's like lightning has a mind of its own."

Bagg was wearing fresh clothes he'd grabbed from his apartment while sneaking in for his passport. Lilly couldn't find any active warrants for him, nor any mention of a police officer having been assaulted by a camera-wielding newspaper reporter. Not a thing inside had changed, other than the mold growing on dirty dishes. Cops had not searched his apartment and had not violated his daughter's room. It was stuffy and the trash stunk. Otherwise, it was as if he'd just walked back in from a shift at the paper.

He'd taken a risk, with the chance some neighbor was holding a business card handed out by a detective, with instructions to call if they saw the dangerous guy from next door coming around. And being tossed in jail would have ended any last ditch attempt at saving the circus. But he trusted Lilly's thoroughness and absolutely had to have his passport.

The plan had sounded slightly more feasible while sitting around an old, beaten-up card table with a group of men eager to say how perfect it all sounded. But here, on an Embraer 190, with its unique "double-bubble" design and single-class configuration of one hundred seats, the plan seemed utterly impossible. Bagg stuck the airplane brochure back into the pouch by his knees, knowing they were going to crash into the side of a mountain and that memorizing the nearest exit was pointless. To convince a twenty-something multimillionaire that a broken-down collection of sickly animals and even more sickly humans would be appropriate caretakers for Fish Head Island seemed ludicrous in the crisp light of the airplane's cabin.

"We have almost three thousand dollars left to offer him," Billy Wayne had said. There on the card table, Bagg briefly tried to imagine what three grand would look like stacked next to fifty-eight million.

"I read the chances of a plane crashing after being struck by lightning is less than one in a hundred thousand,"

Singe said, as the engines roared, pushing the vibrating aircraft down the rubber-streaked runway.

"So it's possible." Bagg gripped the armrests as the plane rose and banked into the clear morning air, a sliver of moon still visible off to the west. Bagg's knuckles were still white as the plane began to level. From the brochure, Bagg knew the plane could go over five hundred miles per hour but hoped there wouldn't be any need for such a rush. The plane could cruise at over forty thousand feet, but he prayed they'd stay closer to the ground.

"Notice how empty the plane is?" Singe lifted himself by the chair in front to scan the cabin. The plane was maybe one third full, probably just the people who absolutely had to get home, or flew enough to believe the old saying about how much more dangerous it was to ride in a car.

"So?"

"It's probably the weather," Singe said, and despite Bagg's churning stomach and clogged ears, he detected something weirdly disturbing in his friend's voice. Was it hope? "The forecast was calling for a pretty bad storm on the islands."

Bagg craned his neck to look past Singe and out the small window, convinced the old storyteller was still just messing with him.

But he wasn't.

Chapter 47

Dr. Frank Pillbright's favorite thing in life was observing the birth of a tropical storm, especially one that grew up strong, made a name for itself, and was remembered long after it had died from the cold. Pillbright could just as easily have become a pediatrician, if only his grades had been a little better and his fear of blood a little less severe. Because he was a meteorologist consumed by tropical storms, Pillbright spent a great deal of his time observing radar maps and satellite images concerning the Sahara Desert.

The Sahara Desert is a big place—almost as big as all of the United States—way over on the other side of the Atlantic Ocean from Pillbright's tiny home in St. Augustine, Florida. His home was also his office, or at least had been taken over by office things. His living room was cluttered by eleven computer monitors, all displaying a highway of sorts, one made of winds that ran from the African continent to North America. It had been as hot as hell during the first week of September in the northern part of Africa, and the North Atlantic had gotten toasty warm, as well. The Sahara had begun its annual custom of sending hot swirling winds out over the warm ocean water, one after another, like a very large game of Frisbee.

One wave of spinning hot air that came out of the desert was promptly named Five by meteorologists in charge of those details, sending the birth announcement out in a National Oceanic and Atmospheric Administration e-mail to news organizations around the planet. It was Pillbright's job to double-check these e-mails for accuracy before they were released, confirming the barometric pressure levels, wind speeds, and that sort of thing. It might not seem like terribly interesting work to most other people, but to Pillbright, it was like the thrill of weighing a newborn baby.

The rotation of the Earth and the flow of the ocean helped keep the spinning alive, as the growing disc headed west across the open water, feeding itself with the warm moisture below, nudged by the northeast trade winds.

The storm had no particular interest in finding land, Pillbright knew, let alone the people who lived on it. Land, as it happened, made the storm feel weak, drained of its energy. But the storm had no choice but to go where it was pushed by more important winds and currents.

Nine days after observing the storm's birth, Pillbright watched it skirt along the Windward Islands of the Lesser Antilles, then spend an entire lazy day moving nowhere, enjoying the bathwater temperatures north of Puerto Rico. After a gentle shove from behind on day eleven, the storm resumed its travels, leaving some of its energy behind in the Dominican Republic, and then a little more as it passed directly over the Bahamas.

The storm wanted to grow, Pillbright sensed, but kept running into clusters of land surrounded by shallow water that couldn't keep up with its thirst. To Pillbright's relief, a subtropical high over the Gulf of Mexico turned it north, helping it avoid the quick death Florida would have caused.

The prevailing westerly winds plotted a new path for the storm, urging it to the northeast and toward yet another speck of land called Bermuda. The waters were cooler up here, and Pillbright knew the storm felt sluggish and exhausted. The cold had that effect. The time to die was approaching, and the storm didn't have the strength to protest its fate.

With all the disappointment of its winds never reaching the magical thirty-nine miles per hour, it did not receive a proper name. No wonder meteorologists called them depressions, Pillbright thought. What could be more depressing for a raging storm—with all kinds of haughty potential—than to be called only by a number? Tropical Depression Five, with just a smidge better luck, might have been known as Dean, as it snuck up on Bermuda, and any airplanes happening by.

Pillbright opened another e-mail from the National Oceanic and Atmospheric Administration, then turned to adjust his computer monitors back toward a lovely, rotating newborn infant over the Sahara Desert. Disappointment was short-lived this time of year.

Chapter 48

If Tropical Depression Five had a little more pep—its winds just a mile or two per hour faster—Flight 1142 from JFK to L.F. Wade International Airport would have been canceled, thus saving a very expensive, well-made Brazilian piece of machinery from being smashed into roughly twenty-seven thousand pieces.

It wasn't the lightning bolt that slammed the nose cone, and then ran along the aluminum skin of the fuselage, that brought the plane down. The bolt burned out running lights and blackened the fresh blue paint on the right engine before exiting through the tail. The lightning damage was mostly cosmetic, what with all the wonderful safety features on the pricey airplane.

Peter Singe, AKA Lightning Man, feeling the power on the other side of the double-paned safety glass, longed for the dreadful, wondrous energy. Lightning Man heard the crash of brutal voltage, ten times the temperature of the sun, and waited for the explosion to take him, like it had so many times in the past. All that rage and energy so impossibly close, yet Singe was denied like a shunned lover; he was a single sperm trapped in a protective condom, so close yet so far.

Bagg eyed his friend's queer expression of near ecstasy, wishing like hell they could pull this thing over so he could get out. His video screen had gone from enthusiastic sneak-previews of upcoming movies to ominous snow, like the tip-off in a horror movie that something was about to happen.

Apparently a result of the lightning strike, little yellow oxygen cups now hung swaying from the cabin roof on shimmering webs of tubing. The plane bounded through the turbulent sky as they began the merciful final approach. The clouds outside, which had devoured the plane thirty minutes earlier, were thick and dark and streaked the windows with constant rain. The clouds lit the faces of the frightened passengers with strobe-like lightning flashes, and there was little talking, not even from the captain or stewardess. The flight crew was busy with this little mess.

"Thirteen." Singe spoke in a spent voice, rolling his head toward Bagg, and turned his wrist to show off the blackened face of his watch. He smiled at Bagg with a tired, satisfied expression. It hadn't been like the other body slamming encounters, and he'd nearly missed noticing the lightning's soft caress. But it was enough. Singe turned back to the jostling window to watch the flashes of light.

☙　☙　☙

The thirty passengers were quiet, perhaps hypnotized by the swaying oxygen masks that nobody was putting on. Bagg and Singe sat in row eighteen, seats C and D, just behind the right wing and engine. Another solid thump, followed by the vaguely familiar mechanical hum of the landing gear being dropped in place, gave Bagg some mild comfort. Okay, Bagg thought, the tires are down, so nothing major was broken by the lightning. This was going to be okay, and now the deceleration had a calming effect, despite his suspicion that they would break through the clouds any moment to discover they were a mere five feet over the ocean and headed directly into the side of a building.

When the plane suddenly accelerated, dipping the passengers back into their soft seats, Bagg assumed the captain had decided to make another pass. Or maybe he'd rejected the ridiculous idea of landing in all this rain and wind. But the acceleration was followed by a weightless drop, as if the plane had stalled and was falling straight down, going for a belly flop into the sea rather than some mundane three-point touchdown on the smooth concrete runway.

The flickering cabin lights went dark, as did the snow on the video screens. Both engines made a gasping noise, reminding Bagg of the feeling when you stuck your head out the window of a speeding car.

"Goodbye, Lennon." Bagg cringed as Singe took his hand in the dark, as if on a first date in a movie theater showing some apocalyptic thriller. Instead of popcorn, Bagg smelled hot wires, the taste of pennies on his tongue. He watched the curious motion of the oxygen cups, dancing at the end of the long narrow tubes, like yellow butterflies playing in the night.

"Butterflies." Bagg shut his eyes, deciding the image was a good one to have when performing a belly flop in an airliner from a mile or so in the sky.

Morgan had once caught a butterfly in a net he'd bought for her in a toy store. It had been for collecting insects and had come with a small plastic container where you could study your finds. She'd been thrilled with her catch, put grass and leaves in the bottom, and added a little bottle cap of water.

"Her name is Tinker Bell," she told her father, placing the container on her bedroom window sill. "She's going to have a dozen babies and I'll teach them tricks."

But the next morning, Bagg had been awakened when Morgan climbed into his bed, snuggling close to him. It had been a regular event if she woke before him in the small apartment, and Bagg was about to drift back off to sleep for twenty more minutes. But the little body pressed to his back was making little lurching movements and he heard the stifled sobs.

"What's the matter, honey?" Bagg rolled over to face his daughter, but she had her chin pressed to her chest, hands cupped by her face, and she hadn't answered through her tears.

"Morgan, what's wrong?"

"I didn't mean to, Daddy." She was slowly shaking her head side to side.

"Didn't mean to what?" he asked, brushing the hair back off her forehead.

Morgan unclasped her hands to show the dead butterfly.

"I let Tinker Bell die."

"Butterflies," Bagg repeated, as the plane continued to fall, the churning, white-capped sea racing up to meet them.

Chapter 49

"Hey, Mack." A brown pelican tried to get Bagg's attention. "You ain't looking so good."

They were bobbing in the churning water, rain falling in fine drops, swept across the surface by swirling winds. Bagg's head and chest rested on a blue seat cushion he'd apparently come across out here, wherever that happened to be.

"Who are you?" Bagg squinted against the salty blowing mist.

"I'm the Ghost of Christmas Past."

"No he ain't!" came a voice from behind. If Bagg knew one bird from another, he'd have recognized this as an American Woodcock, also known as a timberdoodle. "He's just a dopey pelican."

"Who you callin' dopey, Woodcock?" The pelican craned its neck to see over Bagg. "What kinda name is Woodcock, anyway? Sounds like a porn star."

"Hey, coulda been worse," said the flycatcher who'd drifted up next to the pelican. "He coulda picked the name Swallow!"

"Ha, ha, ha! Swallow!" The pelican laughed along with the flycatcher.

"Why you draggin' me into this?" asked the little brown bank swallow, who was floating somewhere near Bagg's bare feet, picking at the swirling white foam.

"Yeah, hey, sorry there, Swallow." The flycatcher looked embarrassed. "No offense."

"So whaddya gonna do now, Mack?" The pelican turned his attention back to the human who was clinging to an airplane seat cushion, miles from where it and the rest of the airplane should have landed on solid ground. "What's your big plan?"

~   ~   ~

Bagg knew he must be dead, stuck in some sort of purgatory reserved for people with unresolved issues. Clearly being lost at sea represented the search for Morgan. The raging storm was his ex-wife? The birds were angels?

Bagg ignored the bird-angel thing's question and resumed his journey to Bermuda by kicking his feet.

"Hey, Mack, you go that way and you ain't hitting dry land for about eight hundred miles. You like lobster, Mack? Man I could really go for some lobster. When you get to Maine, you pick me up one, how 'bout it?"

Bagg made a u-turn on the crest of an enormous wave, and the pelican rose up on the swell beside him, stretching and flapping its wings and began shouting. "Wahoo! Wahoo!"

The sea settled back down for a moment and Bagg got his feet going again. He felt like he was looking through a submarine periscope in an old movie, where the captain was trying to keep from breaking the surface and the lens kept getting splashed by the choppy surface.

"That's better, Mack." The pelican stroked to keep up. "Jeez, if you humans had to migrate to survive, us birds would be ruling things by now."

"Ain't that the truth," added the flycatcher.

"Hey, Mack, one more thing before you go." The pelican had to raise his voice as an especially strong gust of wind drove a wall of heavy rain across the gathering of birds and lone survivor. "There's a little human girl been looking all over the place for you."

Bagg kept kicking his feet.

Chapter 50

The rain was amazing. The gigantic drops sounded like hailstones on metal surfaces and made huge splashes in puddles. The wind swirled in great arcs from different directions, wreaking havoc on small trees.

Morgan stood on the Tucker's Town main dock, but there were no signs of any huge celebration, other than a big flapping banner still attached to a light pole at one end.

The banner said "Welcome," but Morgan felt anything but.

The water surrounding the marina was filled with birds, which Morgan understood was because of the storm. Birds knew when to seek shelter and when to come out of the storm. It was an irony not lost on the little girl who stood on the very last wood plank of the dock, toes hanging ten inside her soaked sneakers. She held her backpack in her arms, trying to shelter it from the rain. But she knew her pictures must be getting drenched.

When it was an hour past the time the boats were to depart for the sanctuary on the VIP tour, Morgan abandoned her vigil. Shivering from the chilly rain, she turned and headed back to a large, dark wood gazebo that offered cover from the driving deluge.

The sky was getting darker overhead, even though it was just past two o'clock.

Morgan sat on the damp bench that circled the inside of the gazebo, cradling her backpack, craving her warm spot back on her beach. There was a long, snake-like hiss from up in the rafters, barely audible over the steady rain.

Squinting into the shadows, Morgan picked out the big eyes that were peering down at her over the edge of a nest.

"Hello," Morgan said, "I'm just looking for my dad."

There was no response, so Morgan let it go. She was in his home, and all the birds were pretty upset by the storm.

"What kind of bird is that?" A voice came from the far side of the gazebo, startling Morgan badly enough she lurched to catch her falling backpack.

"A Barred Owl."

"I thought it was a snake at first."

"Yeah, they hiss when they're upset. They're all freaked out from the storm."

"You know a lot about birds?" Morgan was confused at how she'd missed the man sitting there when she first came in out of the rain.

"My father's a bird. He died when I was a little kid, and I've been trying to find him."

"No luck so far?" The man made no move to come closer. It was just Morgan, the man across the damp gazebo, and an owl keeping an eye on everything from above.

"Everyone thinks I'm crazy."

"Because you're looking for your father? I don't think that's so crazy. I lost my dad, too."

"Mom and my teacher think I need a psychiatrist." Saying the words out loud made Morgan feel very alone. "The kids call me names."

"I'm sorry."

"I know who you are." Morgan looked at the man sideways, her cheek resting on her wet backpack. "You're Mr. Dupont. You came here for the ceremony."

"That's right. What's your name?"

"Morgan Freeman. Like the actor. I came here to see if you could help me."

"Help you find your dad?"

"Yeah, well, I figured if there was anyone who could help ..." But Morgan couldn't finish, her voice caught in her throat and her next breath was a monumental struggle. The tears welled up and spilled over and she clenched her eyes as tightly as she could. Everyone was right. She was crazy. She was a stupid, creepy girl who didn't have any friends and never would. All the kids were right to hate her, and so was her mother.

"Are birds your favorite animals?"

Morgan couldn't answer at first, just a small, strangled cough came out; she sounded a lot like the owl in the rafters. "I wanted to have a bear when I grew up." Morgan wiped her nose on her wet sleeve. "My dad said he'd consider it, but only if it were a really special trained bear."

"Trained to do what?"

"To dance," Morgan had her voice back a little. "What else would you train a bear to do?"

"Like a circus bear."

"Yes, right." Morgan shook her head. "One like in my dad's story."

"A story about a circus bear? I could really use a good story about now. Would you mind sharing it?"

"I'm not as good as my dad at telling it."

"I like stories even if they aren't told all that well." Dupont got up and came forward to sit and face Morgan, across the gazebo's wide opening. "Tell me."

"Okay, well, there once was a circus. And there was a bear named Sadie, who wanted to be a dove and to fly away from the mean owner who sometimes hit her with a whip. Sadie was friends with a magician's assistant, who was practicing and trying very hard to be a real magician."

Morgan paused, remembering her father's soft voice in her dark room. She remembered the comfort in that voice, how every word was meant just for her, secrets kept just between them. A part of her felt like it was wrong to share their story with this stranger, but another part of her was telling her it was okay and somehow very important.

She'd written the story down once, word for word as she remembered her father tell it, but the sheet of paper had disappeared from the top drawer of her bedside table. She knew her mom had stolen it, probably tearing it into little pieces, but she was afraid to ask.

"The magician's assistant was really, really nice and had even made Sadie a pink tutu to wear when she was dancing."

"They were friends," Dupont said.

"Yes, they were very good friends. So, one night, when the magician and the mean trainer were off in town, Sadie went to the magician's assistant and asked for a favor."

"To be turned into a dove?"

"Yes, that's right. But after saying the magic words, Sadie just disappeared under the big sheet and there was no dove."

"It didn't work? What happened to Sadie?"

"Well, after a minute, two little antenna poked out from under the edge of the sheet," Morgan said. "And then two bright orange wings appeared."

"Sadie was turned into a butterfly?" Dupont asked the little girl.

"Yes, a beautiful butterfly that was free to dance in the fields of flowers for ever and ever."

"That's a happy story," Dupont told the girl.

"I miss my dad so much."

"Since you trusted me with such a lovely story, can I trust you with something that's very important to me?"

"Okay."

"Do you have any paper in your backpack?" he asked, and Morgan rummaged for a dry sheet from the middle of the stack and handed it to him. It was an older drawing of a cahow peeking out from a burrow Morgan had made in math class.

Dupont pulled an expensive Montblanc pen from the breast pocket of his jacket, tiny gold-leafed birds sketched into the deep black metal skin, and began writing on the back of the picture.

"I'm not sure how much this will really mean to you right now," Dupont finished his note with the great flourish of a fancy signature and then handed the paper back to Morgan. "But maybe someday."

Morgan read the words and indeed they seemed like a riddle to the little girl. But she loved the man's signature, which she saw included the tiny spread wings of a bird over the letter "i," where a dot should have been. It seemed like something a kid would do, and Morgan made a mental note to try and work such a thing into her own signature, especially by the time school came back in session. If she ever went back to school.

"Keep it safe, okay?"

"I promise." Morgan rolled the document carefully and stowed it in the large compartment of her backpack.

"The rain's getting harder," Dupont said, and the two sat listening to the constant beat of the downpour, the wind whipping damp sheets of mist across the inside of the gazebo.

They sat for a while, not talking, both looking off to the northeast sky, up toward where the lightning was playing tag among the clouds.

Chapter 51

Bagg was upset his forward motion had been so rudely interrupted; his entire body had slipped into autopilot for the last couple of hours, just kicking and kicking. The nearly drowned former newspaper reporter swore at the object in his path, tried to kick his way around it, but then a voice from above caught his attention. Was it God? Was it another wise-cracking pelican?

Just as Bagg resumed his kicking, all five volunteer firemen jumped in to save him and promptly swamped his seat cushion. Bagg sank toward the bottom of the dredged cove in a slow-motion free fall. Underwater, there was no wind or stinging rain and Bagg was relaxed by the sudden quiet, willing to embrace the womb-like calm. His eyes were open to enjoy the beauty of the moment, the dancing bubbles in this fuzzy green and blue world.

Bagg tried to shrug away the hand that had attached itself to his right elbow. He knew the hand wanted him to go back up there, where life was crude and spiteful and windy as hell. It was hopeless up there and this place seemed perfect for him. He'd swim with the fish, maybe find a friend among the mermaids and sea turtles. This was a better place. Sure, you might have to avoid the occasional shark, but life on the surface was chock full of much worse things than circling predators with lots of teeth. Bagg wouldn't mind dropping a wrung or two on the food chain in exchange for the serenity that had enveloped him.

"Let me go!" Bagg tried to shout, but he hadn't even begun to master the art of talking underwater. His divine harmony was cut short, snatched away. The searing pain of his lungs filling with salt water sent his body into agonizing spasms. He turned his fate over to whatever bastard had him by the arm. For Christ's sake, if you want me that bad, then go ahead. I'm done fighting.

Bagg's limp body was whisked back to the surface and roughly shoved on board, where he threw up only a small portion of the salt water he'd inhaled while trying to complain.

"You're gonna be okay, buddy." And Bagg would have laughed at the idea of being okay had his lungs not been filled with what felt like needles and coarse sand. Yeah, thanks, buddy, Bagg thought. I was doing just fine underwater.

There were crackling voices on a radio and more hands all over Bagg's body. Someone shielded his face from the rain with a flapping piece of orange plastic, and Bagg appreciated the gesture. Any remnants of anger over being rescued were forgotten. A brace was wound around his neck, and he was tilted and scooped onto a stretcher for the ambulance ride to the hospital.

There was an upside to falling out of a stormy sky in a large jetliner, left to kick and paddle across an angry ocean, bumping headfirst into a rescue boat still safely docked. Aches and pains aside, his room was filled to the brim with cheerful flowers and cards propped open, signed with lovely little well wishes from people he couldn't possibly know. Nice. Very nice.

Bagg lay on his back, wires and tubes attached to him here and there, as he craned his neck to admire all of his pretty flowers. It was his first foray into consciousness in the two days since his arrival, and every muscle in his body was stiff and aching.

Above the colorful display were other more curious items, which Bagg endeavored to comprehend through his fog. Taped to the soft blue walls were drawings of birds. Some were in crayon, done by the hand of a young child. Others were in pen or pencil, with much more intricate detail. But as little as Bagg knew of birds and art, he got the sense that the same child had drawn them all. Perhaps it was something about the sweeping, rounded shapes of their heads, or maybe it was the uniform tilt of the beaks.

And for just a moment, Bagg thought the little contortionist Amira had slipped into the hospital bed with him. In his right palm was a small hand, about the size and feel of his friend's. Bagg lifted the hand he was cradling and realized it probably belonged to a child. It was incredibly soft, with tiny fingernails bitten and as crooked as his own.

Bagg peered down at the top of the sleeping child's head and found his next breath almost impossible, because he'd suddenly forgotten how to breathe. His chest froze at the sight of her crooked part and the sound of her own raspy breathing, almost a little girl-snore. Her hair was bleached from the sun, and what skin he could see on her forehead was more tan than he'd ever imagined it could be.

But as with most dreams of Morgan, Bagg allowed himself to enjoy a little of the illusion before getting pulled or slammed back to reality. Like being lost in the desert, maybe it kept your sanity around a little longer if you allowed the mirage to linger for a moment, before trudging forward in desperation. Perhaps a quick taste of sweet water before it disappeared back to that place Amira had called thin air.

Bagg let himself smile at his little mirage, who had grown so much since he'd last seen her. When he dared to gently squeeze her hand, Morgan turned toward him, her own dream interrupted. Her eyes fluttered open like butterfly wings, as she tilted her face up to her father's.

Those perfect round eyes filled with all the hope in the world. They were the most beautiful image Bagg had ever seen in his life. And his heart ached. His lost little girl smiled, then closed her eyes again and snuggled close, a slight crackling noise coming from a sheet of once-folded paper trapped between them. With his left hand, Bagg slowly pulled it free, its edges torn and the entire sheet dappled from water damage.

On one side was a picture of a bird, probably drawn by the same hand as those taped to the walls. It looked like a seagull peeking out from a hole in the ground. Did seagulls live in holes? Bagg turned the picture over and was surprised that the writing was entirely done by a heavy, sweeping grown-up's hand, all except for the letter "i" in the signature. Instead of a dot over the letter, there appeared to be the tiny spread wings of a bird. Even more surprising was that the signature had been made by the man Bagg had come to see, to plead the case for a group of people pushed right up against the edge of dry ground, unwanted and undesirable, required to remain invisible until it was time for the calliope to be switched on. Bagg read the letter from the twenty-nine-year-old multimillionaire named Michael Dupont, which gave Miss Morgan Freeman ownership of a little plot of land, a speck of mud and marsh, really, known as Fish Head Island.

The one clause added at the bottom, just under his signature, must have been very important to Mr. Dupont, since he'd written it in all capitol letters:

"TO BE KEPT AS A PLACE FOR DANCING BEARS, BUTTERFLIES, AND MAGIC."

THE END

Cole Alpaugh began his newspaper career in the early 80s at a daily paper on Maryland's Eastern Shore, covering everything from bake sales to KKK meetings. He moved on to a paper in Massachusetts to specialize in feature essays. His stories on a Hispanic youth gang and the life of a Golden Gloves boxer won national awards. His most recent newspaper job was at a large daily in Central New Jersey, where he was given the freedom to pursue more "true life" essays, including award-winning pieces on a traveling rodeo and an in-depth story on an emergency room doctor. The doctor's story ended when the physician brought back to life an elderly woman who had once been his children's babysitter. The essay was nominated by Gannett News Service for a 1991 Pulitzer Prize. Cole also did work for two Manhattan-based news agencies, covering conflicts in Haiti, Panama, Nicaragua, El Salvador, and guerilla raids conducted out of the refugee camps along the Thai/Cambodia border. His work has appeared in dozens of magazines, as well as most newspapers in America.

Cole is currently a freelance photographer and writer living in Northeast Pennsylvania, where he also coaches his daughter's soccer team.

CPSIA information can be obtained at www.ICGtesting.com
Printed in the USA
LVOW121739171012

303297LV00002B/108/P